Eastlick

and Other Stories

www.bookviewcafe.com
Book View Café Publishing Cooperative
Copyright ©2013 Shannon Page

Cover art and design by Mark J. Ferrari.
Back cover and interior design by Matt Youngmark.

"A Bottle of Red, A Bottle of White, ©2013 by Janna Silverstein
"Eastlick," ©2009 by Shannon Page. First appeared in *Black Static*.
"Bane," ©2011 by Shannon Page. First appeared in *Human Tales*, Dark Quest Books.
"Night Without Darkness," ©2012 by Shannon Page and Mark J. Ferrari. First appeared in *Gears & Levers 1*, Sky Warrior Press.
"By the Sea," ©2009 by Shannon Page. First appeared in *Grants Pass*, Morrigan Books.
"Water Proof," ©2012 by Shannon Page and Chaz Brenchley. First appeared in *Buzzy Mag*.
"Embers," ©2012 by Shannon Page and Joseph E. Lake, Jr. First appeared in *The Feathered Edge*, Sky Warrior Press.
"Gil, After All," ©2013 by Shannon Page.
"Oh Give Me Land, Lots of Land, Under Starry Skies Above," ©2011 by Shannon Page and Mark J. Ferrari. First appeared in *Space Tramps: Full Throttle Space Tales #5*, Flying Pen Press.
"The Hippie Monster of Eel River," ©2010 by Shannon Page. First appeared in *Close Encounters of the Urban Kind*, Apex.
"Bone Island," ©2009 by Shannon Page and Joseph E. Lake, Jr. First appeared in *Interzone*.
"Home," ©2011 by Shannon Page. First appeared in *Scenes from the Second Storey, International Edition*, Morrigan Books.
"If This Were A Romance…", ©2010 by Shannon Page and Joseph E. Lake, Jr. First appeared in *Love and Rockets*, DAW.
"Mad Gus Missteps," © 2013 by Shannon Page and Mark J. Ferrari. First appeared in *How Beer Saved the World*, Sky Warrior Press.

ISBN: 978-1-61138-367-6

"There have been great
societies that did not use the wheel,
but there have been no societies
that did not tell stories."

—URSULA K. LE GUIN

Table of Contents

A Bottle of Red, *A Bottle of White*

In the time I've known Shannon Page, I've learned at least two things about her: she likes a good glass of wine, and she likes good company.

Sure, we all like a drink. But for Shannon, native Californian that she is, there's a savored pleasure in the sip, a singular experience that she enjoys for its ownself. She'll take a moment to consider the complexity of the flavor and, yes, like most of us, to enjoy the buzz when the wine hits that sweet spot in the brain. She'll share a glass if it's worth the while. The wine, a pleasure when sipped alone, becomes an embellishment to the social experience when shared. The company makes a difference, and it becomes a sort of collaboration.

Like a good glass of wine, a good short story offers complexity and buzz. When you finish a good story, you take a moment to savor the experience, to let the resonance of truth ring a bit before it fades. I know that, for me, there's nothing like reading a last sentence that just nails the piece: reinforces a metaphor, adds weight to a conclusion. I can't help but lean back and sigh with satisfaction when a piece just works.

What I, what Shannon, and maybe what you get from a good glass of wine, I get from a good short story, too. And this collection brings all the complexity, all the buzz I could want.

With the title story, "Eastlick," a coming-of-age piece with a soupçon of dark magic, Shannon explores the terrible wonder of a girl discovering her own power. There's fearlessness here. In "By the Sea," Shannon goes *there*, that place that a writer has to go, that place where the stakes couldn't be higher. It's the situation that requires characters to make unthinkable choices. They take actions that make readers ask, *Could I do that? Would I?* And there's the inevitability of being human and finding oneself trapped by one's own opportunities. In "The Hippie Monster of Eel River," her protagonist faces the awful potential of responsibility, of knowledge in the midst of a carefree and irresponsible life. It's a gift; it's also a little taste of hell—a lovely bit of dissonance that makes a story worth reading and a character's journey compelling.

And there's more: the power of the well-chosen detail, the universality of human experience, the carefully considered insight.

Shannon also enjoys the process of collaboration—and good writers collaborate with her because she's that good. It's like sharing wine with friends: clearly she enjoys it, but she has no real need for it. She's got powerhouse storytelling chops all by herself. Still, she's worked with some of the best writing partners possible, critically acclaimed authors like Jay Lake, Mark Ferrari and Chaz Brenchley. The results are impressive.

You don't just come to this kind of ability as a writer by accident. I've watched Shannon make a point of working at her craft, hammering the damn thing into shape. These stories are evidence of her success.

I've always thought that reading is a kind of collaboration: a collaboration between writer and reader. The writer offers up thoughts and stories; the reader suspends disbelief and consents to join the adventure. With this collection, Shannon's offering a glass of wine and asking you to collaborate with her, to take the trip with her. Having tasted from the glass myself, I'm here to urge you: accept the invitation, sit down, sip the wine, and turn the page. You'll be glad you did.

—*Janna Silverstein*
Seattle, September 2013

Eastlick

After we fled a failed back-to-the-land commune in the late seventies, Mom rented us a small apartment in town, at the dead end of a one-block street called Eastlick. We did have a neighbor named Dru, and I was an awkward preteen (with a Hallowe'en birthday). The rest is pure fiction. This story first appeared in Black Static *magazine in May, 2009.*

I first see the guy up close when I'm coming home from school. Junior high. I'm wearing purple corduroy pants and a white blouse with lace ruffles at the top and on the sleeves. It itches, but it looks cool, so I wear it anyway.

Although we don't say 'cool'. That's what hippies say, and *I am not a hippie.*

It looks fine.

The guy is working on a mustard-yellow Datsun, or Toyota maybe—modified, with big chrome wheels and exhaust pipes, and a super-shiny paint job. He's taken the badges off the back. It's two-door, with black interior, and looks very fast. I've seen him driving it around before, but this is the first time I've seen him out of the car.

He has dark hair that feathers back perfectly, like Scott Baio.

I smile at him as I walk by. I wish I had books to hold to my chest, but we don't get homework. That's for high school. If I had books to hold, then he wouldn't see my tiny breast-buds, one bigger than the other. Maybe he can't see them under all the ruffles anyway. Maybe they make me look bigger in the chest than I am.

Maybe not.

He doesn't smile back, but he does look at me. I walk a little slower, letting my hips move. I can feel his eyes on me as I go, and I even know when he finally turns back to his car and picks up a crescent wrench. It's weird: I just *know*.

At the end of Eastlick, our one-block dead-end street, I see Dru on her porch, and say hi to her.

"How was school?" She's painting her toenails.

"All right. We get to go on a band trip."

"That's great!"

I linger on our tiny porch, leaning on the metal pipe rail, but she doesn't invite me over. So I get my key out of my pocket and let myself into our apartment.

Mom says we won't live here forever, she'll buy a place once she gets the money from Bruce, but I don't know. I don't know what's going to happen. We moved here after school had already started, just picked up all of a sudden one day and left. We had to leave a lot of stuff out at his place. She keeps saying we'll go back, but we don't.

At least there's Dru. She lives next door all by herself, in an apartment the same size as ours. She goes to the community college. She's half Chinese and half white, and all gorgeous. She's nice to me, when she isn't busy with school or work or stuff. She taught me how to feather my hair, but mine doesn't work like hers does. Hers looks all smooth and sleek and, well, feathery. Mine is lumpy. The best I can manage is some weird-looking rolls down the sides, the shape of the curling iron. Then it all gets messed up in the wind.

I wish I lived alone. I wish I was in college.

~ o O o ~

The guy with the yellow car talks to me the next time I see him. "Hi."

"Hi," I say. I slow down, but I don't stop.

"What's your name?"

"Lara," I say.

He says he's Dana, which I always thought was a girl's name. "How old are you?"

"Thirteen," I say. I've stopped walking now. I'm leaning against a tree, wishing I had the purple cords on. That whole outfit was much cuter. Today it's just jeans and an old yellow blouse from the Salvation Army. But he likes yellow, right?

"Thirteen!" He smiles. "Jailbait."

I smile back. "My birthday's next month."

"Still jailbait." Then he turns back to his engine. He's got a bunch of parts spread out on the sidewalk. It seems like they should be greasy, but they're not.

"Halloween's my birthday," I tell him.

He looks up again. "Halloween? Wow. Are you a witch?"

"No!" I almost stomp my foot, but remember not to at the last moment. That's childish. Instead I slowly spin on my heel, turning to go, flipping my hair behind me. I've seen women on TV do this. I've learned a lot in the month since we moved here. We didn't have TV at Bruce's. We didn't have a lot of things. I know it's better here. But I still hate it.

$$\sim \; o \; O \; o \; \sim$$

I lied to Dana. I told him the truth about my birthday, but I'm not going to be fourteen next month. Or even thirteen. I'll be twelve. It's like I'm almost twelve already, really. And twelve is almost thirteen, which is a teenager. Eleven sounds like a baby. Eleven and eleven-twelfths doesn't sound any better.

My name isn't Lara either. It's Laura. But Lara sounds more interesting, exotic. Like Dru. Dru is short for Drusia, pronounced Dru-sha. Lara sounds like a better friend for Dru than Laura.

~ o O o ~

I'm so excited about the band trip. I pack a week early, gathering clothes and my sleeping bag. I'll put my flute in later, after the last practice. In the bathroom, I pack my hairbrush and curling iron and shampoo and cream rinse, and then I stare for a long time at the pink box under the sink. The one Mom ordered for me. It says "Now You're a Woman" on it, and it's full of all the supplies for when you get your period. A little sample of everything, so you can try them all and see what you like. Should I bring it? I don't want the other girls to make fun of me. I have no idea who's gotten theirs and who hasn't. I'd rather die than ask.

~ o O o ~

I'm not innocent. I'm not naïve. I know about sex, and periods, and boys, everything. I know how much things cost. Mom makes $800 a month, but she gets less than that in her paycheck. Our rent is $250, and the payments on the Subaru are $98. Then there's utilities and water and stuff, insurance, other things. Groceries should be less than $10 a bag, but sometimes they're not. There's never enough money. Gas is almost a dollar a gallon. Mom got a lot of stuff at garage sales, and her boss sold her some old dining room furniture, but we still had to fill the apartment with everything—the beds, dressers, the couch, the TV. You hear on the news all the time about inflation, so it's only going to get worse. There's still a lot more we need—more dishes, pots and pans, a desk.

The roller skates I want are $40. I'll never get them. Or the record player. We listen to the radio a lot, when the TV isn't on.

~ o O o ~

The band trip isn't as much fun as I'd hoped. It's a long ride on a stinky bus, and then we only end up playing one song before the next band gets their turn, and we don't win the competition, and nobody can hear the flutes play anyway. And the whole time I feel gross and tired, maybe carsick from the bus, I don't know. Then we have to stay the night on the floor of a church basement.

The chaperones go to sleep in one corner, and all the kids pretend to, but they don't really. I lie there in my sleeping bag listening to the whispers and giggles. Everyone has a best friend but me.

Then two girls are out of their sleeping bags and sitting in the far corner, near me. One of them pulls out a Ouija board. "Let's play." She looks at me, watching her. "You too, Flute."

Well, I don't know their names either. She's Clarinet, and the other one is French Horn.

Clarinet has to show me how to use the Ouija, which makes her roll her eyes. I put my fingers on the little plastic thing, and she asks it a question, something about her grandmother. The plastic thing moves around a little, not really pointing at an answer, stopping between letters.

French Horn asks about a boy. Same result.

I didn't really believe it would work.

"You ask it something," Clarinet says to me.

"Um…" I have to think. What do I want to know? I want to ask about Dana with the yellow car, but not out loud, not in front of her. "Am I going to get an A in social studies?"

The plastic thing jumps and moves under our hands, whipping out an answer: YES. "You're pushing it!" Clarinet accuses, glaring at me. French Horn gets bored and starts talking to some other girls.

"I'm not!" I protest. It felt like she was. I could almost see her moving it. I could feel it under my fingers, twitching, eager.

"Okay," Clarinet says, "if it's so smart: ask it when am I going to die?"

I ask it, and it's like an alive thing. It quickly spells out: 1-4. Fourteen.

Clarinet glares at me. "Cut it out. That's not funny."

At that moment, in the dark church basement, with all the whispers and sighs around me, the smell of all the kids—their body odors, strawberry shampoo, bubble gum, hairspray—it all just hits me. I *know* Clarinet is going to die at fourteen, I just know it. I don't even know her name, but it's like it's already happened, I know it so strong. I can see it: a terrible car accident, blood everywhere. A severed arm. People screaming, sobbing. Leaves everywhere, and a broken tree trunk.

"Sorry," I mutter, and yank my hands off the plastic thing.

Part of me wants to play with it by myself, but mostly I'm too afraid. Clarinet shoves it back in her bag.

~ o O o ~

In the morning, I go to pee, and there's a dark red smear of blood in my underwear. Oh *man* I knew this would happen. Why didn't I bring the kit? I'm so stupid, I hate myself, I cannot in a million years tell anyone. They'll laugh me off the planet.

I sit on the toilet a long time, trying to figure out what to do. I lean over and open the cabinet under the sink, but there's only extra toilet paper, and Comet, and stuff like that. I look again at my underwear. Then I wipe, and drop the bloody tissue in the toilet, then wipe again. It's not much blood, just a few drops. I take a bunch of toilet paper and fold it up, and lay it in the underwear. I'll go get a clean pair when I get dressed, and hide these.

I flush a couple of times to make sure all the blood is gone, then leave the bathroom and start packing my stuff. I can feel the toilet paper bunched up, moving around when I walk. I try to walk carefully. I just have to make it home.

~ o O o ~

Mom asks if I need help with the kit. I tell her no, but then after a few minutes I call through the door.

She comes in and shows me how to use the belt, how to hook the pad on and fit it around my hips, and position it so it doesn't show over the top of my pants. I walk around the apartment testing it. It's huge, the pad. I feel like everyone can see it between my legs. It slips around, too, though not as bad as the toilet paper did.

I'm sort of thrilled to be a woman and all that, but at the same time, this feels super unfair and gross. And it's going to happen every month till I'm fifty or something.

Mom has terrible periods. She goes to bed and lies on her back and moans. I don't have cramps yet, unless that's why I was feeling so crappy and tired on the trip, but that was before the blood started, so I don't know.

~ o O o ~

"Hey Lara," he says.

I stop, heart pounding. I didn't know he was there.

He's sitting on the porch of his house, hidden in shadows. Then he grins, flashing bright teeth. "Hi, Dana," I say, leaning on the grubby picket fence, letting my bag slip down off my shoulder. It's heavy, I have three library books today.

"Come sit?" he asks. There's a couch on the porch, a real furniture-couch. Doesn't it get wet when it rains? He pats the place beside him.

I glance down the street, but of course I can't see if Dru is out. I'm self-conscious about the big lump between my legs too. "I gotta get home," I say, but I don't move.

Dana grins at me, and he's so cute, I can't stand it. I squeeze my knees together, holding the pad in place.

"Aw, come on," he says. "Just for a minute."

"Okay."

I push open the gate and walk up the cracked concrete path, then climb three wooden steps and sit down next to him. He's in the very middle of the couch, and I take the side closest to the steps. A smell of dust and mildew rises up as I sit. At least he won't smell my period.

"You want a Coke or something?" he asks.

"Sure." Mom never buys Coke.

He gets up and goes into the house, brushing against my knees as he goes by. The screen door slams behind him, and doesn't close all the way at the top. But it's a house, anyway, and it's not small. Do his parents live here?

I wonder how old he is, I should ask him. He got to ask me, didn't he?

But when he returns with the Coke, I just take it and sip the sweet fizzy bliss.

"You're quiet, for a girl," he says, after a minute or two.

"Uh-huh." I grin at him over the Coke. Oh *man* he's cute.

"I like that, I like quiet." He smiles back at me, and again I notice how bright and white his teeth are, in contrast to his perfect dark hair.

He doesn't know I can scream and sob and wail, and sing along to Donna Summer at the top of my lungs, and holler at my mom. He doesn't know the power in me. He doesn't know what happened on the band trip. I might as well pretend to be meek and quiet. I can be anyone I want.

I keep quiet and nod at him, and drink. "Your birthday's next week?" he says.

"Yep."

"I guess you're too old for trick-or-treating," he says.

I try an eye-roll, like Clarinet. "Yeah," I say, my voice all sarcastic.

"Ah, too bad," he says, and now he's grinning in a sort of wicked way. "It's fun to go out with a big old gang of folks. We get candy, then just hang around, make a little trouble. You should come with us."

"Really?" I ask.

"You bet. We take off after dark. It's a blast. Be here at eight, we'll go."

"Um... okay."

Now I'm all nervous. I want to go, I want to be with his gang, whatever that means. And now I've been here too long, I'll be late getting home, and that makes me even more nervous. Dru will notice, she'll tell Mom. And how in the world am I going to ask Mom for permission? She'll want to call Dana's mom! No way. This is crazy. He's going to hate me.

I finish my Coke and hand him the glass. "Thanks. I gotta go." I get to my feet and linger at the top of the steps. He gets up too, and stands really close to me. He smells like his own Coke, and car engine, and man. Not boy: man. I know what man smells like.

"I'll see you later," he says, and touches me along the side of my cheek.

I'm still shivering when I get home. And for the whole rest of the

evening, every time I remember the touch on my cheek, I shiver again, with
a shimmery delight.

~ o O o ~

Mom was going to take me to the shoe store after she got paid on the
first of the month, but we're only going now. "It can be your birthday present," she says. I don't protest, even though this way it won't be a surprise.

We walk into the store and I immediately see what I want. Tall Frye
boots, in a rich brown color. They have a stacked wooden heel, and a braid
up the side. They're stunning, gorgeous, amazing—and, better still, they are
just like a pair of boots Dru has.

They're also a hundred dollars.

A little gasp escapes me as I see them. Mom is already looking at the
sale rack, at the low Oxfords with black laces.

I don't even know what to do. We can't afford a hundred dollars. That's
a car payment.

"Mom—I want these," I say, before I can stop myself.

Mom doesn't hear me. She's talking to the sales lady, who gets out the
little metal measuring device. "Come here," Mom says. "Are you a seven or
a seven and a half?"

"*Eight* and a half," I say, with the tired whiny sound I hate in my own
voice but that I just can't help.

She's holding the hideous oxford. I walk over holding the Frye boot.
The sales lady is holding the metal device. We look like we're ready for
battle, each with our chosen weapons.

Mom barely glances at the boot, but she sees the price. I knew she
would. "No," she says, without hesitation. "Sit down, take off your shoes."

I brandish the Frye. "Why not?" I know damn well why not, but I want
to make her say it. I know she doesn't want to, she's embarrassed in front of
the sales lady, embarrassed to be divorced, poor, a failure. But I can use this,
maybe. I can make her buy them; she doesn't like to look bad.

"I said no. Sit down." She's frowning, and her forehead is scrunched up and wrinkly. I glance at the sales lady. I know she wants to make a sale, maybe she can help me. She looks bored, but I suddenly catch a thought from her. Almost like she said it out loud, but she didn't open her mouth. *Another brat whining at her mother.*

I sit down, dropping the Frye. Mom leans over and unlaces my right shoe, yanking it off my foot. I don't help, but I don't resist. I'm too freaked out. I heard what the sales lady said, clear as day. She's not on my side. But she didn't speak, I know she didn't. I can't read minds.

And I didn't move the Ouija thing.

We buy the oxfords. I barely say another word, just the essentials, and I shut myself in my bedroom when we get home.

$$\sim\; o\; O\; o\; \sim$$

Dru lets me hang out with her on Saturday. She does my makeup, smoothing pretty blue eye shadow on my lids and sparkly blush on my cheeks, and then fixes my hair. Hers is perfect, of course, but she lets me learn how to do French braids on her. Her hair is so soft and smooth in my hands, and it slides away, out of my clumsy fingers. She just laughs, and brushes it out, and tells me to start over. She says I'm not holding it tight enough, but I'm afraid of pulling, of hurting her. But I keep trying, and after a while I produce something barely passable.

"It's great," she says. "Now we'll teach you to do your own."

No way. I'll never be able to do my own. How can you do it, if you can't even see behind your head?

I fiddle and struggle and swear at my hair anyway, because she's helping me. "This is stupid," I finally say, dropping the mess.

"You have to *want* it," Dru says. "Focus. You can do it."

I look back at her, helpless. What is she talking about? Of course I want it! She nods at me in the mirror. "Go on."

So I try again, wanting it. And I braid my hair. It looks pretty good.

Dru smiles now. There's a gleam in her eye I haven't seen before, and it makes me a little scared. Then it's gone, and she's herself again. "So—big birthday plans?" she asks.

"Nah, not really," I say, starting on the second braid. But then I have a fantastic idea. I could tell Mom I'm hanging out with Dru! Then I could go with the guys down the street... well, with Dana down the street, and whoever his friends are. It would be so much fun. And Mom knows Dru, she wouldn't have a problem.

I open my mouth to ask, but then don't. Dru wouldn't lie for me, she just wouldn't. Mom trusts her. It's no use.

Dru must see my face light up and then shut right down again, as she watches me in the mirror. "What's the matter?"

I shrug, continuing to focus on the braid. "Nothing. Just—nothing."

She watches me for a minute, then says, "No, a smaller piece. Then wrap it under. See?" Her eyes stay on my face, in the mirror.

$$\sim \; o \; O \; o \; \sim$$

Halloween is my birthday, but we're going to do the family celebration on the weekend, when Dad is in town. At least I hope he'll be in town. But, never mind. I don't care if he is or not, actually. It doesn't matter.

"Is your friend coming by?" Mom asks. "What's her name again?"

I'm standing in front of the full-length mirror in her bedroom—the only big mirror in the apartment—fiddling with my costume. It isn't anything like I'd hoped it would be. I wanted to be a witch, because of what Dana said that once, but I don't look scary at all. Dru loaned me a tall black hat, and I'm supposed to be wearing black stockings, but I could only find grey nylons. My "long black dress" has little white flowers on it, and barely goes past my knees. I keep tugging at it, but it's not going to get any longer. And underneath I'm wearing a small pad, the kind that sticks to your panties. My period should be over by now, but it kind of dribbled on, stopping and starting again. Mom says it does that, before it gets going for real. Having a blood stain on my clothes has suddenly become an obsessive fear.

"Kristin," I lie. "No, her mom's picking me up at the end of the block." My cheeks flush as I say this, so I turn and pretend to inspect something on the side of my face, away from her. I'd told her I was going trick-or-treating with a friend from band over on the nice side of town, where the rich houses are.

"I don't know why she can't drive one extra block," Mom says.

I turn back to her and give her a long look. If I roll my eyes, she won't let me go, but oh, how I want to. I want so hard for her to stop asking questions. I envision her shrugging, and then...

Mom frowns, and shrugs. "Okay. You'll be back by ten, right?"

"Right."

After she goes out to the kitchen, I stare at my reflection a while longer. I don't have a wig, and my hair is way too blonde to be witchy. The heavy makeup is good, but I look more like a hooker than anything else, come to think of it. And the Oxford shoes don't help one bit.

Well, this is as good as it's going to get.

I pause by the bowl of candy at the door—icky things, like suckers and Jolly Ranchers and stuff like that. Cheap stuff. I don't want any of it.

Not that anyone gets all the way down to the end of Eastlick. None of the houses along the block have their porch lights on, and who trick-or-treats at an apartment complex anyway?

"Bye," I say, my hand on the doorknob.

Mom's cooking a package of Rice-A-Roni, stirring the melted margarine in the pan with the noodle bits and rice, the hot water already measured out and waiting. "Come here, let me look at you."

This time I do roll my eyes, but not where she can see. Then I walk into the kitchen, which isn't really a separate room, except that it's got linoleum instead of carpet.

Mom eyes me up and down, hesitating at the nylons for a moment. I stand there, looking back at her. Then she sighs, and smiles, although she still looks sad. "Have fun."

"I will."

Outside, it's cool and dark, and now the thin dress seems like not enough. But I won't go back and get a jacket. It would ruin the costume.

I'm at Dana's house in a minute. His porch light isn't on either, but I go inside the gate and up onto his porch, and ring the doorbell before I have a chance to talk myself out of it.

Then I wait a long time, my heart pounding, my mouth dry. I can hear people inside, laughing and talking.

I ring again, and knock.

A guy opens the door. He's ugly, with lots of pimples, and greasy blond hair. He might be Dana's age, or maybe older. He's not in costume, unless he's dressed up as a hillbilly, or a mechanic. "Sorry, we don't have any candy," he says, still laughing at something behind him.

"Is Dana here?" I ask, before he can shut the door on me.

He pauses, looking over his shoulder, then seems to hear me. He turns back to face me. "Dana? Yeah, um—who are you?"

"Lara."

The guy looks blank, then gives a wide smile. His teeth are not as white as Dana's, but they're not bad or anything. No, he's not in costume. This is how he looks: just a dog of a guy. "Lara. Well, come on in, Lara!" He throws the door open wide.

I follow him in. There's sort of a party going on. I see a lot of beer, and I can smell hard liquor, and dust, and cooking oil. There's only guys in this room. No one's dressed up, nobody has Halloween bags or anything. Are they going to go trick-or-treating like this? I pause two steps into the house, looking around, fear tightening my chest. It's not too late. I could turn around and go home now, say Kristin never showed up. Or just wait outside two hours, then go home and say I had a great time.

Then I see Dana. He comes in from some back room, his face lighting up in a gorgeous smile when he sees me. "Lara! You made it!"

Now it's a whole lot better, although I still feel stupid in my costume. I smile at him as I yank the witch hat off my head, holding it behind me. "Yeah."

He crosses the room and puts an arm around me, and starts introducing me to people. I forget the names at once, there's too many of them, and I'm just loving the feeling of him touching me. I notice another girl here. I think I recognize her from school, but she must be one of the eighth graders, or at least she's not in any of my classes. Anyway, I don't talk to her, as Dana moves us along to meet more people.

"Here, for you." The guy who answered the door is in front of us, holding out a plastic cup of Coke.

"Thanks." I take a sip, but it's got some alcohol in it. Rum, I think. It gives the Coke a bad taste, but I take another sip anyway, because I don't want to look like a nerd.

Dana leads me to a couch and pokes at two guys. "Hey, scoot over." They do, sort of, and then he sits down in the corner and pulls me down next to him. I have to almost sit on his lap, and my other side is leaning into the guy next to me, but he's talking to the first guy and ignoring me, so I guess it's all right. Dru's hat is getting crushed, so I set it on the floor and take another sip. The Coke and whatever is sloshing around in the cup. If I drink it down lower, it won't spill.

Dana is talking fast, his dark eyes moist and pretty. No, that's wrong. Guys' eyes aren't pretty; they're handsome. I'm not listening to what he's saying, because I've never been this close to his eyes before, and I just want to look at them.

It's not very long before my cup is empty. Did I drink that whole rum and Coke? Maybe I spilled some. I'm feeling very warm, and very happy. I can't believe I was so nervous earlier. Everyone's so nice. Now a couple of guys are standing before Dana and me, in front of the couch. Dana has his arm around me, and he's touching my shoulder in a really sweet way. I lean over to put my cup down, but then one of the other guys grabs it out of my hand. "Another drink for the lady!" he says, and skips off to the kitchen.

That strikes me as super funny—he's like a comedian on TV, he said it in a real silly high voice. I laugh, and then Dana laughs too, and then the guy is back with a full cup. I take it and sip it. This one tastes more like Coke. Good, I don't want to get drunk.

I lean into Dana. It's so nice to be near someone. Near him.

It gets warmer and warmer. There's a lot of people in the room, and they're all drinking and talking so loud. Maybe we could open a window? But I can't seem to say this, I'm confused, and sleepy. I suddenly wonder what time it is. There's a clock on the mantel, but it's stopped, it says three-thirty, and it hasn't moved since I got here. Lots of beer bottles and empty cups are on the mantel too. Again I wonder who lives here with Dana, but now I can't ask him, he's talking to one of the other guys, even as he's holding me really tight against him and stroking my shoulder and the top of my collarbone.

Now I'm glad the dress is thin.

But I guess we're not going out trick-or-treating?

I suddenly have a thought: Mom's going to want to see the candy I got! Oh man! What am I going to do? They don't have any candy here. I lean forward, pulling away from Dana, frightened. Mom's going to kill me, she's really going to kill me. She'll know I lied, I'll be in trouble forever.

Dana pulls me back to him, and then turns to look at me. "Hey, I never even gave you a house tour. I bet you want to know where the bathroom is!"

For some reason, everyone thinks this is super funny. So I laugh too, and then it is funny. Of course! A house tour!

Dana gets up from the couch and pulls me to my feet. I'm holding tight to his hand, but still I almost flop over. Maybe I am drunk? The room is so hot, I feel giddy. I feel like I do when my favorite song is playing, like Black Water or something, but more confused. The room spins, then settles back to normal. I got up too fast, that's all. Yeah, maybe I do want the bathroom.

Dana leads me through the crush of guys—there's even more guys now than when I got here, I think—and into a hallway. There's still more guys in the hallway. We push past them and he points to a closed door. "There's the john—someone's in there, though. Come on." He pulls me along down the hall, and I follow. It's like playing Crack-the-Whip—he just drags me along. It's nice.

Most of the doors are closed, but the last one is ajar. "Here's my room," Dana says, pushing the door open. It's dark, but he doesn't switch the light on.

He leads me into the bedroom and sits down on the bed. He's still holding my other hand so I just fall down, landing in his lap. I'm giggling too. It's all so funny!

Then he's holding me and he's kissing me, and it's the sweetest thing ever. At least until he sticks his tongue in my mouth.

I try to pull back, startled. His tongue is huge, and his hand went up my skirt at the same time. But he just holds his tongue in there deeper, rolling it around mine. I've never French-kissed before, and I don't know what to do. I can't breathe all that well, either—just through my nose. And his big hand is squeezing my thigh, he's squeezing too hard.

Suddenly he stops the kiss and pulls away, smiling at me. "Very nice." But he doesn't take his hand off my thigh. He's pushing my skirt up really high, to where you can see the top of the nylons, the ugly part at the top. His fingers keep pulling, reaching. Searching.

I think this is the first time I'm really afraid.

I start to try to get up, off Dana's lap, but he holds me tight, one hand on my thigh, one arm wrapped around my shoulders, his hand on the back of my head. "Uh-uh, don't run away now, Lara," he says, and leans in for another kiss. My mouth is open to say no, so his tongue just marches right in. He holds my head against his, with his fingers clutching my hair, and his other hand reaches further up my skirt, all the way to the top. Now he's touching me—through the nylons and through the panties and through the thin pad—but I can still feel it, like an electric jolt. He's rubbing his finger back and forth, and it feels good, and creepy, and I want to get the hell out of there. I never said he could touch me there. I never said he could kiss me or touch me anywhere.

I struggle harder now, trying to pull away, to get his tongue out of my mouth, his hands off me. But suddenly he twists and pushes me down on the bed, on my back, even as he's still all over me, his tongue in me. He's way too heavy, too strong, too big. I can't move. I'm trying to, but I can't.

Dana pulls his tongue out of my mouth long enough to say, "Don't waste your energy fighting." Then he settles over me even more. His knees are between my legs, prying them apart. My dress is hiked all the way up, so that the top of my nylons shows, and my naked belly button above it. Dana's hand snakes down into the tight nylons, into the underwear. He can feel the pad. He laughs, breaking the kiss again, and says, "Hey, a bleeder," before he puts his mouth right back on mine.

At the same time, he pulls his hand out of my panties and reaches up on my stomach, higher, pushing aside my bra. He touches my nipple, then squeezes it hard. It hurts, you can't touch them like that.

"Mmph!" I try to cry out, twisting my head as hard as I can. I yank my mouth free of his, tasting blood, but I still can't twist my body out from under him. He's too big. "No!" I say. "Let me go!" I don't feel drunk or warm or happy or anything any more. I feel sick, and I have his blood in my mouth, I cut his tongue with my tooth.

"Little cunt!" he says, reaching a hand to his mouth. The blood pools at the corner of his lips, and it's on his fingers, and it's dripping down on me. "You bit me!" he says.

The blood scares me, and energizes me. And still there's Dana, Dana in front of me, on top of me, bleeding on me, swearing at me.

I have to get out of here.

I want so much for this all to stop. I want it worse than anything I've ever wanted in my whole life: more than the Frye boots, more than Dad coming back, more than anything. I want him to stop hurting me. I want him to—

Dana suddenly screams and peels off of me, falling to the floor, holding his head. I scramble to my feet, pulling my dress down, trying to cover up. Dana is screaming, and looks up at me. His eyes are all bloodshot, red. What happened? Something's wrong.

Dana starts sobbing and lying on the floor, curled up like a baby, holding his head. What's wrong? Is he having a heart attack or a stroke or something?

Then I know I did it. I did something to him, I hurt him. I did magic on him, I wished for it and it happened, like with the Ouija board. I wanted him to hurt, like he'd hurt me. And it happened.

All this flashes through my mind in a second, and then I turn and run from the room.

~ o O o ~

I don't stop until I get to the street, and then I still don't stop. I'm half-way down the block before I realize I can't go home like this. I have blood on my face, and I lost Dru's hat, and my clothes are all messed up. And I don't have any candy. I make myself stop in between street lamps. I'm panting, breathing so hard, but I can't get enough air.

It doesn't matter. I'm safe now. Nobody has come out of Dana's house. I can see from here, nothing's going on. Well, the party is still going on. Maybe nobody knows what happened in his bedroom. I didn't even look at anyone when I pushed my way out of there. They're probably all too drunk to notice.

I'm still standing on the sidewalk remembering how to breathe when Dru's car turns the corner. She pulls over, rolling down the passenger window.

"Get in," she says, even though we're a half a block from the carport. I do, and she bites her lip, looking at my face, at my dress. Then she shakes her head. "Come on. Let's get you cleaned up."

In her apartment, she doesn't speak for a while as she sits me down at her kitchen table and wets a soft cloth. Finally, she says, "It wasn't supposed to be this way."

I wonder what she means, but then I kind of know, and I wish I didn't.

"He was supposed to be gentle, but he blew it," she goes on. "I'm so sorry. He shouldn't have been drinking."

I stare at Dru, then shake my head. "No," I say. "I don't want this. I wish everything was like it was before." I don't want to have any magic, I don't want any powers. I want to be normal. I wish this as hard as I can, harder than I've ever wished for anything in my whole life.

"Even though it saved your life?" Dru asks, although I didn't say that last part out loud. Then I stop wishing.

"You know it, you know it all," I whisper. "You made that all happen."

She gives me a sad look. She's washing my face, washing away Dana's blood, the smell of him. "No, Laura, you did. You're much more powerful than I am."

Now I'm terrified. I open my mouth to start screaming for my mom next door.

Dru stops me with a small smile and a raised finger. "You don't want to do that. What are you going to tell her?"

And I cannot speak—I clamp my mouth shut, without actually deciding to. No, she did it. I feel my throat closing, and I panic. Then she puts her finger down, releasing me. "Just sit here a while. Just listen to me. Let me tell you how it is. Let me tell you about wishing, and hoping."

"I want it to stop," I say, in a tiny voice.

"You can't wish it away. But I can help you."

I stare back at her. I *am* more powerful than her, and I know it. Before she can do anything, I push away, push her down, throw her to the floor, hard. I fling the door open and run out into the night, away, away.

She can't teach me anything. I already know too much.

From far behind me, I feel Dru trying to pull me back. But she can't do it.

I run, out the end of Eastlick, into the dark. And as I run, I start to understand that nobody can hurt me. No creatures of the night. No boys with yellow cars. No Ouija boards.

I run, and I laugh. And when I realize how alone I am, I laugh even harder, so that I won't weep.

Bane

Editor Jennifer Brozek wrote me one fine afternoon basically saying, "Help! I've got an anthology that's short a story, can you write one in a few days?" "Of course!" I said, delighted to be asked to pinch-hit, even though I was leaving for Australia the following week. She told me what she wanted: a fairy tale turned on its head, told from the monster's point of view. Human Tales *came out in August of 2011.*

The fiery orange padparadscha sapphire lay glowing at the cave's entrance.

A torment. A reproof.

A caution.

$$\sim\ \text{o}\ \text{O}\ \text{o}\ \sim$$

Once upon a time there was a dragon. She was fierce and brave and wild. Her sinewy coils stretched longer than the fat man's house in the village where the sheep-keepers dwelled, longer than the span of river that ran through the valley at the foot of her mountain, longer than the hottest day of summer and the coldest night of winter.

The dragon called herself Granletten, when she thought of names at all. She had not seen another of her kind in many, many turnings of the world, since her sister Persille had taken flight, seeking her own path far beyond the mountain, in the way of dragons. Solitary creatures, dragons are, despite their penchant for deep thoughts, and for clever repartee with like-minded (or, even better, contrary-minded) souls.

~ o O o ~

This morning had started like any other. Granletten had shifted her great bulk toward the front of the cave, shielding its contents from the rising sun. She thought about the clouds on the horizon, the turning of the seasons, and the time when she was a half-grown dragonlet and had first flown through a waterfall, just to see what would happen. She was just preparing to think about moving her right front claw a few inches, to cover the pile of gold coins that lay there, when her great eye was caught by a movement on the path.

Oh, is it time for another human already? Surely it hadn't been all that long since the last one. His bones were around here somewhere… She cast an eye back to the far reaches of the cave, but did not see them in the gloom.

By the time she looked forward again, the man-child was nearly at the cave's mouth.

~ o O o ~

Granletten kept down the numbers of brave fools who came waving their tiny swords in her scaly face by the simple expedient of distance, living as she did in a large cave on the wild side of her mountain.

The humans satisfied various purposes of their own by sending her their most dispensable fools: younger sons of large families, troublemakers, petty criminals—anyone who needed weeding out. Then they would wait a decent interval before sending another, leaving her to go about her dragonly business unmolested. Every once in a great while they would send a clever rogue. At those times Granletten enjoyed some smart banter before killing him. It was really a favor she did for the humans, relieving them of these unwanted burdens upon their fickle society.

~ o O o ~

"Good morning, fierce and terrible dragon," the man-child sang out, his voice only trembling a little. In his small and pale hands, he rather inexpertly held a sword. A large satchel was slung across his back.

Granletten rolled her enormous eyes. Somehow the humans had gotten the idea that she needed to be told who she was, as though she might perhaps have forgotten; now every fool who came by recited the same tired lines.

She sent him a puff of smoke from her nostrils, because that's what he would be expecting her to do.

The man-child held his ground. She could almost taste how badly he wanted to turn and run.

What would be his story? A quest, a dare, a princess's hand in marriage? Ah, humans and their petty concerns.

The man-child suddenly set the bulky sword on the ground, then dug into his satchel and brought out a small bundle.

"I have come bearing a gift."

Granletten perked up her ears. This was different. Usually they came to steal from her.

~ o O o ~

When not fending off stray humans, Granletten spent her time amassing, sorting, cleaning, and organizing her treasure. Dragons are the keepers of the world's brightest, loveliest artifacts, holding them safe and secure. She was pleased to honor the fiery spirit of the earth by collecting and safeguarding its elements, resting the cool length of her body across as much of the bounty as possible, like a hen atop her eggs.

As the weak and tender jewels such as opals and pearls stay supple when given regular contact with the thin, watery oils of human skin, so do the bolder gems—rubies, sapphires, diamonds—crave the touch of a dragon. Gold and platinum come to life in the fire of a dragon's breath, singing out the reflected glory of the earth's fires below in an answering song, thrilling to the heat and wildness. Treasure stolen by humans, to be worn by their interchangeable kings and queens and princes and sultans and rich men's daughters, or hoarded in their counting-houses gathering dust and slowly dying inside—this was treasure that wanted rescue. That wanted tending by the world's dragons.

The rest of her time was for deep, solitary thoughts.

When you live a double dozen centuries or more, you have plenty of time to ponder. And dragons lived longer than any other of the earth's creatures. It was all part of the ancient bargain, the balance that held the world together.

A balance that seemed to be shifting.

It began with the humans. Granletten could not recall exactly when the first flickering spark of animal essence coalesced into something greater, something finer, prouder. Animals were clever enough; the mountain goats had long since learned to avoid her smoky cave entrance, lest their young vanish into her great maw.

But she could not place precisely when the clever animals became *really* clever; when they developed the ability to think.

The ability to speak.

It had happened so subtly. Fits and starts. Long stretches of no progress at all. Then one day, she realized she could talk to them.

They would talk back. Sometimes they would even make sense.

~ o O o ~

"A gift?" Granletten tried to form the words, to speak back to the man-child, but her voice was long-unused, and it came out more like "Grr-grft!"

This frightened him, clearly; he took a step back, stumbled over his own sword, and almost fell.

Granletten blinked at him, waiting for him to recover. Then she tried again, after clearing her throat (and sending another gust of smoke and ash in his direction). "A gift? For me?"

"Y-yes, your highness, oh mighty dragon..." He flushed and looked down at what he held, as if reminding himself of it. Of his resolve. Why *had* the humans sent this one? He wasn't like the others—neither brave or foolhardy enough to be on a dangerous adventure, nor calm enough to be one of the clever ones.

Granletten leaned forward, resting her jagged chin on her scaly front limbs and peering at him for a closer look. "Tell me your story," she rumbled.

~ o O o ~

What joy it was when the first humans began to talk to her! It wasn't as though the dragon had been lonely—no, not that. "Lonely" was a pale, small, human emotion, a concept it had taken her some time to grasp. "Of course not," she had laughed, when the first clever man-child had gotten it through to her powerful, long-thinking mind. "My sister Persille is just beyond those mountains, over there." She'd waved a sharp-clawed forelimb in a generally sunward direction.

No, loneliness was not the problem. But to have someone to listen to one's ideas, to argue back? Ah, sweet treasure.

The problem came clear when that first man-child had brought his clever mind to her, had gone away again (for she did not kill this one, out of amusement and a desire to speak with him once more), and then, by the time she had thought about what he had said and looked for a continuation of their conversation... well, he was gone.

Granletten had roused herself, secured her cave and treasure, and ventured down to the village, searching for the small, fair-haired youth that had so delighted her just a short while ago.

After all the screaming and panic and general hubbub had subsided, and she'd had to dispense with a few particularly foolish-brave warriors with little pointy metal weapons to wave at her, a trembling elder had approached her.

"What... what do you want, noble dragon?"

Granletten had sighed, sending a gust of fire breath to singe the man's hairy ears, without exactly meaning to. "The boy, who came to me: Emmon, his name was? I would speak with him once more."

"Emmon?" Confusion, consultation with other elders. Finally, from another, even more ancient one: "That was my great-grandfather, dead these hundred years or more."

No. One couldn't have a satisfactory discourse with humans, when they came and went like so many mayflies.

So Granletten the mighty dragon kept her own council. She enjoyed the greater and lesser fools who came her way, thought her deep thoughts, and tended the earth's treasures.

~ o O o ~

"M-my... my story?" The man-child had a smear of dirt on his face, dust mixed with sweat. Granletten resisted the urge to wipe it away—even if she could wield a claw so tenderly across his fragile flesh, he would surely not take the gesture in a friendly manner.

"Yes. Your story." Her voice was warming up now, the words coming more easily. "Why do you bear me a gift? Nobody brings gifts to dragons. If you're trying to play a trick on me, please remember that no one has ever actually succeeded at that."

"Oh... n-no trick, I promise. No trick. Um... your th-things are so beautiful..."

She raised a scaly eyebrow. "How do you know what my treasure looks like?"

"Everyone knows. I found something beautiful, too beautiful for anyone in the village, or the city, or across the whole country. They said I should bring it to you." All this without stammering.

~ o O o ~

Two things the humans did: they made the jewels lovely, and they made them portable. By digging and cutting and faceting and polishing the raw, bulky stones that made up the essence of the earth's magic, they made the gems far easier for the dragons to collect.

It was perhaps ironic that humans did this with no actual understanding of what it was they were working with. Of the value of their finds, the true treasure of their play-pretties. Oh, there were various self-styled witch-kind and sorcerers and the like among the humans, who claimed to find powers and echoes and spirits and other such nonsense in precious stones. Granletten had quickly discerned that this was all smoke and ash; that these holy folk were just as greedy as any other clever monkey or bright-eyed magpie who spies a shiny bauble and seeks to make it his own, to hold it close.

No, the humans had no clue that the blood-red rubies with which they adorned their fairest maidens or worthiest kings were the literal blood of the earth; that the deep green emeralds that graced the plump fingers of a rich man's wife held the spirit of the forests and marshlands within every sparkle; that the rare golden-orange sapphires of the tropics were the manifestation of the very passion that kept the earth vital, and propagating, and alive.

They just thought the stones were pretty.

Granletten didn't mind. Portable suited her; the fact that the humans had gathered so many jewels actually made her work easier, saved her the trouble of hunting them down in the depths of the earth herself. And beauty pleased her. Even a dragon has a sense of style.

~ o O o ~

Granletten narrowed her eyes at the man-child. He no longer looked afraid, now that he'd gotten around the tangle of his words. "Did your king send you?"

He shook his head. "No, not the king; not even the mayor of the village. They're fools." He paused, seeming to consider the import of his words, but then pressed on. "The holy man sent me, because you are more powerful than the mayor or the king. You're the one who should have this." He opened the bundle.

The dragon, like all of her kind, was a cold-blooded creature. Despite this fact, the ichor in her veins ran hot and excited when she looked at what the man-child brought forth.

It was a single perfect enormous padparadscha sapphire, bright orange, flaming like the center of the sun. Some human hand had cut it, shaped it into a faceted oval, as if to be set in jewelry—but it would be a bauble for a giantess, for the thing would weigh down any woman's finger, would leave a bruise on even a strong man's chest.

Yet it had never been set to metal; Granletten could see that at a glance. The fiery essence of the stone sang out to her, even as it reached for its brethren in the hoard behind and beneath her. Yearned to be returned to its companion-stones.

Granletten looked at the man-child's face, assessing it. He appeared both proud and certain of himself, without doubt, and without any of the fear he'd shown earlier. What was his game here? What did he want in return?

"Where did you find this, youngling?" she asked instead.

He shrugged, then set the heavy stone down on the ground before the cave's mouth. "Our holy man is wise, and would not tell me where it came from. He said you would want to know, and that you could not be told."

"All the treasures of the earth are mine to guard and tend; you humans merely take custody of them from time to time, without leave." She said all this without threat in her voice. The words were clear enough.

He gazed back at her, still unafraid. "And so I give it to you."

This had gone on long enough. "And what do you expect in return?"

The man-child smiled. "He told me you would ask this too."

~ o O o ~

Sometimes, the humans would come to her, not seeking an adventure or the solution to a quest, but offering a bargain. They would have noted her great size and power, the terrible fire of her breath, her powerful wings and sharp teeth and claws, and would ask her to destroy some neighboring village, or burn down a particularly stubborn stand of trees, or haul some great structure from one place to another. In return, they would offer her a grubby handful of stones—paste, usually—or shiny metal-things of no value whatsoever.

Granletten would patiently explain to them that they had nothing that was of any worth to her, and if they had, she would take it without doing them any favors, other than leaving them alive. If she felt generous.

This never seemed to please the humans all that much. But it would make them leave off bothering her a while, anyway.

Until the next generation came along, in a heartbeat, as they did; and they would forget the lessons of the last time. Oh well, at least it made for an interesting distraction, every once in a while.

Long life could be tedious.

~ o O o ~

"Of course I would ask that. Who gives a gift to a dragon without asking for something in return?"

She tried not to snort too violently; the flames would crisp the man-child's face, and then he would only be screaming, incapable of further conversation. And she really did want to hear what he had to say next.

The thought helped draw her attention from the astonishing sapphire, anyway. She hadn't even known there were such stones in the world—so large, such concentrated masses of pure earthly essence.

So much passion.

"Well." Now the man-child drew himself up, self-important. "I do. I need nothing from you. I am merely offering up the most impressive jewel mankind has ever known to the most impressive beast in the land."

Now she did snort with all the gust of her fire-breath, turning her head slightly to spare the life of the foolish creature before her. "And did your holy man not warn you about excessive flattery? Did he not tell you how clever I am?"

The man-child danced away from the edge of the fire, a small ember smoldering at the edge of his pointy boot. "Of course he did, your grace. He told me you are the cleverest dragon in all of the land. Cleverer than your sister, Persille. Cleverer than the he-dragons who perished in the last turning of the aeons. Cleverer than even the great dragons of the Antipodes, whose very sweat can ignite ancient forests as they sleep." He watched her carefully as he went on.

Too bad for him that dragon-emotions did not play out across dragon-faces.

"I suppose you fancy yourself clever as well." She was playing for time, and she knew it. Because she could not take her eyes off the padparadscha sapphire. It was… awakening something in her. Something she could not explain, could not define.

Yes, it was lovely—all jewels were, in their own way. And large, well-cut, flawless jewels were lovelier. And the jewels of fire—rubies, sapphires, the yellow diamonds—were lovelier still. All this was perfectly understandable, perfectly reasonable.

So this, being the biggest stone she'd ever seen—it made sense that this jewel would stir her passions.

But still, there was something more at work here…

Then she heard the words of her own thought. "Passion," Granletten whispered. "This is a stone of passion."

The man-child gave a hesitant grin. "Yes, your highness: it is a very pretty stone."

"No." Understanding dawned on her. The humans had no idea, no concept of what minerals meant to the earth, though they were drawn to them all the same. They didn't grasp why they—humans—felt compelled to collect and refine, purify the gems. Clever though they might be, they lacked this fundamental awareness.

Which was why dragons were the true keepers of gems.

But dragons were meant to be immune to their stirrings. And yet Granletten could not deny the quick beating of her heart, the steaming of the fires in her belly… the heat in her loins.

For the first time in centuries, Granletten felt aroused.

Close on the heels of this discovery was the terrible knowledge that this was something she was not meant to feel. There was no purpose for this arousal, no possible outlet for it. It was as the man-child said: there were no male dragons, hadn't been in many centuries. Never would be any more.

All the dragons that would ever exist in the world were here already. When and if they died, they would not be replaced.

This was the bargain dragonkind had made, ages past. One can have long life, or one can propagate, leaving one's children behind to carry on.

Not both.

Something broke inside Granletten at that moment—her soul, her will, her resolve—something vital, something sharp. She cried out, sending flames and fire everywhere, scorching the cheaper jewels and melting great gobs of gold, thrashing her long tail back and forth. The man-child had fled; he was halfway down the mountain by the time she recovered enough sense to even wonder about him.

But he had left the bedamned jewel.

It sat in the entrance to her cave, glistening, glimmering. Inflaming her. Lust poured through her loins once more at the sight of it. "Throw it away!" she bellowed to herself, reaching out a long claw to grab it.

Touching it was worse, though. As she drew it to her face, she knew she'd never, ever be able to let it go.

It would stay here, in her sight, torturing her. Forever tempting, forever withholding. Forever promising something she could never have.

~ o O o ~

A dragon is always alone.

But until this terrible gift, she had never been lonely.

Granletten lay in her cave, staring at the padparadscha sapphire. Large tears rolled down her face as a dragon-sized heat boiled through her body.

Unquenchable. Intolerable.

Forever burning.

Night Without *Darkness*

By SHANNON PAGE *and* MARK J. FERRARI

I love collaborative writing, as you'll notice throughout this collection. To me, collaboration combines everything I love best about writing (creation, imagination, that indefinable spark) with everything I love best about editing (figuring out another creative person's mind and working out how best to express it). Plus, it's just fun to play together. This story was written for Gears and Levers Volume 1, from Sky Warrior, April 2012.

In which the lamentable Wendell Shrewsbury, Esq., proffers his astonishing recollections regarding the spectacular events which transpired on the evening of December 7, 1886, in the Cambridge manor laboratory of Rupert Collin, Baron Frost.

…The laboratory in flames, generating ever-larger flashes of blinding light and searing heat. The terrible din of exploding bottles and jars assaulting his ears. Tinctures and potions combining as they were never meant to do, filling his lungs with noxious fumes. The high, choking screams of Lord Frost… suddenly silenced.

Shrewsbury stands, frozen as always, held within this horrifying scene by guilt and remorse—real or imagined, he no longer knows—unable to avert his eyes as Lord Frost bursts from the conflagration, a man aflame. The doctor's nearly vanished lab coat is a shriveling, blackened wick, billowing up on gusts of heat as it is consumed. His sizzling skin sends a cloying stench into the air... "Shrewsbury!" With that anguished, accusing croak, Lord Frost pitches forward, perishing for the thousandth time at the feet of his horrified protégé.

A dark, flitting presence begins to mock Shrewsbury from within the flames and smoke, from behind Lord Frost's ruined face—from inside Shrewsbury's very mind. As it whispers sins—of commission, and omission—he is appalled to realize that it has been there all along, hiding in his thoughts, his dreams, slyly driving him... to this.

"Officious fool!" it hisses triumphantly, as if borrowing voice from the flames themselves. "What would England be without its dreams—and us to shepherd them?"

~ o O o ~

An insistent knocking brought Shrewsbury to what remained of his senses. He bolted up in bed, gasping for breath, pulling the covers up against the chill of the deep February night. Had he been shouting? Very likely; his throat felt dry and sore.

He looked around, blinking in the dimly lit room. It was not his own; he was abed in a well-appointed guestroom at the home of barrister Ian Rutherford, Esq.

An old friend from college days, Rutherford had made significantly better progress in the world than had Wendell Shrewsbury since their graduation together some twenty years before. Rutherford's warm if unexpected letter inquiring into Shrewsbury's strange elusiveness these past few years, and inviting him to come and rekindle their old friendship, had drawn Shrewsbury hesitantly out of hiding, hopeful that a change of scenery and some social interaction might relieve his... difficult condition.

Apparently not.

"Shrewsbury? Shrewsbury! Are you quite all right in there?" The knocking grew a little gentler, if no less insistent.

It was the first night of Wendell's visit—and, he feared, after this display, his last.

~ o O o ~

A quarter of an hour later, the two men sat downstairs in Rutherford's book-lined study. A coal fire had been laid and lit by Rutherford's aged, live-in housekeeper, Mrs. Sapphira Lamblittle, and was now begrudgingly bestowing some small warmth upon the room. This elusive comfort had been augmented by the half-drained snifter of brandy at Wendell's elbow. He took another sip and adjusted the belt and lapels of his dressing-gown self-consciously. He could not meet his old friend's eyes, choosing instead to watch the low flames, despite their dreadful evocation of his fiery dream.

"I am terribly sorry for waking you—and Mrs. Lamblittle," Shrewsbury ventured at last.

"Not at all!" Rutherford cried, too cheerfully. "I am only glad that you happened to be here and not alone while suffering so terrible an episode."

"Ah..." Wendell gazed into the fire. "Well... Yes. It can be quite troubling..."

"You've had such fits before?" his friend asked gently.

"I have." Wendell took another sip, nearly finishing the snifter, and set it down on the mahogany table beside him, only to have Rutherford reach for the decanter and pour him another generous glass. "Almost... every night."

"Every night?" Rutherford blanched and took a healthy draught of his own brandy, then shook his handsome head. "What devilish torment! Is there no one of sufficient expertise in such matters to offer you hope of relief?"

"There was," Wendell lamented. "There was..." The liquor was beginning to affect him; that, and the terrible paucity of sleep. Despair crept ever closer. "But he is lost forever now—and... I fear this torment I endure is all too richly deserved."

"The devil you say!"

"The devil, indeed." Wendell teetered on the brink of indecision. He could make his excuses and leave tonight—or on the morrow, more politely—to continue bearing this burden alone. Or...

A sudden resolve prodded him to speak before he quite knew he'd decided to. "Oh, Rutherford, dear friend, I cannot contain it any longer. I must tell someone, though it leave me in as much need of your legal assistance as of any medical counsel. Yet, confess I must, if only in the desperate hope that guilt acknowledged and justice satisfied may rid me at last of this endless nocturnal scourge. May I burden you, old friend, with a dreadful tale—from which I dare hope our long friendship might emerge intact?"

His friend stared back, blue eyes glinting in the firelight. "After such an introduction, how am I to sleep now without hearing it?"

"I fear you'd best not count on sleeping either way," said Wendell. "Does the name Rupert Collin—Baron Frost—mean anything to you?"

"I've heard of him, of course. Who hasn't? Such a titillating catastrophe!" Rutherford leaned forward, keen interest on his ruddy face. "Did you know him?"

"More than that," said Wendell. "I was his research assistant for some years."

"You jest! How can I have failed to hear of this before?"

"I have taken pains to see the fact unadvertised." Wendell did not entirely succeed in keeping his voice steady.

"Surely," Rutherford said, "you weren't there when..."

"Oh yes," Wendell whispered, lost in painful memory. "I was there. I am not sure I have ever truly left that night behind. It has not left me. That much is certain."

Wendell accepted another refill of his brandy, cleared his throat, and set out to confide at last the lurid truth of Lord Frost's spectacularly fatal attempt to rid England forever of nightmares.

~ o O o ~

"You know, of course, that Lord Frost was a brilliant man of science."

"Of course," Rutherford murmured. "Sleep research, was it?"

Wendell nodded. "And not merely sleep—he was also enquiring into the anatomy and possible uses of dreams."

"Yes," said Rutherford. "I read his *Systems and Practices of the Nocturnal Mind* with great interest. A seminal tract. Quite revolutionary."

"You cannot begin to know... how revolutionary," said Wendell.

"Do tell." Rutherford settled more comfortably into his chair. "I am awash with curiosity."

Wendell knew that he was stalling for time, considering his approach, as though just the right combination of words might somehow sanitize the awful truth.

He took another swallow of brandy, then stared again into the fire as he spoke. "Though it's been scarcely more than whispered beyond certain inner circles since his... horrific demise, Lord Frost believed that night-mares might not be merely dreams at all, but invasive psychonomic para-sites—an entirely new and utterly uncatalogued form of life which preys upon, or engenders some malevolent symbiosis with, the dreaming human mind." He kept his eyes firmly upon the low flames, anxiously awaiting his friend's response to this outlandish assertion.

"Please, go on." Rutherford's voice was low and calm.

Wendell risked a glance at the barrister, finding him apparently at ease. "During my employment with him, Lord Frost did, in fact, invent, and was perfecting, a series of ingenious devices capable of extracting these parasites from the minds of numerous tormented subjects. In fact," he ventured tim-idly, "we had managed to imprison a fair collection of these... creatures... in hermetically sealed glass vacuum bells for study and extermination."

"Fascinating."

Wendell sighed. "It's likely treason to be telling you all this. But I don't care... Not anymore. What can they do to me that could be worse than what I suffer now?"

"Treason! Good God, man! Why?"

Wendell considered his worldly friend, wondering how he of all people could fail to grasp the implications. "Imagine our advantage over other nations, were the sleep of all English citizens—and theirs alone—never troubled by such anxieties and terrors; if every head in England woke well rested each morning; if England's children grew up free of the subconscious fears that so distort and disable young minds elsewhere in the world. How many fewer criminals might we have to cope with? How much more fearless confidence might this country's future generations take for granted in the course of their endeavours?"

"You don't mean that he intended to keep such a boon secret from the wider world?"

"Indeed. He was commanded to do so by none other than the prime minister."

"What of Scotland?" Rutherford asked, a slight resentment creeping into his heretofore encouraging tone. "And Ireland? Would all of Her Majesty's subjects have so benefited, or only those closest to the throne, if you take my meaning?"

"I do not know, old friend," Wendell said, shaking his head. A lump of sorrow—or anger—settled in his chest. "Nor shall we ever know. Not now..."

$$\sim \; o \; O \; o \; \sim$$

Rutherford soon proved so engrossed, that, against all expectation, Wendell found himself warming to the task of describing Frost's ingenious devices. Chief among them, he explained, was a massive piece of sealed headgear rather like the helmets worn for deep sea diving. This 'extraction bell', as Frost had called it, was encrusted with smaller mechanisms cleverly contrived to produce, through the highly pressurized release of steam from tiny pinholes, ultra-sonic frequencies inaudible to human subjects but extremely unpleasant to the fiendish parasites. Upon penetrating the subject's brain, these frequencies had compelled the ethereal creatures to flee through various orifices in the victim's head. From there, sonic devices had moved along tracks attached by a series of minute airlocks, generating a moving pulse which forced the fleeing beasties through a network of complexly valved and insulated vacuum hoses sealed to the headgear. In this way, the parasites had been conveyed into large glass bell jars, instantly vacuum-sealed by pumping out their atmospheric contents through a sonic barrier which the creatures themselves would or could not pass. The gaseous parasites alone were left inside to be observed through various filters and lenses, and experimented upon by numerous other means and mechanisms of Frost's invention.

Describing these marvels gradually transported Wendell back to the happier days of his mentorship under Lord Frost. As a man of science himself, Wendell could not help but admire the genius behind such a truly elegant system. He even began to recall some of the pride he'd once taken in his own contributions to their work. "We were going to change the world!" he declared, waving his empty brandy glass expansively. "Top government ministers—I mean *top* ministers"—he fixed Rutherford with a knowing gaze—"visited our laboratory every week, eager for our latest reports and demonstrations. And rather ready with support, if you take my meaning... Lord Frost's fortune, though vast, was not inexhaustible, and groundbreaking scientific research is not for the financially faint of heart."

"I can well imagine," his host said, replenishing Wendell's drink once again.

Shrewsbury took another fortifying swallow. Confessing himself had clearly been the right decision. He already felt his awful burden dissipating. How much torment might have been avoided had he found the courage to try facing all this sooner? In fact, he wondered what had kept him hiding all this time. Could even that be laid to the pernicious influence of...? But no. Those were the musings of a madman, alone in the dark with his thoughts. He was not that madman, and not alone tonight.

The thought returned him to his surroundings. The fire was nearly out, and the coalscuttle was low; Mrs. Lamblittle must have retired once more.

"A truly fascinating tale, Shrewsbury," Rutherford said, pouring a bit more brandy into each of their glasses. "But I find no evidence within it to explain your earlier assertion."

"What assertion do you mean?"

"That this nightly torment you endure is well deserved?"

"Ah yes, of course," Shrewsbury muttered, gazing downward. His prideful reminiscences collapsed and fell away. "I shall hasten to the point, then, so that we may both have hope of at least a few hours slumber before dawn."

"Do not rush on my account!" Rutherford leaned back in his overstuffed chair. "But tell me: did you not undergo the experiment yourself? Or was Lord Frost unable to perform this extraction of your own nightmares?"

"Ahhh…" All unknowing, and from entirely the wrong way 'round, his host had hit upon the dark heart of it. "No, more's the pity; I never did. Had I experienced anything resembling an overt nightmare during those last fateful months, I'd doubtless have been bolted into Lord Frost's collection device as fast as you could say Wee Willy Winkie, and that would have been the end of it."

"The end of what?" his old friend asked with visibly rekindled interest.

"If only I had seen the truth in time," Wendell lamented, "I'd likely enjoy a station far loftier than yours by now." Rutherford's smile dimmed somewhat, but Shrewsbury gave it no thought as he fell deeper into reverie. "Alas. No such happy fortune is accorded me." He took a larger draught of brandy than good manners might have countenanced, and heaved a sigh of resignation. "Here's the awful truth of it, then."

Rutherford set his brandy down, and leaned forward in his chair to listen.

"I must assume," Wendell said, "that one of these fiendish creatures somehow glimpsed the nature of our activities while sorting through the contents of my own mind at nights. Not only that, but it apparently then had the cunning to conduct itself in ways not recognizable to me as nightmare… Not *then*. No…"

"I am… not sure I take your meaning," Rutherford said, in a stiff voice. Wendell glanced up at him. The shadows of the dying fire played upon his old friend's face unpleasantly, though Rutherford smiled as if anticipating some reassuring explanation.

In for a penny, in for a pound, Wendell thought, gripped now by the determination to unburden himself completely of this dreadful secret. "I believe it infects me still."

"What?... One of these parasites you speak of?"

"The very creature whose tender ministrations you so mercifully interrupted earlier this evening," Shrewsbury acknowledged.

Rutherford withdrew into the shadows of his plush chair, and raised the snifter to his lips, obscuring his expression.

"Once they are housed in the skull," Shrewsbury explained, "such creatures can live and grow, apparently, watching and waiting, biding their time..."

"You speak of these... parasites... as if they had intelligence," Rutherford observed.

Wendell leaned forward, gazing at his friend. "But they do—it does! These are no mere automatons, mindlessly feeding and breeding and dying like so many other members of the animal kingdom. They think. They plan, and scheme," he whispered, half forgetful of his friend, "but subtly, oh so subtly."

"So this nightmare you've been suffering is not just a living organism lodged within your mind, but actively contriving some enduring plan to harm you?" Rutherford asked.

Shrewsbury nodded miserably, aware that he had finally outpaced his host's credulity.

"But why?" Rutherford pressed. "I too have nightmares from time to time. Who does not? They do not remain after waking to keep waging some campaign against me. Even if you are correct, and these dreams really are the work of some elusive organism, what purpose could a parasite have in persecuting the host from whom it presumably benefits?"

"Revenge, I assume," Shrewsbury replied with a desolate shrug. "We persecuted others of its kind, and would certainly have done as much to it if we had guessed in time that it was there. Having used me to defeat my mentor, it now seems to derive more pleasure from my extended torment than from just dispatching me as it contrived to do to poor Lord Frost."

Rutherford set his snifter down abruptly and lurched forward in his chair. "Surely you're not claiming that this insubstantial... *insect* is some-how responsible for Lord Frost's death!"

"It... *and I*," Shrewsbury murmured, once again unable to look any-where but into the dying fire.

"I do not believe it," Rutherford said. "I would sooner think you mad, old friend, than a murderer of any kind. I will help in any way I can, finan-cially if necessary, and, of course, you may count on my absolute discretion, but I think you must seek help immediately in regard to this delusion that you suffer."

"That is very generous," Shrewsbury said in disappointment, "but I am quite certain that this is no delusion. Would that it were! I am well aware of how incredible these claims must sound, but the entity of which I speak is, sadly, all too real. You have not seen its cousins in the laboratory as I have. You... were not there... that night..."

Elsewhere in the house, Wendell heard footsteps and the muffled thump of a closing door. Mrs. Lamblittle, no doubt, up again for something. He hoped she might consider coming in to replenish the coal.

"What did happen... *that night*?" Rutherford pressed, if less enthusias-tically than before.

That night... Wendell thought despondently.

"It started well before then," he said at last. "Having discerned the threat we posed to it before we discerned its threat to us, the pernicious demon refrained from inflicting any overt nocturnal terror. Rather, it simply hid within my mind, subtly manipulating both my thoughts and dreams to induce within me a growing urge, first to prove and later to aggrandize myself before Lord Frost. It exploited my propensity for pride, my vanity and weakness for conceit. No gentler description is merited, I fear. I found myself increasingly compelled to pretentious displays of zeal for meticu-lous detail and obsessive perfection in my work, not that I found anything strange in such behaviour. What young man does not seek the attention and approval of his employer in hope of advancement? Unfortunately, this new proclivity soon proved so insatiable that I began inventing opportunities to demonstrate my usefulness by fixing things that were not broken—first between myself and the lesser members of Lord Frost's staff and household, then between myself and Lord Frost himself, and eventually presuming to *improve* upon the lab's equipment and devices themselves…"

"What sorts of improvement?" Rutherford asked.

"Small things. Trivial, in fact… at first." Shrewsbury sighed. "Needless attention to parts I thought wanted lubrication or polishing to remedy some rough edge or improper motion. Things meant to have no real impact beyond that of impressing upon Lord Frost what a careful, knowledgeable, *important* resource I was. Indeed, Lord Frost was initially delighted by my industrious attention to detail—which just encouraged my evolving mania." Wendell gazed bleakly at his host, who stared back in silence. "How is one to know he builds a weapon, Rutherford, if he never sees more than the one small piece he's given to contribute at a time?"

"I… could not say," his friend answered carefully.

"They are diabolic creatures, these nightmares," Wendell said. "This one, anyway. By this excessive maintenance, it learned at least as much as I did about our equipment's every part and function. I saw nothing then save my own *good* works, and cannot say, even now, exactly when I shifted from inconsequential meddlings to more significant attempts to usurp both the direction and implementation of Lord Frost's research. No longer content merely to magnify myself as his assistant, I now hoped to engineer recognition and reward as a peer and co-author of the breakthroughs we pursued."

"Had you even any medical degree yet?" Rutherford asked.

"I… am still accorded the MA (Cantab)," Shrewsbury admitted with chagrin. It was as if the tale were telling him now, rather than the other way 'round, but Wendell felt compelled to make Rutherford see this was no mere madness to be coddled and contained at some gentle sanatorium. If even his old friend could not be made to see the truth, then what purpose had there been to this whole exercise?

"Under the devious influence of my invasive parasite, I had become convinced that practical experience trumped any mere certificate bestowed by tired old wine-soaked dons. I imagined myself Lord Frost's *right hand man*, and merely sought to help others, including himself, recognize the fact." He shook his head in self-disgust.

"On the fateful night in question, I arrived at the laboratory hours earlier than necessary—as had been my overeager practice for so many months by then—and, predictably, found myself alone there. I lit the lamps, reviewed Lord Frost's most recent notes, and set about preparing the materials and devices for that evening's procedure. It was to be a challenging extraction. The subject was a deeply troubled young woman." Wendell shook his head sadly. "She had sought us out on the advice of Lord Frost's cousin in Dorset where they both resided. Her dreadful and relentless nightmares had brought her to fear sleep itself. Much like…" He trailed off with a small shudder. "We were, of course, earnestly determined to free her of this affliction.

"As I ignited the device's engines, and adjusted output levels, it suddenly seemed to me that stronger frequencies than normally applied were surely called for in a case of this severity." As the dreadful reminiscence grew more vivid, Shrewsbury became all but unaware of his rapt audience. "I can still recall how the machine hummed to life under my fingers, as if eager for my commands… I turned the knobs higher, strangely convinced that the apparent strength of that night's quarry demanded strength in return, and that my employer's usual practices were overly cautious, perhaps to the point of endangering our subject." The recollection filled Wendell with an urge to sob, which he manfully suppressed. "I assured myself that Lord Frost would examine the machine himself, once he arrived, and override my decisions if he chose to.

"My preparations were barely concluded, however, when I heard a tentative knock at the laboratory's inner door. I went to see who it could be and found Miss Ingleside, our unfortunate client, arrived at least an hour early. The housekeeper, it seemed, had simply escorted her up and left her at the laboratory door. I remember thinking she should be reprimanded for such conduct. In retrospect, Miss Ingleside's premature arrival seems uncannily well timed to facilitate what was about to happen. I have sometimes wondered since if these creatures may be capable of some communication over distance with others of their kind. Could her parasite have conspired with mine?" Wendell bowed his head. "This is yet another question we will likely never answer, now." He sighed deeply.

"I recall that Miss Ingleside was dreadfully pale. There were dark, greenish patches below her sallow eyes. Her dress hung off her thin, brittle frame as if off a broomstick. She asked timidly if I were Lord Frost, and I told her, no, that I was his associate. Flooded with compassion for the poor creature, I invited her to sit down in the room's only chair, to which she would be later strapped for the procedure." Wendell reached once more for his brandy glass, which Rutherford had quietly topped up. "She sat there shivering, though the laboratory was quite comfortable. Only when she declined the offer of a blanket did I realize that she was trembling with fright, if not exhaustion too, rather than from cold.

"My heart filled with the tender, urgent desire to assist her at once. I felt bizarrely certain that Lord Frost would heartily approve of my decision not to make her wait a moment longer for relief. I had performed this sort of procedure countless times by then, or at any rate assisted Frost in doing so, which seemed much the same thing to me at that ill-fated moment."

Rutherford made a small, apprehensive noise, and rose to set the last few coals onto the fire, nudging them into place with a long wrought-iron poker.

"Have I been wrong to tell you this?" Shrewsbury asked.

"Of course not," his host replied, settling back into his chair. "It is just… not the kind of tale to be listened to in darkness."

"Of course. Quite right," said Shrewsbury. "It was foolishness. Utter madness. Lord Frost was a meticulous researcher, always careful to maintain precise records and complete control of each experiment. Though I'd been permitted to maintain and calibrate the engines and delivery systems, and pump out the collection jars upon capture of an organism, there was never to be any hand but his on that final switch… He had made that very clear." Shrewsbury gripped his glass, fairly quivering with outrage at his own disastrous arrogance. "Yet, after months, I now surmise, of my nightmarish handler's grooming, I somehow felt myself perfectly qualified to help this poor girl without waiting for Lord Frost, whom I did not expect for some time yet."

Rutherford sat in silence, his face blank of any readable reaction to such hubris.

"I bade Miss Ingleside make herself as comfortable as possible, and adjusted the chair's restraining belts to her small frame, then fastened her delicate arms into the leather straps upon its own. Lord Frost and I had quickly discovered how forcefully the distressed parasites could cause our subjects to thrash about in pursuit of escape once the procedure began.

"She quavered a bit, as I finished my work, but I had explained the treatment to her very carefully before strapping her in, so she did not complain. I placed the extraction bell over her head, and sealed it around her neck, made sure her breathing-tube was functioning properly, and, after giving her a final, reassuring pat, stepped to the controls."

Shrewsbury put his head into his hands in abject misery. "I wish I could claim to have hesitated before placing my hand upon that lever… but I did not. All was ready and checked two or three times over. I was fully confident of all my calculations.

"I threw the master switch.

"Steam billowed from exhaust portals just outside the laboratory windows, as usual. Miss Ingleside gave a small shriek, muffled by the diving bell and breathing tube, which, as I've mentioned, was not unusual either. I cautioned her to be still, but she responded by writhing even more aggressively against her constraints. Seeing how mercilessly the beast within drove her, I surmised it must be very powerful indeed. Motivated by this speculation, I increased the frequencies yet another notch—hoping to drive her tormentor out the faster."

"I do not think I like where this tale seems to lead," Rutherford murmured.

"Nor should you," Wendell answered sadly. "As you've clearly guessed, guided by my own still undiscovered passenger, I kept finding reasons to turn the dials further up, just the merest nudge. Miss Ingleside began to thrash about so wildly that she actually managed to free one of her wrists from its strap, and, a second later, her upper arm. *So much strength in such a tiny frame!* I thought, rushing to stop her as she began to rip the other straps away with her freed hand. I grappled with her, but her strength proved truly superhuman, and I found no way of gaining ground against her efforts without risking harm to her myself. I had no idea what to do.

"Even more unfortunately, the panel of controls was close enough to the chair that as we struggled with each other, she was able to reach out and slap frantically at its knobs and dials, apparently attempting to stop the procedure. All she succeeded at was boosting half the frequencies to levels I would never have employed in any state of mind. Worse yet, as they were knocked completely out of calibration, the sonic instruments began to generate dissonant vibrations that rattled half the objects in the room, including my own teeth.

"I still see that moment, with such dreadful clarity, as the bell jars began to shatter from the sound."

"The nightmares!" Rutherford gasped. "Did they escape?"

"Oh yes. But not just to flee, I soon discovered. Abandoning the struggling woman, I leapt for the collection of vibrating jars, attempting to contain the damage, but had hardly started before the air seemed filled with terrifying sounds." Wendell brought his hands up to the sides of his head. "I barely heard Miss Ingleside begin to scream anew as the room filled suddenly with monstrous forms. I felt pressed about with filthy, sweating, stinking bodies. I cried out, trying to push them back, but they simply pressed in harder.

"Panic turned to terror in my head and chest. The air became rank, entering my lungs like viscous, septic syrup. I no longer saw the laboratory at all—but the interior of a crowded passenger-coach, loaded with convulsing corpses. It careened down a narrow, winding street, rocking wildly as all of us inside it cried in panic, gouging, scratching, kicking to get out. I tasted blood, felt it coat and clog my throat!

"Gasping, I groped desperately around me for a pull-cord to alert the driver—but everywhere I reached, I just felt more putrescent flesh, more rotting, blood-drenched clothing, matted hair, ragged fingernails… When my hand at last found what I was sure must be the cord, I yanked upon it with all my strength, and was rewarded with a flash of light and heat, as if the very coach around me had exploded.

"Amidst this maelstrom, I heard the shouts of my employer. As if punctured by his voice, the illusory coach vanished, and I found myself lying on the floor as Lord Frost struggled nearby to free the now unconscious Miss Ingleside from her remaining restraints. The laboratory was engulfed in flames! Hoses had been torn away, spewing the highly combustible experimental fuels we used to heat our boilers all about. These had somehow ignited. Gazing about in horror, I saw that all of the laboratory's accoutrements had been scattered and demolished! Had I caused all this damage flailing at imagined corpses?

"Lord Frost bellowed something at me, seeming angry and confused. I drew breath to explain myself, but my lungs were stung by smoke and searing heat, and I was merely wracked with coughing.

"'Get up, man! Help me get her out of here!' he cried, trying to drag me to my feet.

"Still influenced by my internal foe, I heard only blame and outrage in my mentor's voice. After all my efforts to win his admiration, he clearly now felt nothing but contempt for me. I found his censure quite unfair. He had no idea of the trials that had befallen me. With his help, I pulled myself upright at last, still intent upon explaining. But before I could, his face became that of the Devil itself—twisted, red and leering. I shrieked and scrambled back, shoving him away... quite forcefully..." Shrewsbury's restraint failed at last, and the anguished sob that had been building in his chest—for years—erupted. "I pushed him... straight into the conflagration!"

"Shrewsbury!" Rutherford exclaimed. "Calm yourself!"

"*Oh, dear God!*" Shrewsbury wailed, rising from his chair. "*Dear God, I killed him, Rutherford!*"

"It is but a memory!" Rutherford shouted, rising now as well to grab Wendell's arms as if to keep him from destroying the study as Wendell knew he'd ruined Frost's laboratory in his panic. "No one seeks to hurt you here! Be calm, old friend!... Be calm."

"I could have saved him, Rutherford," Wendell sobbed, collapsing into his friend's bewildered embrace. "I could have saved them both, but I just stood there, frozen, immobilized by the sudden understanding of what I had done—not just then, but all along." He wrenched himself from Rutherford's arms, and staggered back to fall into his chair. "That is when the demon within me finally made its presence known. It started whispering accusations, audibly gloating at how easily I had allowed myself to be manipulated—as it still does... to this very night."

"How could you have known?" his friend insisted, trying feebly to comfort him.

"How should I have not?" moaned Wendell. "In all the world, I was one of just a handful who *could* have known... Who *should* have known..."

"Shrewsbury, dear friend," his host insisted, "what is gained by such self-torment?"

"I saw him die," Shrewsbury whimpered. "It was too terrible... I ran, Rutherford." He buried his face in his hands again. "I left them both, and ran to save myself... It is only right that each night now I am required to return... Unable to run... Forced to watch..."

"There are doctors who can help you," Rutherford insisted. "There is no demon in your brain, my friend. Only guilt and horror, for which no one, least of all myself, could blame you after such an ordeal."

"They are free!" Shrewsbury rasped. "Do you not understand? With cause to fear us—no, to hate us even—and the only man who might have stopped them dead! By my hand!"

Rutherford seemed about to speak again, but they were interrupted by a loud banging at the front door of his residence. Startled, Rutherford looked at Wendell, as if wondering whether it were safe to leave him there, then headed for the study door. Before he reached it, however, Mrs. Lamblittle burst in, followed by two burly constables.

"There he is!" the housekeeper cried, pointing at Shrewsbury. Wendell made no effort to resist as the men hurried past her to seize him. Well-drunk on brandy, and quite depleted from so many months of such badly interrupted sleep, he just collapsed into their grasp.

"What is the meaning of this?" Rutherford demanded. "Unhand him! He is my guest here."

"He's no proper guest, Mr. Rutherford, no he ain't!" Mrs. Lamblittle broke in shrilly. "It was treason he were talking! Said so himself. Treason and murder. I heard him, I did! I were listening in the hall the whole time, and glad of it." At the scowl this brought to her employer's face, she added, "I'm saving us all, and you'll thank me for it later, I've no doubt."

Wendell watched his host struggle to frame some response, and lose that struggle. *Quite wise, old friend*, he thought. *An up and coming barrister might not want to be heard defending a murderer caught in the act of treason. And just as well. If I am lucky, they will hang me now. Then again, to sleep, perchance to dream... Aye, there's the rub...*

As the constables hustled Wendell toward the door, he felt the thing within him seize his body, and a shrill, unnatural laughter burst involuntarily from his mouth. Wendell screwed his eyes shut, trying to suppress this violation of his sovereign self, but to no avail. The thing inside him pried his lips apart once more, and a voice that he had never heard before outside of dreams screeched, "Self-destructive fools! You think yourselves so wise, your science so indomitable, but without *us* there can *be* no dreams! And what will England be without its dreams?" it cackled. "What will England be?"

By the Sea

This was my first invited story—a huge thrill. The post-apocalyptic anthology Grants Pass *was looking for stories about people's responses to the hope of a new start, in a safe place, after the world ended—Grants Pass, Oregon. Some of the stories were to involve people believing the story and trying to get to Grants Pass; others were to be rejections of that dream. The character of Elizabeth popped into my head, and the rest of the story just... unfolded.* Grants Pass *appeared in the summer of 2009 and won an Australian Shadows Award for best horror anthology.*

Elizabeth Barnett stood on the veranda, lifting a wiry hand to shade her eyes as she watched Christos sail away. The sun gleaming off the Mediterranean assaulted her, but the light was beautiful all the same. Sometimes the loveliness here made it hard to remember how thoroughly everything had gone wrong.

Or maybe she was just being an old fool. Sunlight, kilometers of pale beaches thrust against bright blue water, hills covered with scrubby brush, khaki-colored rocks, and the occasional dark green cypress tree—it was not enough to hide the fact that she was very likely the last person left on the island. The last living person, anyway.

She snorted and turned away from the sea before Christos, in his little white sailboat, had moved out of sight. No point in watching him go. He wouldn't be back. She'd seen to that—they'd fought for weeks like rabid dogs. Or plague-infested weasels, more like. In the end, she'd set her teeth and scratched his lovely face with her long fingernails until the blood touched his chin. And still he stood, pleading.

"Beth, come to Grants Pass, I know it's real."

"It's a lie, and you're never going to get there on that damn fool thing anyway."

"This is our only chance."

"We have no chance."

He'd simply stood there, looking at her.

"I have no chance," she'd finally added, her voice bitter and dry. "I'm seventy-eight years old, and you know my health. I'll die out on the water."

"You'll die here." He'd leaned forward, almost touching her, but holding back.

That was when she'd scratched him, digging in with every last shred of strength she had. It was either that or touch him in a different way, and she'd held on to at least that much dignity, through it all.

Now she would not watch him go. The world had died; what difference would one more person make?

~ o O o ~

"Kayley's journal," Beth said out loud as she heated a slab of halloumi over a wood fire she'd built in the stove. Bitter as it still was, at least her voice had lost its edge of testy near-panic, she thought. Three days Christos had been gone, and although she was growing accustomed to the terrible silence, she still felt the need to speak to the air from time to time.

She'd made this batch of the cheese herself, and she was proud of it, even if it didn't have the tenacity of the stuff she'd been able to find at the market when she'd first bought this property, fifteen years ago. Or even the weaker but still salty-sweet cheese that Christos had come up with, using the thin milk they'd managed to glean from the last goat.

"Bunch of adolescent fantasies."

She might as well talk aloud. There was no one to hear, no one to judge. No one to answer.

… No one to brush her thinning grey hair, to stroke her hard and ropy shoulder muscles, to clear the weeds from her front walk. No one to argue back to her. To bring her a drink when the sun went down. To glance up from his work in what passed for her garden, his dark eyes smoldering at her as he…

"Stop it, you stroppy old cow," she muttered to herself. She finished toasting the cheese and then stood over the stove, eating it with callused fingers that hardly felt the heat of it.

Then she stood, staring unseeing out the window as she remembered.

~ o O o ~

Elizabeth Barnett, international best-selling author of *The Caged Sword* series of dark and twisted romantic fantasy novels. Elizabeth Barnett, the toast of London, New York, and Prague literary circles—at least, those circles civilized enough to consider the genre of romantic fantasy. Elizabeth Barnett, who shocked the world by retiring at the height of her fame and purchasing a three-million-pound estate in the hills outside Larnaka, Cyprus, with her third husband, James—seventeen years her junior and famous in his own right as the developer of those ridiculous computer games that children played, instead of reading decent fantasy novels.

"The writing was on the wall," she said to the window. The sea shimmered far below her, and Christos was not coming back.

~ o O o ~

James had been one of the first to die. Maybe he had even brought the plague back with him, from his last trip to France… but if he hadn't, someone else would have. The plane had been full of people, and there had been ten more flights after that, before all air traffic had stopped. Beth had sat with him in the Apollonion Hospital on the Greek side of Nicosia—even then, with the wall down, the city was still deeply divided between Turk and Greek—holding his hand as he coughed blood, sobbed, and finally choked out his last breath. The sad-eyed doctors had searched their stub of what remained of the Internet, pumped him full of expired antibiotics, anti-inflammatories, and steroids, and mopped up the effluent that had poured from her beautiful husband. He had died all the same.

"You filthy bastards! You swine, you cowards, you Mediterranean cretins!" she had shrieked at them, wailing and beating at the chest of the infuriatingly calm chief resident. He'd stood and listened to her, blinking his large dark eyes, waiting for her to wind down.

It was those Greek eyes that had prompted her to move here in the first place, when she could finally afford it. Not this doctor's eyes per se, of course; but dark Greek eyes in general, remembered from some long-ago junket she'd taken with her editor and her agent. Three middle-aged British women on holiday, slumming in a sea of sweet Greek manflesh. Beth had always remembered that trip, long after she'd married reedy blond James. She'd always intended to end her life here.

Just not like this.

Beth shook her head, still standing at the window, the fire gone cold in the stove, the uneaten bits of halloumi sticking to her fingers, cloying. She felt sick to her stomach, and wondered for the thousandth time if the plague had finally found her as well.

"No, nothing can kill you, old loon," she said aloud, half-affectionately. She turned away from the window, taking the greasy pan from the stove. She set it in the sink without rinsing it. There wasn't much water left in the bucket anyway; she'd have to go to the stinking well for more.

Instead she went to the basement, or what passed for one. It was a low space half-dug into the rocky hillside, intended for a wine cellar. But Cypriot wine was harsh and sour, and her English palate had never adapted.

She stood blinking in the dim space, waiting for her old eyes to adjust, and pulled down a fresh bottle of Bombay gin. She stocked the large bottles—1.75 litres—even though they were hard to maneuver above her glass, especially as the evening progressed. Before leaving the cellar, Beth counted the bottles. There were eighteen, not including the one she had in her hand.

"That's all you've got," she said. "After that, it's all over." Her words were swallowed by the earthen walls.

~ o O o ~

Seven weeks after Christos sailed away, Elizabeth Barnett sat in a leather chair with one of her own books in her lap—book seven of *The Caged Sword* series, and her personal favourite: *Man and His Weaknesses*. She could hardly stand to read books written by anyone else. They were never written as she would have done; they were over too soon, or too late; the relationship between the hero and heroine never rang true; and the endings were always contrived, seemingly invented merely for the purpose of making a good story.

Well, of course they were, she knew that. But other people's imaginations, to Beth, just seemed… inferior.

So she read her own work. And certainly there was plenty of it. When twilight fell, she lit a fire in the hearth and a small candle by her chair, refilled the glass of gin, and picked up the book again, chuckling to herself as Larion prepared to storm the Fair Castle Rhuligel and save Marleena. Naturally, Marleena would refuse to be saved; that was when the fireworks would start. "Oh, you minx, you little vixen," she murmured.

That was when she heard the crash from the back yard.

Beth froze, holding the heavy hardcover on her lap. What was it? Definitely something large. Another goat?

She heard another noise, not a crash this time, more like a bump. It was closer to the house.

She slowly got to her feet, leaving the book on the chair. A goat would be good news: it would mean milk, or at least meat. She walked over to the doorway and peered down the hall, craning to see the back of the house, but it was too dark inside. A small window was set high on the back wall of the living room for cross-ventilation.

She sidled over to the window and stood on tiptoes, but could not reach to see out.

She could hear, though. She heard footsteps.

"Who's there?" she called, making her voice strong, projecting to the rear of the audience as she had done for years.

The footsteps stopped.

A goat would have kept on, ignoring her in its desperate search for food. What other animal could it be? The dogs were all long dead, eaten mostly by one another, and then by the remaining people.

And the people were long dead as well. Most of them, anyway. If one in ten thousand humans had survived the plagues, that would have left Cyprus with a population of eighty. Not counting tourists, of course—but the tourist trade had slowed greatly before the final plagues. The last ten flights in had been matched by as many flights out before the planes were grounded for good.

Moving quietly, Beth left the living room and went into the hallway that led to the back door. It was darker here, and there was still a little light outside. She made her way to the window in the door, staying back a bit so as not to be seen.

A man stood in her back yard. He was staring at the house, the roof. The chimney. He must have smelled the smoke from her fire.

Ignoring the clutch of fear in her chest, Beth studied the man. He looked terrible; he was clearly starving, and filthy. But he didn't seem plague-bit. He was about fifty, maybe, though it was hard to tell in his condition—no, she corrected herself. It was impossible to tell. He could be thirty or seventy, who knew?

Anyway, he appeared weak. Frail as Beth was, he was likely not a significant threat.

By the looks of him, he was not Greek or Turk or Armenian or any of the other more customary inhabitants of the island. He could be at least as English as she was.

What were the odds?

As she watched, the man suddenly became animated. She sucked in her breath and pulled back farther from the window. He took a step toward the house, then stumbled and pitched forward.

"Oh," Beth said, as the man landed on his face on her cobblestones.

~ o O o ~

He lay on a narrow bed in the guest room, still unconscious. Beth cleaned and bandaged his bloody forehead, and brought in some more halloumi—the last she had, it would be canned food after this unless she found more milk—in case he woke up. He was breathing, but unsteadily; his temperature seemed high, but she was no doctor. Beth had never been a mother either, had never wiped a fevered brow as people did in her novels. Maybe he was plague-bit. But no, there were no buboes, there was no swelling. And the only blood was from his cut.

She sat in a hard chair beside him, biting her lip. It had taken much of her strength to drag him here, and lift him up onto the bed. She wouldn't have been able to do it at all if he hadn't been so emaciated.

The man's eyelids flickered and he gave a small moan.

Beth leaned forward, peering into his face. "Are you awake?"

"Ah…" One eye fluttered open, then shut. He gave a long, sour exhale.

Beth touched his shoulder, giving him a light shake, and touched his forehead again, next to the bandage. "Wake up."

He was silent a moment, then both eyes opened. "Wh… mou… uh…"

"Do you speak English?" she asked.

Now his eyes opened wider. "Yes."

"That's good." Beth stared into his face before looking away. "But then of course you do, everyone does."

The man blinked, staring at her. He asked, "Where… where is everyone?" His accent was flat, broad—American, perhaps.

"What do you mean?"

He swallowed and glanced around the room. His face filled with fear. Terror, even. "Nobody's here, are they?"

"I'm here." Was the man a fool? Quite likely. Most people were fools, and if they hadn't been before the world fell apart, they certainly were now. Or, rather, they were dead now, the vast majority of them. And the fools like Christos had sailed off to follow a dream, a computer hoax, a cruel fantasy someone had written, about a place called Grants Pass, where society would begin again. As if there was any chance of that.

"You..." The man struggled to sit up, and Beth didn't stop him. He leaned against the pillows and shivered in the heat. "Who are you?"

"Elizabeth Barnett." She watched his eyes as she said her name, but he gave no flicker of recognition. "Who are you?"

"Tyler." He blinked and swallowed, and she stared at his throat, but saw no swelling. "Tyler Anderson."

"I am pleased to meet you, Tyler Anderson," Beth said, slipping into the tone she would use when greeting over-eager fans.

Tyler closed his eyes, leaned against the headboard, then opened them again. He had already smeared the white coverlet with his filthy, stained hands. But without water, she'd have no way of washing them. Everything was just going to get dirtier and dirtier from here on out, until everything was the color of the sun-baked earth. Including herself.

"Is it true that California...?" His eyes appealed to her as he broke off, then started again. "Is San Diego really ruined?"

Now Beth stared at him. "That was two years ago."

~ o O o ~

She was not a nurse, she told herself that she didn't care if he lived or died, but for some reason she fed him and cleaned him up a bit, and changed the bandage on his forehead. The bleeding slowed and stopped; the wound would heal.

Once he was cleaner, she saw that he was even younger than she'd realized. Probably in his twenties, though he'd lived a hard life during those few years. Well, who hadn't, lately?

He slept a lot, and ate the halloumi she brought, and the canned foods. Beth began to wonder if she'd need to make another raid on the neighboring houses, or even—God forbid—venture down into Larnaka again. Christos had packed the small cellar full before he'd left, even as he'd continued to beg her to change her mind. But an old woman didn't eat nearly as much as a young man.

Within a week, Tyler was able to walk around a little, and a day or two later, he washed himself, using most of a bucket of brackish water. Beth brought him pants and a cotton shirt that had belonged to James, handing them to him without comment.

Tyler dressed himself, then came and found Beth in the living room.

"Drink?" she asked, indicating the bottle of Bombay on the sideboard.

"Oh my God," he said, his blue eyes glittering with a touch of madness. Or at least that's how she would have written it, as she thought about it later. In the moment, she only thought, *Now, there's a healthy young man who appreciates quality gin.*

He poured himself a full three fingers of the stuff, his arms shaking as he lifted the heavy bottle with both hands. Sitting in the second leather chair, he raised the glass and smiled at her.

She lifted her half-empty glass, and they clinked.

He took a generous swallow of the gin, closing his eyes as it went down, and turned to face Beth, grinning. "Oh, man. That's incredible."

She lifted an eyebrow. "I take it it's been a while?"

"Ha!" It wasn't a laugh; more like an ironic bark, and a bit too loud. "Yes, it has. I'd say two years, at least."

Beth leaned forward, holding him with her eyes. "So, Tyler, tell me: what do you know of what has gone on in our world these last few years?"

He took another drink, not quite as gulpish as his last, but she still noted it. *If he drinks like that, eighteen bottles won't be near enough,* she thought. "Not a whole hell of a lot, to tell you the truth."

"What's an American boy doing in Cyprus anyway, now, knowing nothing? If I didn't know better, I'd say you've been in prison."

Now he did laugh, though it was as bitter as before. "Why, yes, as a matter of fact, I was in prison." He finished the glass of gin, setting it quite deliberately on the table beside his chair, next to the cut-glass coaster.

o O o ~

It turned out to be the usual story—young tourist arrested for drugs in a country with little patience for such things, thrown into prison to teach him a lesson. It would have had the usual outcome—his parents sending money or coming to retrieve him, a whole lot of nuisance and no lasting ill effects—except for the unfortunate timing of the apocalypse.

Tyler spoke no Greek, no Turkish, nothing but English. His parents had presumably died in the initial earthquake, but he didn't know for sure, as communications went down almost immediately thereafter. The plagues had come then, sweeping across the world. He had known almost nothing of this as he languished in prison, waiting for rescue, for anything. His guards changed weekly, then daily, with no explanation. Then one died right in front of him, and he finally, belatedly, understood.

"How did you get out of the locked cell?" Beth asked him, swirling her drink.

He shrugged, looking down. "Reached out, took the keys from him. I thought for sure I'd get the plague then, but I guess not." His words were casual, but his face was bleak. There was more to the story. If he wanted to tell her, he would.

He was vague on the timing—how long he had been out of the prison, surviving on the rough countryside. But that was because he didn't know, Beth felt, not because he was trying to deceive. It had obviously been a while. He must have wandered the entire island before finding her. Christos had come to her in the first few weeks after the initial devastation, when the few survivors were banding together. And Christos had stayed with her when the others had left the island. Until he, too, could no longer resist the empty promise of a dream.

~ o O o ~

Tyler's strength grew, and soon enough he was poking around the place, exploring neighboring houses, trying to figure out ways to improve their lot. Just like Christos had done. Beth was pleased enough to have the help, although she'd been doing perfectly well on her own, thank you very much. Tyler began talking more, yammering on to her in the evenings about everything and nothing—his boyhood in California, girls he'd liked, his world travels on a shoestring. She took to retiring early, going to her room with a book and a candle where she could read in peace until she felt like sleeping.

"What's this?" he asked one day. Beth was in the kitchen, trying to decide whether to light a fire to heat up the canned lakerda or just eat it cold. She turned around at the sound of his voice. He was holding a sheaf of papers.

Beth recognized them at once. "Where did you get that?"

Tyler shrugged. "I was cleaning up, I found them. Is it true?"

"Give me those." Beth reached out for the papers, but Tyler held them away from her. "I asked you where you got that."

He stared at her, his eyes wide and needful. "We could find other people. We could go; we don't have to stay here!"

"Put that down. You're a goddamned fool, do you know that?"

He started to say something else, but she interrupted. "I said, *put that down*, and don't speak of it to me again."

He paled and set the papers on the counter, backing out of the kitchen.

Beth took the Grants Pass email hoax, intending to put it back in her bedroom, where Tyler had had no business snooping in the first place. She had made it perfectly clear that her room was off limits, yet where else had he gotten it? It was the only copy.

She stopped at the doorway, thinking for a moment, and then went back into the kitchen to light the fire.

~ o O o ~

But once he'd read it, he wouldn't let it go. He was worse than Christos. "We can be saved!"

"You go ahead if you like," she said. "I'm fine here."

"I can't leave you here. You're, um, you'll die." He was shaking his head, stubborn, desperate. "Please!"

She laughed in his face. "You were going to tell me I'm old. I *know* I'm old, and I know I'm going to die. And therefore, I'm not going anywhere."

"We can take a boat—there's plenty of boats left in the harbor."

"And petrol?" She sneered at his naiveté. "Do you know how many people already left the island? You don't think they left a lot of petrol lying around? That's why Christos sailed, you idiot American. And now he sleeps with the sharks."

He bristled. "You don't know that for sure. And yes, I am American—what of it? Why shouldn't I want to go home?"

She waved at the harbor. "I am not stopping you."

~ o O o ~

That night, she heard him sobbing in his bedroom, long after she'd gone to her own. "Mom… Oh, Mom…"

So that was it: he missed his mommy. And he'd fixated on Beth, in some sort of perverse mother-complex way. She snorted to herself. "More like a grandmother."

But the next morning he was at her again. She had to shout at him again to get him to stop. He stormed out without eating breakfast, and spent the day somewhere else. Down at the water, if she was any judge.

He returned at twilight, calm, not mentioning where he'd been. She offered him a glass of gin, and they sat on the veranda, drinking together.

After two drinks, he said, "I found a boat. I think it could make it across the ocean. And it's got a full tank of gas. So I know I could find more."

"I'm not leaving," she said, without turning her head. The sun glimmered red on the water as it sank. "I hate America. And I forbade you to speak of this." She set her glass down, got up, and went inside.

She walked all the way to her bedroom, then through it into her small private bath. Of course she didn't use it as a bathroom any more—the septic tank was overfull, and there was nobody to call to come and clean it out—but it had other uses. She opened the medicine cabinet, first looking, then rummaging, then yanking everything out. But they weren't there.

He'd not only stolen the email from her bedroom. He'd also raided her stash of narcotics, carefully hoarded from James' final illness.

Beth stood before the ransacked medicine cabinet, shaking with anger. She had to make him leave. He was not like Christos—he was worse, far worse. Bad enough that he would harangue her, try to control her. But that he should steal from her—that he should steal *drugs* from her—a man who had already gone to prison for drugs—oh, this was not good. A man whose life she'd saved.

"Not good," she whispered.

She felt a prickle on the back of her neck and wheeled around. He was standing in the doorway of the small bathroom. She hadn't even heard him come in.

He was pale, and shaking. Now that she knew, she recognized the signs easily. He must have taken several pills, and then two—at least two—glasses of gin on top of that. "Beth," he started, taking a step towards her. The name was a bit slurred, the consonants softer than they should be.

"Get out of here," she said.

He took another step, and now he was right in front of her. He reached up and took her shoulders in his hands, hard, and shook her. It hurt. She pushed back against his chest, trying to twist out of his grip, but he was decades younger than she, and very strong. "We... have... to... go," he said, staring at her even as he rattled her thin bones. His eyes were too liquid, too glossy. "I'll *make* you go."

She pushed harder, and he abruptly let go, staggering back and bumping into the wall behind him. He didn't seem to notice. "You're drunk," she said. "Go and lie down. We'll talk about this in the morning."

He looked at her, wary. "You mean it? We'll talk about it?"

She shrugged, resisting the urge to rub her throbbing shoulders. "You are in no condition to talk now."

He kept staring at her, then turned and went to his own bedroom. She stood in the bathroom a long time, shaking, listening as he fell onto his bed. He was snoring within a few minutes. Only then did she pull her shirt open and examine the bruises, peering into the mirror. He'd crushed her shoulders so hard she could almost see the imprint of his fingerprints.

Beth re-buttoned her shirt and left the bathroom. She knew what she had to do.

~ o O o ~

She stood over his bed as he snored. He looked so helpless and frail, lying there. Almost innocent. Though she'd never had children, sometimes she could understand the appeal. Having someone to love, someone to take care of… Of course, she'd had James for that.

Tyler was somebody's son. His mother and father had loved him and raised him, and had let him go, had watched as he had flown the nest. He'd flown far—all the way across the world, where he'd gotten in trouble and caught up in the terrible things that humanity had done to itself. Maybe he'd deserved better. Maybe not. Who knew any more?

But it was too late now. There was no better to be had, and if he was going to refuse to understand that, there was nothing she could do about it.

She raised the knife, leaning over him to reach the far side of his neck. In book 8 of *The Caged Sword* series, *A Clutch of Posies*, Marleena finds she must murder the Lord of Terror, using only a dull kitchen knife. In her fear and hesitation, she botches the job at first, and he awakens and threatens her, but in a stroke of luck, as he is leaping onto her, the knife nicks his jugular and he dies. Then all the Sisters are freed, and the land rejoices.

Tyler's white, exposed neck was surprisingly tough at first, despite Beth's knife being as sharp as it could be. She remembered slaughtering the goats, and pushed harder. When she thought of it as butchering meat, it came easily. She even knew to step back so as not to get soaked with his blood.

The covers, of course—that was another story. Tyler's blood spurted at first, another rush with every beat of his heart. Impossible to believe there could be so much; but the goats had been even worse. Soon it ebbed out more slowly, flowing down his body as he twitched, gurgled, and stilled. It spread across the white cotton coverlet, pooling and sinking in, threading fanlike out along the folds of the fabric. Beth watched it for a long time, unmoving, and finally turned to go.

She shut the door of the guest bedroom behind her, turning the latch that would keep it fast. The corpse would smell at first, but she knew that in this hot, dry climate, it would soon desiccate, even mummify. In any event, she could put a towel under the door if she had to. She wouldn't need that room any time soon.

She walked down the hall to the kitchen, washed the knife, and laid it on the counter to dry. Then, she went to her bookshelf and pulled down the final book in her series: *Alone at Heart.*

Night fell as Elizabeth Barnett sat on the veranda with a tumbler of warm gin, the book unopened beside her, and waited for her world to finish ending.

Water Proof

By SHANNON PAGE *and* CHAZ BRENCHLEY

As I mentioned, I love collaborative writing. I adore the process of bouncing my words and thoughts off another writer's brain, and coming up with something greater, sometimes weirder, than either of us would have done alone. I've long been a fan of my friend Chaz's lush, gorgeous prose; when he agreed to write a story with me, I was overjoyed.

Though this appeared online at Buzzy Magazine *in August of 2012, we wrote it several years before that—before Chaz married Karen Williams. I did ask him if we should change the main character's name. He assures me that Karen loves the story as is.*

O f course Karen was the best woman for the job. That went without saying. In fact, if Melanie had claimed it, Karen would certainly have argued her own case. In front of Grant, if necessary. Karen wasn't afraid of Grant. Not one little bit.

But that wasn't how it had gone down. Instead, Melanie had taken it upon herself to get the chains and the knife and the reinforced table, had secured the warehouse and the whiskey, had even lured the man from his downtown hotel at midnight and dismissed his driver. Okay, fine, carry on.

Then, without batting a false eyelash, Melanie had handed the knife to Karen.

Who had not hesitated, not at all. No. She was competent, well prepared and—what was the word—unflappable. She was unflappable, yes. Not susceptible to flap. Which meant handling what came, whatever came, however unexpected or unrehearsed.

Like the knife. That was unexpected.

Not to mention unpleasant.

Afterward, while they were cleaning up—rinsing hairs and blood off the blade, hosing down the table, picking stray gobbets of offal off of each other's clothes—Karen struggled with her emotions. It took her a while to even figure out what was bothering her, exactly. Melanie had handled the situation flawlessly, all the way through to the end there. And putting an end to it had properly been Karen's task; she was senior, after all. It was just… well, there was something more than insidious, inappropriately dominant about the way Mel had slapped the knife into Karen's hand and stood back, hands on hips, that sly *show-me* grin on her face.

It made Karen mad all over again just to remember it.

At least the grin had vanished, once the blood began to splatter.

"What?" she grunted, holding the knife two-handed as she tugged it down from sternum to groin. "You weren't expecting blood?"

It was hard to cut cleanly the way she'd been trained, when he was bucking and writhing beneath the blade and the point kept catching on what must be vertebrae deep inside. Still, she lifted her eyes from her work just for a moment, just to see Melanie's mute shake of the head.

She grunted again and made the transverse cut, and thank God he was lying still at last; her hands were all-over slimy now, and she struggled to keep any kind of grip or direction on the knife. She'd been aiming to slice straight through his belly button both ways, and missed both ways. Not by much, though. And she felt the moment when the blade severed his spine; function mattered more than form.

Now he was just meat. Rank meat, spoiled. And smelling like it. She was glad to let the knife fall and step away from the table.

Melanie was still stuck on that question Karen had flung at her. Rubbing her spattered arms mechanically with a tissue—no, one of those moistened hand wipes, the chemical scent of it burning even through the reek of slaughter—she shook her head. "I didn't, no. Not blood. I thought, I thought they were… not human anymore. Not on the inside."

"Bodies don't change, just because something else possesses them." Karen uncapped the whiskey, reached out a long arm, and poured a libation into the man's gut, where she had opened him up so extremely. It was a gesture, but not meaningless. Tradition matters. They hacked the spirit out of him; they poured the spirit into him.

Did she imagine the hissing scorching sound, as spirit met flesh? Perhaps. Perhaps she did.

She tipped her head back, lifted the bottle, poured a steady dribble down her own throat. Didn't imagine the fierce bite of that, spirit on her own flesh, oh no.

"Oh, that's good."

She held the bottle out to Melanie. Waited a moment, nudged the other woman's shoulder with the butt-end of it. It was tradition again, this ritual drink after.

Melanie still didn't move to take the whiskey. She shook her head against a question not asked, muttered, "I've never killed a man before. Not, not a *human* man…"

Lady, you still haven't. Aloud, Karen said, "Melanie. Take a drink."

~ o O o ~

She did, at last. And then they cleaned up, and Karen reran it all through her head and got mad again, and then cocky again, the taste of triumph like the taste of whiskey, hot and savage inside her—*I did this*—and then shrugged all of that away. Cocky or angry or defiant—none of that would do a body any good at all. Or a spirit, either. Not when it came to facing Grant.

Time to put the bottle down, and turn her mind to water.

They left the body for Colin and his team. Wanting a shower, Karen let her mind drift as Melanie drove the van through the night streets. A sheen of moisture clung to the pavement: not quite mist, heavier than fog: a strange clammy dew, slick under the worn tires. Even the weather was shifting, it seemed. Laying something down, skin on skin, like a declaration: *What passes for normal, lady? That's not normal now.*

She knew it. If it had been possible only to know one thing, that would have been the one. As it was—well. She knew too much. And had done either too much—way too much—or else too little, depending.

It's usually a mistake, she thought, *to peer beneath the skin of things.*

$$\sim \text{o } O \text{ o} \sim$$

Melanie had slowed almost to a crawl on a narrow road overhung with trees darker than the city night. They loomed above, vehicles of emptiness, leaning across to touch one another like shadow-memories of shape.

"Where is it?"

"Grant's?" Karen stared out the windshield. Where *were* they? "Southside. You *know* that."

"No. The proof. You were meant to gather the proof. Where did you put it?"

Questions tumbled in Karen's startled mind like oils in turbulent water, clouding everything: How did Melanie know about the proof? And what did she want with it here, now? Or at all?

This wasn't the time to challenge her. Karen was uncomfortably aware that Melanie had reclaimed the knife.

There wasn't time to be clever, either. There never is.

"Oh, fuck it. I just... There was so much mess everywhere, y'know? I just forgot. Do you want to go back?"

"God, no," Melanie said, shuddering. "No, I don't. Besides, someone might be there by now." *It might be Colin.* "We'll just have to 'fess up and hope that Grant will trust us." *It's your head on the block.* She said that too, or she tried to—but it's harder to lie in body language. There was something else that concerned Melanie, and it was nothing to do with Grant.

After a minute, she shrugged and drove on: a little slowly, a little distracted. Karen took careful note of turnings, and of street signs as soon as there were any. Just in case it turned out to matter, later.

They had to cross the river to get to Southside. Halfway over the bridge, Karen said, "Pull over a second."

"What for?"

"Just do it. There's no traffic; we're safe enough. Right here, over water."

She could feel it, the flow of it deep inside her like a bass note thrumming, copper at the back of her tongue. Her skin tingled.

Melanie stopped the van, turned in her seat: her turn to stare. Karen held her hand out.

"Give me the knife."

"Wait, what? No! No, it's my—"

"It's got my fingerprints all over it."

"No, we wiped it."

"Not literally." *Numbfuck.* "The steel remembers. Do you think any blade ever would forget what we—what *I* just did with that knife? Come on, give. Grant will buy you another."

Blankly, Melanie handed over the knife. Blade first, like a threat. Karen pricked her finger as she took it, then opened the door and stepped out, went to the railing, and tossed the knife over.

Black water glimmered, too far below. Between the dark and the distance and the reflected city lights, she hadn't a hope of seeing the blade break water. Even so, she felt it. She thought she did. Felt something, at least: a satisfaction.

Perhaps it was only relief—but steel remembers, and steel is only an expression of water. Water has a long, long memory.

~ o O o ~

"I don't get it."

That was Melanie, driving them away.

"Call it an offering. Or a debt repaid." *Or just a precaution. Next time,*

I'm bringing my own knife. "Best not to forget who we work for." And then, a sharp response to bewilderment, "Oh, for crying out loud! Do you think we're some kind of free agents? Rebels on the edge? Down these mean streets a girl must walk who is herself as mean as they come? Get real, Melanie. We're clerks, is all."

"We work for Grant."

"Grant is just a bureaucrat." A bureaucrat with connections, but still. "It's the big picture that matters, is what I'm saying."

And whose picture you chose to stand in, and whether you had a foot in one frame and a foot in another, and…

~ o O o ~

"… And you brought the proof, of course?"

Karen didn't want to guess how much Grant had paid for the desk. Really, she thought, he should fit it with a glass top. Something that would wipe clean.

"Of course," she said, smiling, hoping that Melanie would see it reflected in his shades. "How else would you know it was the target that we killed, and not some poor innocent regular guy?"

She reached into her pocket—these coveralls were so foul already, nothing mattered—fished out the revolting thing, and tossed it very deliberately onto the pristine oxblood leather surface of the desk.

You shouldn't have doubted me. Old man.

If he was old. If he was a man. Who could tell?

Behind her she could almost feel Melanie's silent gasp, and the hot anger close on its heels. Karen let the smile linger on her face as she lifted hand to mouth and sucked the index finger slowly.

Grant's eyes widened; Melanie lost it altogether. Karen drew the finger out of her mouth and swallowed, relishing the sharp tang. It was mostly her own blood anyway, from the knife-prick on the bridge. "Don't get any on my shoes, please."

Doubled over, Melanie emptied the contents of her stomach onto

Grant's Kashmir carpet.

Karen took a small, deliberate step away and turned back to Grant. "So, about payment…"

The gray-haired man gazed at Karen a moment longer, then brought forth an oversized white handkerchief trimmed with a thin line of embroidery. He unfolded the cloth slowly, almost making a ritual of it, engulfed the slimy thing in fabric, and drew it up.

Blood soaked immediately through the white cloth. Was a fine linen barrier enough to protect him? Karen didn't know; the depth of her own ignorance hit her like a punch to the stomach.

Or perhaps that was just the sound—and the reek—of Melanie's misery behind her.

Karen shook her head. No distractions: not here, not now. She must focus on Grant. He was lifting the thing, bringing it closer to his face. His fingers seemed to absorb the ooze as soon as it touched his skin.

She had wagered wrong, then.

Just as well she had thought to add her own blood to the mix. She might actually live to see the dawn.

"Very interesting." Grant turned the bloody mass in his hand, glancing over at Karen. The dark glasses hid any expression, but his hand trembled. Age? Weakness? Or the other thing, too much power, barely controlled?

Or… was her own power somehow finding a way?

She blinked back at him, covering her thoughts as best she could. Melanie moaned. Karen could almost feel sorry for her.

Almost.

~ o O o ~

There was so much pretense in this room, masks beneath masks. Karen pretended to be baseline-human, normal, mercenary. Melanie pretended to be competent, experienced, loyal—though she'd given herself away quite thoroughly by now, and not only on Grant's rug. Karen hadn't forgotten that detour into unfamiliar streets, or the abortive demand.

And then there was Grant. The gray hair, the dark glasses, the thousand-dollar suit—he might be anything, almost, except what he appeared to be: a mature businessman with clean hands.

The only honest thing they had between them was the proof, that little worm of pseudoflesh he'd masked in his handkerchief. That at least was nothing more than it seemed to be.

When the public talked about worms, they meant the victims, the possessed: *They worm their way amongst us, seeming human, seeming just like us. Corrupt, demonic, deadly…*

You could always trust the public to confuse themselves and each other, blame the victim, burn the innocent. This time, though, burning the innocent was unavoidable, Karen's own job. There was no cure for the possessed. These twists of matter she cut out were a residue, a seedcase, something left behind; excision was always fatal. She'd stopped trying to be careful. Quick was better. Whether anything of the host abided, some deep-buried sense of horror, she had no idea. And no way to learn. Grant's people were presumably experimenting—why would they collect these proofs so assiduously if not to find out what they were, what they were made of, what they signified?—but Grant would never tell her anything. Whatever else he was or might be, he was an old-fashioned bureaucrat at heart: giving orders, sharing nothing, keeping his juniors in ignorance.

It was her private pleasure to be keeping her own secrets. He no more knew the truth about her than she did about him. Less: he didn't even know that there was more to learn.

She hoped he didn't know. It would be folly to underrate him.

He said, "I have another task for you. You'll be paid when it's done."

Of course. There was always something more. A mask beneath the mask, a task beneath the task.

Still. Every man contained his own proof. It was only a matter of finding it within him.

She said, "What do you want of me this time?"

~ o O o ~

At least he didn't make her bring Melanie. Karen drove the van back into the city, wondering if she'd ever see the other woman again. Carpets could be cleaned; it was the stained soul that was more problematic. Grant understood that.

She turned off the highway into side streets that narrowed into lanes. Here were trees again; she was miles from Melanie's detour, but here too they edged into the roadway, their wide roots cracking the sidewalk, their branches dropping leaves and seeds onto parked cars.

Trees. Why was she noticing trees so much? *Because they are another expression of water, fool.* Tonight was all about water, and what it brought. The icy depths of the river; the invasive fingers of the mist; the tap she and Melanie had run and run, to clean up after the extermination.

Near the end of the block, she slowed the van, searching for a number. There it was: a small pale house cowering underneath a huge and ancient willow. The tree with the closest affinity to water…

She left the van at the corner, blocking a fire hydrant. Let them try to give her a ticket.

A voice whispered from the shadows, "Ill met on a dark night."

Karen didn't shift her head or her pace. "I am not here to meet you, minion."

The house was only gently protected; she barely felt the touch of power as she climbed the steps, put her hand on the doorknob, waited three breaths and went inside.

Colin nodded at her from where he waited before the fire.

"No," Karen whispered. This was wrong, and more wrong. "Not you."

He was on his feet fast, his hands in her hair, his tongue in her mouth.

Her mad hot dumb lust flared up as it always did, every single goddamn time.

She didn't even fight it anymore. What was the point? It would only take longer, and she'd lose anyway. Moaning, she leaned into his body, pulling him close.

He kissed her harder, then reached for the buttons on her coveralls.

It was only then that he noticed all the blood.

Karen had to swallow down a smile as he pretended not to recoil. It was drying now; he didn't get much on his own clothes, but she could feel the revulsion in him, in the hesitation of his hands. Then he shrugged quickly and bit into her mouth again, masking it with lust of his own.

Just for a moment there, he had made her think of Grant again; but pretense became reality again soon enough, as their bodies followed well-worn pathways in the firelight. This was Grant's opposite, all down the line: urgent and immediate, naked and truthful and exposed. Nowhere to hide, and nothing left worth hiding…

~ o O o ~

Karen buttoned up the rank denim garment without washing herself first. Whatever she might take away from this, whatever she could keep: she knew its value. Long past any plans or dreams—only keeping her eyes open, her back covered, her mouth shut—all she could do was collect what might be useful, and try to stay ahead of the falling blade.

Mike… All unbidden, his sweet, uncertain face came back to her as she reached for her boots. She pushed the image away—and thought how strange it was that she could do that, where she couldn't thrust aside her simple animal need for Colin, her thrall to his desire. Mike was opposite again, orthogonal to this whole dark world of hers; and he would only stay safe so long as she kept him so. And that meant keeping on as she was going. Never pausing. Never doubting.

Never regretting.

Colin came back from the bathroom, buttoning his jeans. Not a word from either of them about what had just passed: some moments lay outside words, beyond reason.

"So," Karen said. "What did you do with him?"

Colin nodded to the darkened hallway at his back. Karen could see water-stained lavender wallpaper, curling up where the seams didn't quite meet. A door ajar, halfway back. Now that she was paying attention again, there was a low, fetid smell.

"Do I even need to look?"

He shook his head.

"All right." She was on her feet now, boots laced as tightly as her soul. It was all about control, in the end. Exposure and control. What you showed, and to whom; what you kept for yourself.

~ o O o ~

She drove slowly through the predawn streets, aimless, worried. Not about Grant. He would be angry, perhaps, that Colin had gotten to the body first, but it was hardly her fault. She'd been following procedure; he was the one making changes, late, too late. She thought likely it was blood that he wanted. He'd just have to look elsewhere. There was enough of it about, for pity's sake, in this city these days.

Pathways of information were as convoluted as city streets; she wanted a map, and didn't believe there was one. Any more than there was a single city, that a single map could chart. What Grant knew was not what Colin knew, far and far from whatever Mike might know.

And then there was what she knew herself, layers beneath layers…

She drove without purpose, just keeping the van on the move, winding through the streets. After a time, she pulled over and parked, rubbed her eyes, sighed. Only then did she realize what she was about: waiting for the sun to rise. Not returning to Grant while the night sky held sway overhead, cold and compressed. While the streams and eddies of power favored his kind, and not hers.

First light of dawn would be soon enough, to go to him. No matter that she was lost, and killing time; she wasn't too proud to admit even to herself that she was only roaming the streets at night for fear of…

Fear of what? Something indeterminate, something inchoate in the back of her head, in the corner of her eye: a whisper in the fog, a shadow astray, a touch of chill. She couldn't tell, except that there was something. It had been nagging at her all night: more than Melanie, surely, though thinking of the other woman made Karen mad all over again. Had it all started with the knife, the way Melanie had just handed it to her?

No, before that: when Grant had sent the two of them to do one woman's job in the first place. Belatedly, Karen wondered if she was meant to be training Melanie. Of course Grant wouldn't come right out and tell her so: she might think she was training her own replacement. She might be right…

Karen felt a faint tingle at the back of her throat and glanced out, suddenly aware of her surroundings. She was on the west side of the city, down by the river, after passing warehouses and parking lots and rusty, abandoned cargo containers with weeds growing tall around their bases. Dawn would be here soon, and she was a good twenty minutes from Grant's.

She turned the engine back on, hauled the van into a wide U-turn across the deserted quay, and drove.

~ o O o ~

The guards seemed hesitant, or distracted; or perhaps that was just Karen's night mood carrying forward into the cold gray sunless morning. She noted it and disregarded it, nodding back to them as she drove up the long lane to the main house. Just one more piece of information, useless without context.

Useless like her side of the bed tonight, her pillow, empty next to Mike. That had a context, but it was all evidence of absence.

Useless like his gentle sad sigh when he awoke alone—again!—that she could almost hear, clear across town.

She shook away the thought as she killed the headlights before they could shine in through the front windows of the house. Sentimental! Moping over Mike. As if that would do either of them any good. There was no room for sentiment here. For weakness. For doubt.

She hesitated, though, on the wide front porch, her hand already on the doorknob. Something was different; something made her doubt.

A new scent in the air.

A female scent.

Here? In the seat of Grant's power, his control...?

Stifling a sudden urge to flee, Karen stood taller and opened the door.

~ o O o ~

Well, at least the smell of vomit was gone.

In here, though, it had been replaced by the deep and pungent reek of blood. Not just any blood: the terrible, sour tang of the old ones. Grant's own, unless she missed her guess.

Well, that was information.

She stood just inside the front door, easing it closed behind her, keeping alert. Seeking. Listening, smelling, tasting the air.

Her eyes showed her only the palatial and familiar house, beautifully decorated, unthinkably expensive. A veneer over an ugliness beneath, fooling nobody. The broad, high-ceilinged atrium in which she stood gave off into a double set of hallways. Leftward lay Grant's private rooms, a focus of rumor and ignorance, the breath of fascination and the breath of terror intermixed. Karen had never been that way, and didn't need to go there now. She could follow her nose into familiar territory, rightward, to Grant's office suite.

Her nose didn't actually want her to go that way, wise nose; nor did any other part of her anxious, rebellious body. Her feet were very much against it.

Still. Here too there was fascination, as well as terror. All her life she'd been drawn toward the screamingly dangerous; why else would she do this job? For Mike's sake, she was meant to be working on that, but...

Putting her pricked finger in her mouth, Karen bit down hard and tasted blood, fresh and vigorous. Salt is the taste of life, the taste of hope; salt and water are the prime constituents of the tale of blood; and water—well. Water has a memory of shape.

Karen pulled an air of confidence about her and strode down the right-hand hallway toward Grant's office.

The door was closed. Oddly for such a private man, that was new. He used to keep his secrets within his skin. Now the heavy, fetid smell of death and possibility lay everywhere; the air was gravid with it.

If she once let the door check her, she would never find the nerve to open it. She didn't pause, then—just worked the handle and walked on in.

Melanie stood behind Grant's desk. Karen began to sigh with relief—*Oh, only her*—before she understood any of what else she was seeing.

Grant's body lay sprawled on the floor before the desk. The Kashmir carpet was history by now, to be sure; a great quantity of his dark oily blood had saturated it and was no doubt soaking down through the floorboards. And that was somehow easier to look at, easier to comprehend than the remade woman who was, no, not *only* Melanie, not that at all. Melanie entire, all falsehood stripped away: smiling at Karen, mocking her silently, glimmering almost with an aura of focused knowledge, of terrible strength.

She leaned forward, resting the palms of her hands on Grant's desk. Smearing it deliberately with the gray man's blood, making it abundantly clear that she had slain him with her bare hands. Which meant that the ritual mattered to her as much as the slaughter, and maybe more. Which meant...

"No," Karen whispered—not because it could not be true, rather because it made all the sense in the world. All the sense in any world. All she really wanted to deny was her own naiveté: tricked by the apparent foolishness, the sudden eagerness to stand aside, the squeamish reaction to a little spray of blood. Why in the world—in any world—would Grant have employed such a woman on such a task?

Karen had been too caught up in her own annoyance to see it. Stupid. Fatally stupid.

"Yes," Melanie said, enjoying herself thoroughly. Letting her own true self show through, a rippling power like Damascus steel at the core of her. If she'd only had the time, Karen could have run through the catalogue to find the place where Melanie fitted—night witch? necromancer? something on that order, surely—but time was a luxury, out of reach. Courage too, perhaps.

Unless...

Karen shook her head, banishing the thought. She would not throw her lot in with this… woman. Some fates were quite literally worse than death.

At least death brought an end to suffering.

Sparing a moment of rank envy for Grant, Karen stared back at Melanie. The sorceress was watching her with faint amusement. "You might want to rethink that," Melanie said, seeing altogether too clearly what Karen had not even dared whisper. "Working for me might not be pleasant, but it is certainly better than the alternative." Her eyes flicked down beyond Grant's desk, to his marauded body.

It was that glance that decided Karen. Under Melanie's rule there would be no benefit, no reworking of the power in the city… no healing from these desperate wars.

Had Melanie merely been waiting for the lesser powers to wear themselves out destroying one another before stepping up to harvest what remained?

Karen swallowed, trying to chase down the terrified lump in her throat.

And tasted her own blood there, from her bitten finger… and something else.

Oh, she thought, *Colin…*

Something of himself he had left in her. Residual, essential, seminal.

Something to work with, that was not her own.

There were two of them in this fight now, and that made all the difference.

Water holds a memory of shape, and a man is mostly water, after all…

Karen dropped her shoulders into a slump, dropped to her knees in ritual humiliation.

"Hold, there." Karen watched through her eyelashes as Melanie stepped out from behind the desk. The witch's clothes were clean, unstained, though her hands remained ostentatiously blood-soaked.

"There," Melanie went on, standing over her. "Go ahead. I just wanted to watch you from here."

Karen lowered her body, arms spread out in a token of submission. She was hanging just above Grant's sprawled corpse, the slick foul nastiness of him. Cold now, the blood, the fluids: she could feel that, so close she was. Too quickly cold, inhuman.

She waited, breathing. Gathering.

After a long, heavy moment, she felt the pressure of a hand on the back of her neck. Melanie's sticky fingers pushed her down until her own hands had no choice: they had to lie in the gore of Grant's spillage.

Again that touch of something more, the memories of water. Three of them in this fight now.

She wondered if Melanie would force her all the way down, rub her face in foulness: but not, apparently, or not today. The cold hand left her neck; the cold voice said, "You may rise."

Karen drew herself up, seeing Melanie's satisfied smile, not a trace of anxiety around the corners of Melanie's eyes. Confidence never thinks to look for betrayal: not until the blow is landed, the city fallen, the queen unthroned.

Karen rose up, up and up; and the blood her hands were dabbled in, all the leakage of Grant's death—all that chill wet came with her.

Blood is mostly water, after all.

Karen was given to the water, long ago. Only hours earlier, she had given the knife to the river, to the dark shapes stirring under city glimmer; given it with her own blood on the blade, and kept that small cut open, fresh and wet.

Water holds a memory of shape. The knife was in her hands now, shaped of blood, all the weight of a man's life held within it. Another man's strength behind it, in her body, through and through; and her own power to drive it home, her will, her willingness to act.

The blade of the blood-knife took Melanie in the gut, where she was wettest.

~ o O o ~

Flesh is just a bridge above a river.

Steel and blood, they are only expressions of water.

Blood is a blade.

Blade seeks the darkness, down and down.

Something down there is *waiting…*

A hot rush over Karen's hands, liquid body, death exemplified. Melanie and Grant, foul together, dead together. Wet together, fluids intermingled: he'd keep the witch down if she tried to rise.

Karen cleaned up as best she could, gave up as soon as she wanted to, took the van and was gone. The guards on the gate waved her through; she waved back meaninglessly. Driving home through the morning fog, she sucked on her finger and thought of a hot shower, thought of Mike.

He was right. She really needed to get a different job.

Embers

by SHANNON PAGE and JAY LAKE

Another collaborative story. I wrote a lot of stories with Jay; I've included my favorites in this collection. Some day, I may write a novel (or a series...) in Magical Alt-History Renaissance Italy. Until then, here is "Embers", which appeared in the anthology The Feathered Edge, *edited by Deborah Ross, in 2012.*

Firenze, 1498

I peered around the rough-edged corner of the Palazzo Martelli, searching down the long, night-shadowed lane but seeing nothing save the muddy path to the river Arno below. The Ponte Vecchio glimmered in the distance, lit by a single torch at the near end. On my shoulder perched Fain; I hadn't trusted him to this task, so he murmured and cooed his dismay in my ear.

My nose caught the scent of lavender and the musk of men. Or rather, a certain man. Which made me curse quietly and draw back into the shadows.

Fain burbled at this.

"There is no humor here," I muttered. "For someone who claims not to use our magic, he's sore adept at getting to places before me."

The dove could not speak, not in the usually understood sense of the term; but as with many long-held familiars, our communication was subtle and unmistakable. And at the moment, Fain was clearly disagreeing with me.

"All right," I whispered. "You call me wrong. But if Piero *does* cast, then why has he been working against us?"

Fain had no answer to that.

I waited until the bells sounded for Lauds, the last of the night's prayers. The man I sought did not reappear, and I dared not follow where he had gone. Only then did I slip through the first cold glimmers of dawn back to my small room in the rafters of the Palazzo Medici Riccardi.

~ o O o ~

As it is sometimes easier to hide amid a crowd than on the deserted streets of night, I spent the next afternoon in the markets and piazzas of the city of my heart. Despite the best efforts of the mad priest Savonarola, Firenze remained a vibrant metropolis, full of traders bringing commerce from every land. These far-eyed men tempted all with silks and spices and fine-worked leathers and, to a lesser degree, glittering gold and jewels. I permitted myself the luxury of admiring the pretties for an hour or two as I searched for the man Piero, though in truth I knew he lurked closer to the Arno.

Nestled in my bosom, hidden by the folds of cloth I had drawn around me to keep out the new-spring cold, Fain seemed to whisper, *Last night you avoided him; today you hunt him.* Or perhaps the dove merely slept, and those were my own thoughts.

At any rate, the point was well taken. I was of two minds about this entire business, to be sure.

Finally, as the late shadows pointed ever eastward, I made my way towards the river. I was forced to steel my sensitive nose against the assaults of the butchers who made their killings in the little shops lining the Ponte Vecchio. Why they perched here over the water was no mystery. Why folk downstream still drew from this river was the question.

Of course, ordinary folk did not know of the bad magic of drinking water tainted with the blood and offal of murdered beasts. They blamed night humors for their various ailments, or the curses of the vengeful departed. They weren't wrong in this, necessarily; those were certainly at work in the world as well. But the poisons in the Arno carried off more children and old women than any curse fomented by uneasy ghosts.

It was no truck of mine, I supposed. And there were fewer people to die of starvation.

Gathering my suitably bleak thoughts, I approached the foul waters.

I stood on the packed clay of the bank a long while, staring into the moving path of the river, seeking to see anything of the bottom of it. Divination by water was a tricky art at best, and the winter rains had been formidable this past season. They were not finished yet, I was certain, though we were having a small respite these recent days. Merely mud, not deluge.

His presence spoke to me from across the river long before I raised my eyes to him. Rising over the odor of the waters with the improbability of our kind, musk met my nose and I knew, yet I would not give him the satisfaction of my gaze. Not until I was ready.

Finally, I looked up. Piero stood on the opposite bank amid a little forest of boats drawn up to shore, surrounding him like disciples ready to spread his message across the four corners of the world. He was too far across the rolling water for ordinary conversation. His black hair fell in curling waves to his shoulders, and it seemed as though I could see the light of his soul deep in his eyes, though even my powers were not so great. Especially not at this distance. In my bosom, Fain stirred, fluttering a soft wing against my breasts. I touched a hand to myself in order to gentle the bird as I spoke to the man across the water. My voice barely rose above a whisper.

"You know this shall not pass. You conceal yourself away from me, yet we all know your game."

Piero smiled, catching every word, as I knew he would—just as I had caught his scent. "Lucrezia, your faith in me warms my mortal heart."

Your heart is not mortal, I thought. *And my faith is as nails driven through flesh.*

But that he would even stand and speak to me, even across the width of the Arno: this was progress, to be sure.

"You have been warned." I raised my voice slightly as the wind rose to push it downstream. "Join with us, and we will make this right." Prayers and the focus of my power rode upon the words.

His smile grew, or perhaps that was just the glint of the westering sun on the water rendering odd shadows. "Sorceress, my path is clear."

The response he would have to give, of course. But I had my own path as well, and my task. Again, I summoned my truest voice. "Three nights hence we meet under the full moon, atop Fiesole. Join with us."

He took a step back. I had kept my words casual, but if I spoke the command for him to join with us a third time, he would be compelled to obey.

Piero reached for his pocket. The scent of his musk rose, blocking out the reek from the ancient bridge downstream. The aroma tangled the threads of my thoughts and caused my hand to slip within my robes, feeling for the softness of my own skin.

A nip from Fain returned me to my senses.

I opened my mouth to speak the thrice-uttered compelling words, but Piero was gone. "Join with us," I whispered anyway. The wind carried the spell off harmlessly, compelling the boats to nothing at all.

$$\sim o\ O\ o \sim$$

In a small forgotten room in the basement of Il Duomo, I met with the Lady. She had been my superior since the last turn of our order, and it amused her to meet here, in the cradle of the god of men. We sat amid bolsters of glittering silk and a great rack of gilded beams once intended for a festival altar, or perhaps a bishop's folly. The room smelled faintly of incense, wine and sweat; surely odors brought in the last time these playpretties were folded away, before they had been banned.

"The city is restless tonight." She stroked the fur of her own familiar, a golden ferret she called Mani.

I waited for her to continue. The Lady did not speak idly, though oftentimes her words journeyed a route opaque to my comprehension.

"The man of San Marco stirs the mists in complicated ways."

Savonarola.

Nodding, I let my mind trail back over the events of the past year. The mad priest's passion had attracted the attention of our kind, for its purity and its fury. After his burning of the vanities, however, we'd lost interest. Just another zealot, riding the wave of his time.

And miscalculating, ultimately. As they always did. So why did the man's activities concern us, any more?

"He has touched on something that we might wish to see to," the Lady said, to my unasked question.

I continued to listen. Fain sat on my shoulder, casting a suspicious eye on Mani while holding his peace.

But the Lady stopped there, instead asking of my meeting with Piero.

"I do not know if he will come," I admitted. "I was unable to bind him."

She nodded, her face a mask of pale beauty and dark power. "Try harder. You have two more days."

~ o O o ~

Whether from fear or inattention or over-confidence, I had wasted far too much time. I did not even know where Piero spent his waking hours, much less where he made his bed.

Now I had to find him and bring him into our midst. No longer the luxury of avoidance for me, of ambivalence: the Lady had spoken her command. I complied.

It was easier thusly.

Or so I told myself.

A return to the river would be a waste of time. Like the Virgin Mary, he would not appear in the same place twice. So I turned to magic.

In a quiet alley intersection, witnessed by none but a nervous cat, I burned three sticks of rosemary and a twist of cinnamon bark under the blue cross of the sky above. I spoke the incantation into the scented smoke, then closed my eyes and followed my nose.

Lavender. Musk.

East.

Fain clucked like a tiny agitated chicken. I steadied him as best I could with a trembling hand, then lifted him to his perch within my robes. "We go."

The bright sunlight of false spring shone as we walked, fast drying the mud of the streets. It was very nearly pleasant. Yes, something was certainly amiss.

Eastward we went, following the scent of the man. The scent that tugged at the very heart of me.

No: I would not harbor these thoughts. My path was clear.

$$\sim\ o\ O\ o\ \sim$$

I found him in a field of grass outside the city, halfway to the Palazzo Pitti. He had spread a dark green blanket upon which he sat, sipping from a tiny porcelain chalice that steamed like a cup of sin itself.

My heart thudded in my throat as I approached. His black curls glinted in the sun, bright from the natural oils and unguents with which he would anoint himself. A small spray of lace at his breast was mostly hidden by a blood-colored tunic. The eyeleted paleness was tickled by a few dark hairs peeking around the edges, the merest hint of a solid masculinity underneath. Fain kicked out with his claws, scratching the tender skin of my breast and sending droplets of warm blood down to my navel even as I walked.

Reaching within, I pressed my shift against the blood, praying that the stain would remain hidden under my robes as I approached the edge of the blanket.

"Come," he said. His eyes were dark dying suns as he lifted a silver pot over a second chalice. "May I?" Steam rose from the spout.

"Thank you." I folded my legs beneath me, sitting on the grass with what I hoped was an elegant motion. Fain murmured and settled, poking his beak out of the folds of my robe to gaze bird-mad at Piero, fooling no one.

He carefully poured out three teaspoons of a beverage darker than rock oil, then handed it to me.

I sipped. It was delicious: bitter, and hot, and full of fantastic magic. Coffee.

"You know this is forbidden!" The African beans would not come to this country for another hundred years or more.

"I do know that. Which is why I partake far from the city." He sipped the last from his own chalice, then poured another measure. "But you did not come here to debate mage law with me."

"No." I took another sip, rolling the beverage on my tongue before swallowing. It burned, but did not hurt.

"Come here." Piero patted the green blanket next to him. "It is not a binding; just a soft place away from the ants."

I watched his face: he spoke the truth. Besides, he would surely have already noted the aroma of my spilt blood, even from where I sat. I risked no further harm in coming closer to him.

Except for the lure of his sweet flesh, the thrilling of his musk-and-lavender breath, the black song of his eyes.

"No," I said, even as I moved onto the blanket beside him. "No."

Fain quivered against me, mewling and cooing. The breeze blew overhead, and the sun caressed my own dark hair, and the skin at my ankles. Far below us, the river Arno passed along its own path.

~ o O o ~

Back in my room, I cursed myself for such terrible weakness. Then I poured icy water from the basin onto the dried blood on my belly, not even permitting myself to gasp with the shock of it. I abluted my body thoroughly, until the porcelain vessel was red with my essence.

And still I could not sleep.

I would have liked to blame the noise from the street, for the crowds roiled and shouted below with the strength of madness and god-blinded passion and rebellion, but in truth, this was no different than so many recent nights. It would end badly for the priest, this much I knew. Whatever the Lady's game with him, I hoped she would bring it to bear soon. This tension would not hold for long before breaking.

Nor would my own.

Sighing, I rolled onto my side, gently so that Fain moved with me. The small comfort of his feathers and quick-beating heart did nothing for me.

I wanted Piero.

"No," I whispered to the darkness.

Yes, the darkness whispered back. *Yes*.

~ o O o ~

"Again you did not bind him."

"I am sorry, my Lady."

"In fact, it rather appears that he has bound you, in a manner of speaking."

That I could not argue with. I hung my head.

When I finally met her eye, I saw that she was smiling. And I recognized the look she wore.

Handing her a shade of a smile in return, I said, "I understand."

She nodded. "But hurry. We gather tomorrow at midnight."

~ o O o ~

I lay naked in the moonlight upon the softest bed in which I had ever rested my unworthy bones. Not *my* bed, to be sure; it belonged to a cadet daughter of the Medici family. She was on an extended holiday, taking the healthful waters in a small convent outside of Trieste, in an attempt to cure herself of an inconvenient swelling about the mid-section. Given enough time—she wouldn't need nine months, not this far along—the problem would resolve itself, and she would return to Firenze.

By then, my work would be long done.

Fain perched on the footboard, curling his clawed feet around the ornately carved wood. He held his head so as to keep one eye on the open window and one on me. I settled even more comfortably among the many silk-covered pillows and allowed myself a small sigh of pleasure. The feeling of the young Medici's linens against my skin made me question my very path in this life.

A gentle breeze sent me a breath of the night air and stirred the gauzy magenta fabric with which the girl had adorned the marges of her window. Queens' coronation gowns had been made with less fine stuff. But even this marvelous cloth could not keep out the smell of the street below: mud, horse shit, sour cooking oil… as well as lavender and musk.

Piero was at the window, and then he was in the room.

And then he was in the bed.

"I knew you would fall to me," he whispered as he covered my traitorous, willing body with desperate kisses. "I knew you would come here."

No matter that the note had been mine. I do possess some small magic, you know.

I writhed and turned beneath him, welcoming him to me, luxuriating in the feel of his leanness against my body. He had been in the fields recently; his skin smelled of grass, tasted of crushed sage and a hint of dust. I bit his arm, gently, savoring the lushness of him. Seeking to know him.

He growled and tumbled me over onto my belly, then clutched my thighs, moving his hands slowly and deliberately up to my rear. Cupping its roundness, he leaned in and returned my bite: first on the flesh, then dipping a quick tongue to my nether eye.

The mark of a sorcerer.

But then, I already knew that.

"Not so fast," I murmured even as the pleasure threatened to blind me. I allowed him one more sip at my pot of dark honey before I twisted around. In one swift motion, I turned him over and climbed up to top him, holding him down with strong hands.

Piero grinned up at me, even as he tried to hide the flash of shock in his eyes. He hadn't known me to have such strength.

I leaned down and kissed him, filling his mouth with my own tongue.

He tasted of me, of course, but beneath that he was fresh-baked bread and more of that cursed coffee. I could get used to kissing this man.

Pulling away, I reached down to untie his pants. "We are at an imbalance," I said. "I am bare and you are clothed."

"We can fix that." He wriggled out of his trousers and linen drawers beneath, while his shirts fell away almost of their own accord. The dark hairs of his chest were even lusher than I had imagined. I buried my nose in them, then kissed his ruby nipples, one after the other.

I still sat astride him, holding his hips with my knees. His eagerness strained up to meet my sweetpocket, which I kept just out of reach, smiling down at him as though I was playing a game.

Finally, I lowered myself a fraction of a measure. "Join with me."

"Oh yes," he whispered.

And I lowered further. "Join with us." Then I took him into me, with the oldest binding magic of them all.

In the corner, Fain cooed and put his head under a wing.

$$\sim o\ O\ o \sim$$

The morning light found me alone in the tangled blankets and crushed pillows. I smiled as I allowed myself to remember our night, moment by moment, a slow, savoring retelling. After I'd bound him, he was my plaything for many hours, rough and tender both. And even though he had escaped with the dawn, I knew he would appear at midnight.

The Lady would be pleased.

With reluctance, I got out of the Medici daughter's bed and found my clothes and my familiar. Fain slipped into my robes, clucking at the lovebites and bruises on my satisfied flesh before he settled into place.

Then I left the room as it was. Maids would tell stories of witches and sorcerers haunting the night, and they would not be wrong.

I spent the day sleeping in my hidden chamber, conserving my strength for the ritual to come. So I missed the commotion in the Piazza della Signoria—the shouts of the crowd, the nailing together of the giant cross, the dragging of the chains. The sickening, mouth-watering smell of roasting flesh finally woke me.

Rushing down to the piazza, Fain fluttering about my head, I arrived in time to see Savonarola and two of his acolytes fall to the flames.

On the far side of the fire, Piero's gaze caught mine—a cruel and fiery echo of our first meeting across the Arno. He shook his head, gentle and sad, before he vanished. Such an audacious working…

~ o O o ~

"He *was* bound," I said.

"Yes." The Lady gazed at me, her face even paler under the moonlight. "I have to think on this."

"He cannot loose his magic in the world." I paced the small circle we had built with the stones of Fiesole, looking down on the valley of the Arno and the sleeping farms, each with their wary watchlight guttering to keep the likes of us at bay. The rest of the order would be here soon, and what would we tell them?

"I think he shall not," she answered, speaking slowly. "To pull himself from your call—he had to undo *all* his bindings. Not just the most recent one. And he was forced to unleash a great terror upon the entire city in order to do even that much."

I stared at her. The flames, the mad priest brought down, the vanities of piety burning brighter than even gilt and paste jewels. "Of course." Excitement and relief flooded through me. "So we *have* defeated him!"

The Lady chuckled. "Oh, no, Lucrezia—I am afraid we have done no such thing. Set him back a bit, perhaps; bought ourselves more time. But he will return."

At the bottom of the hill, I could see a small group of women beginning their climb. "What can we do?" I asked. "What happens next?"

"Be patient," she whispered. "Be vigilant. Wait and watch." Then she turned to greet the others.

~ o O o ~

I stood below the Medici girl's window. The bells of Lauds had rung not long past; dawn would invade the world soon.

It was dark within. The shutters were drawn. I could see no tender fabric, no welcoming bed. Fain slept unknowing against my aching breast.

One more glimpse. Just one more scent of lavender, and his sweet, sweet musk. That's all I ask.

The night air returned to me only mud and offal and the faraway reek of the Ponte Vecchio butchers.

If this was defeat, I feared victory. I turned and walked slowly back to my room, my feet heavy on the rough cobblestones.

Gil, After All

This story is the only one in this collection appearing for the first time. It was commissioned in 2009 for an as-yet-unpublished Gilgamesh anthology from Morrigan Books (publishers of my novel Eel River*). I imagined Gilgamesh transported to modern times, trying to make sense of everything that happened to him. I'm quite proud of the results, and happy that, at last, I get to share this story with an audience.*

Gil gazed across the table at Esther. The light from the candles flickered on her pale cheeks as she reached for her wine glass. Gil wanted to see the effect as lovely, but Esther's face was hard and closed. Even the soft glow of the flames was helpless against the flood of her anger.

"I can't believe you." She put the glass down hard, the wine untasted as she raised her brown eyes to his. "You really are completely worthless."

"I…" He paused, waiting to see if she would leap to her feet and storm out again. When she stayed, he went on. "I'm sorry. I apologized already, a thousand times. What more do you want me to say?"

"It's not what I want you to say," she spat. "You've *said* enough. Now you need to *do*. Did you even find a job yet?"

Gil smiled. At least she was talking. The job stuff—that wasn't important. If he could get her talking, the battle was half won. Now he could ease his way into her heart again. She'd wanted him before, but he had been following another. He'd never expected it would end the way it had… but no matter. That was all behind him.

Now it was over and he had returned home, and Esther would put out all the raging infernos in his heart. She would light a new flame there, one that burnt low and steady, not searing the hillsides and leaving none alive. One that a man could live a long and happy life by. He understood this now.

He just had to get through this dinner.

~ o O o ~

In fact he had to do more than that. He'd been sore disappointed, when he'd first returned and found he wasn't treated as the conquering hero he'd expected to be. He had done his best, against mighty odds, yet his welcome home had been… Well, it had been a real kick in the teeth.

But he wasn't going to hold it against Esther. She had every right to her feelings. And now Gil was more than happy to let her go through whatever she needed to make it right. He would help her, even.

She wasn't all that interested in hearing about his adventures, though. She wasn't all that interested in hearing what he had to say at all. Half the time, it was as if she didn't even believe him, and the rest of the time, she just didn't seem to care. But what did she want him to do?

~ o O o ~

Gil excused himself to go to the men's room. The restaurant had grown crowded, hopping with dressed-up diners laughing over their pomegranate margaritas and seven-dollar beers, and he had to wait in the narrow hallway for the one-holer to free up. While he stood there, leaning against a bus table, he could smell the spices swarming in the steamy kitchen. *Better than inhaling the putrid odor of the john,* he thought.

There were cinnamon and cardamom, those he was sure of. But what was the astringent undertone? He closed his eyes and breathed more deeply, searching, traveling back…

It was a crowded spice bazaar, every flavor known to man and then some, jumbled with the rank smell of unwashed humans and never-washed animals from the farms up the coast; plus monkeys, green papayas, tall sugarcane stalks, and the salt of the ocean.

There was a pull on his garments, a tugging, followed by a sharp pain just below the back of the knee. He whipped around, then looked down.

A small hairy thing crouched at his heels. Matted seal-dark fur, really, covering the creature head to toe. It was shaggier on the boy's head—was it a boy? Yes, had to be—but did not let up anywhere, did not show any skin.

More to the point, the thing was jabbing a long knife into Gil's leg.

"Stop that!" Gil reached down and snatched the weapon from the boy, who began to wail, his voice deep and rich with the agony of the ages. Shopkeepers up and down the aisle looked up at the other-worldly shrieks of the creature, and a burly spice dealer reeking of star anise began to step forward. Without a thought, Gil picked up the surprisingly solid youngster and sprinted off in the opposite direction.

"Dude? You're up."

Gil snapped back to the present as the guy behind him in line nudged him in the back. "Oh, sorry." He stepped into the foul john and closed the door behind him. The lock wouldn't slide; the bar sat too high to enter the loop on the facing. Why did these things never work? Well, the fellow outside knew he was in here; he'd keep others away.

He unbuttoned the fly of his Levi's, bumping his elbow on the greasy wall as he adjusted himself to pee. For such an expensive restaurant, their facilities were, well, crappy. The toilet looked like it hadn't been scrubbed in a month, and there were no paper towels. He'd have to warn Esther. He hoped she could hold it till after dinner.

In fact, he hoped she'd come back to his place, where his bathroom was fiercely clean, as were the sheets on his bed; and a bottle of pricey champagne waited in the fridge.

Gil finished his business, buttoned up, and contemplated washing his hands despite the lack of towels. He could dry them on his napkin, back at the table. But what about the door handle? No, he was clean. This would have to do.

He nodded at the guy waiting—was it the same guy?—then hurried back to the table.

Esther was gone.

~ o O o ~

Gil ran with the monkey-creature in his arms until his lungs stung with the effort, until his legs felt as though they would fly from his body, until the spice bazaar was miles behind them. Then he collapsed by the bank of a river, arms and legs splayed, insensible.

The creature, now tall as a man, sat watching him while he recovered, his black eyes revealing nothing.

Gil had dropped the knife some ways back, but his companion did not clamor for it. Nor did he try to run away. He seemed to sense that he was in the presence of something more powerful than himself. As if he knew he had been taken up by a hero.

After the moon had inched its way across the sky towards the far horizon and Gil's breath had returned to him, he sat up and looked back at the creature.

"Well?"

The strange child-man stared back at him, sitting poker-straight, eyes unblinking. Gil looked into that gaze, and knew he had found a brother.

~ o O o ~

"I suppose you thought that was very funny, leaving me with the check."

It had taken him three days to get Esther to answer his calls. He stood in the doorway to his kitchen and squirmed, holding the tiny cell phone to his ear. "I didn't leave. I told you. There was a line."

"For thirty-five minutes?" Her voice dripped acid. "That's when you come back and tell a person. That's when you give up. That's when you alert management that someone's died in there. You don't just *wait*."

He had no response to that. She was right.

"Can we try again? Come over here, I'll cook."

She sighed, heavy, almost liquid. "I don't know why I bother."

I do, he thought, hope rising in his breast once more. "Come tonight. I'll make..." But then he couldn't think of anything he knew how to cook. "A surprise. I'll make a surprise, something special."

"No," she said. "No more meals. I'll tell you what: meet me after work tomorrow. Bring a gift that shows me you're sorry, and you want to make it right. Bring me something that shows me you've listened to me, that you know me."

"What do you mean?" He hated the shrill panic that crept into his voice. A gift! He had no idea what she might want! Well, jewelry, sure, but he wasn't about to spend money on jewelry unless...

Her laughter interrupted his thoughts. "Yeah, a gift. Something from your trip, maybe. You did bring interesting things back from your trip, didn't you?"

"Sure I did. Sure I did."

"So. Give me something you brought back."

~ o O o ~

Gil and Kiddo—for the creature would take no other name—lay wrapped in one another's arms, lost to the world. Lost in each other, flesh melding into flesh, sleek hair caressing pale smooth skin. Brothers, lovers, soulmates—there was no word for what they were. Just: one.

Of a day, they roamed the land, slaying monsters, pillaging cities, raping women, carrying off spoils. But they often as not had no use for the spoils; they'd cast them into the deep black pools that littered the forest, laughing, for they knew they'd take more tomorrow, and tomorrow, and tomorrow.

They were two halves that made a whole. It was beyond love, beyond happiness. Kiddo knew Gil like none other had, not his mother, not his lovers, not his teachers. Words were hardly necessary.

Kiddo knew.

~ o O o ~

Gil stood at the bathroom sink, staring at his reflection in the mirror. He'd been having the visions again, he knew he had. If only he could remember them better. Obviously, that was what had happened in the restaurant, he knew it at once. But losing thirty-five minutes: that was frightening. It had been bad enough when the fugues had lasted a few seconds: the bright, solid visions, all the scent, the color, making this world seem pale and faint by comparison, leaving him shattered and confused when they vanished again. But this: this was going to interfere with his life, if he wasn't careful.

In an hour, he would see Esther. He had only one thing to give her, as she had asked. Despite all that had come before between them, he did not know if she would appreciate it.

~ o O o ~

She was a few minutes late. He stood outside on the street, watching the door to her office from a respectful distance.

People exited the building and rushed down the street, mostly strangers, but he recognized a few of her co-workers. Fellow goddesses of industry, he'd called them, joking but serious. Esther had laughed. But that was before.

Now she appeared, glancing around, looking for him, a look of impatience already threatening to take over her face. He waited ten or fifteen seconds before pushing himself off the lamppost and walking towards her.

She saw him and half-smiled, then her eyes flashed to his empty hands. He could almost read her mind: *No flowers, no wrapped gift? Bastard. Unless gift fits in pocket: good, good.*

He grinned at her. "You look gorgeous."

She allowed him to kiss her, not turning away. He took her arm, and she fell into step with him. "Where are we going?"

"My place."

He glanced at her sidelong, watching her mind shift again. *I told him no, not his place. WTF? Gift too large to carry? Should I say no?*

She must have decided to go with it, as she did not protest, but walked alongside him.

~ o O o ~

Gil dreamed, strange and terrible things that brought fear and a sick cold trembling to his arms and his legs and his scrotum. He cried out in the night, wailing for release, and soon Kiddo embraced him, as ever. "Do not fear, dear brother, the dreams are not bad omens," the hairy man soothed. "Nay, they bring good tidings. The monster is no enemy of ours. We will prevail."

Limbs entangled, the men found their comfort and Gil forgot his terrors.

Yet every night, Gil dreamed anew, each dream more horrifying than the last. "Kiddo—we shall all die! I know it! We must change our ways."

The lustrous fur enveloped his skin, calming his panic, inflaming his desire. Kiddo taught him the many ways of pleasure, and then many more. Gil was a faithful student at his master's knee, and his heart was gladdened.

And so it went.

~ o O o ~

"Well?" Esther's voice held a smile, though she kept her face steady as she stood in the entryway to Gil's apartment, holding her suit jacket by one finger.

"Well, come in!" Gil urged. He motioned to the living room, the sofa. "Drink?"

Esther hesitated a moment longer, then hung her jacket on his coat rack. She took the easy chair, crossing one slender leg over the other, keeping the top leg raised ever so slightly, so as to avoid an unsightly bulge of the thigh. "Sure—sparkling water, thanks."

He almost poured her champagne anyway, but decided against it. Must step carefully here, delicately. "Ice?" he called, from the kitchen.

"No, thank you."

He returned with two glasses of fizzy water, handed Esther hers. Sat on the couch, grinning at her.

She lifted her glass in a mock-toast. She was not smiling. He could almost smell the expectation wafting off of her, the last-chance-ness of this. He tasted her air of incredible generosity—for even coming here, letting him do whatever it was he was planning, whatever stupid, foolish, worthless thing. He could already hear her crowing words: *I knew it.*

He wanted to shrug his shoulders. Instead, he sipped his water.

~ o O o ~

Then Kiddo had the bad dreams. The awful nightmares, from which he would wake screaming, shuddering, sweating. Gil tried to comfort him, but the visions were too terrifying. Blood, death, destruction. One of them must die.

"No, that is not the meaning here," Gil protested, remembering his brother's words. "It is as you told me before. Dreams, like the divination cards, are never literal. Death only means a completion—such as the completion of our task. It points the way for a new beginning."

"One of us must die!" Kiddo wailed. He would not be consoled. Gil touched and soothed him in the hundred ways, and then the second hundred ways, but solace did not come to his brother.

Gil became afraid.

~ o O o ~

"It's very simple," Gil said. "Come sit by me, and I'll explain it."

Esther had finished her water, declining a second glass. She leaned forward in her chair, poised, ready to flee. He could see her eyeing her jacket, the front door, the outside world. He'd never see her again if she left. He knew that. "I can hear you perfectly well from over here," she said.

"No, you can't."

They stared at one another. Gil tried to read her intention, the story behind her eyes. Tried to know her like he had known the other. She was the key to his future, she would complete him...

As he watched her, suddenly the tension in her body relaxed the merest inch. "I don't know why I'm doing this," she said, joining him on the couch.

"Champagne?" he asked, sliding an arm around her shoulders.

She held herself rigid under his arm, not leaning into the embrace, not pulling away. In the kitchen, the ice maker rumbled, going through its cycle, dumping fresh cubes into the bin. "All right," she said, and he knew he had her.

~ o O o ~

Gil lay prostrate over Kiddo's dead body, and wept.

~ o O o ~

He gazed up at Esther through drunkenly hazy eyes. Much as he wanted to see what she was doing, the room kept spinning, and his lids drooped shut time and again. He felt as though his veins had champagne in them, tiny bubbles fizzing and popping in his blood, making him tingly all over, but not in an altogether good way. In fact not good at all.

She straddled him on the bed, her strong thighs pinning him down, pinching his hips together a little too forcefully. She was down to her bra and panties—both in frothy black lace, matching, and quite sexy. He'd smiled to himself as she'd stripped, earlier. A woman doesn't dress like that underneath if she doesn't think it's going to be seen, and appreciated.

Gil just wished he could concentrate better. His head lolled to one side, then back again. He tried to focus on her once more. Had she had anything to drink, beyond the first glass?

Oh shit, he'd opened a second bottle, hadn't he? He groaned and closed his eyes, just for a second.

Bereft, lost, friendless, abandoned. Gil wandered the endless desert and then crossed the seven seas, and was destined to be forever alone.

"And so you have come back to me, is that right?" Esther loomed above him, her dark hair falling forward to shade her eyes. *Kiddo fluttered through his vision—sweet, downy seal-fur, strong limbs holding him, caressing him.* Esther's strong legs squeezed him tighter, too tight. Sweat dripped from her chin, landing on his chest. He couldn't move his arms to wipe it away.

He smelled spices, and the manure of goats. He felt the alcohol swarm through him, smelled his laundered sheets. His stomach burned and ached, and his groin felt tight, constricted. Desire? Fear? He wanted to reach up and kiss her, or shove her off him. He wasn't even sure which. Both.

"You, who called me selfish and greedy and single-minded?" Esther laughed, and the sound was terrible. It grated against his spine; Gil shivered on the bed. *She had offered him jewels and riches beyond his wildest dreams, she had promised to love him forever, she had invited him into her temple, blessed everything he owned. And he had pushed her aside, pushed her away and left.*

"You, who said he had to go *find himself*? Is this the gift you brought back to me? Your lousy worn-out *body*?" She grinned cruelly down at him, a face with no love, no compassion, no understanding. Was this what he had returned for?

The hundred and the second hundred ways of love worked on everyone—man and woman alike. Kiddo had taught his brother Gil well.

But they did not work on the goddess.

"You were going to show me some *sex trick*?" She squeezed even harder. Gil stared up at her with frightened eyes.

He was at her mercy. He had always known that.

$$\sim\ o\ O\ o\ \sim$$

Kiddo dreamed beneath the soil, and although Gil journeyed to the farthest lands, he could still hear the dreams.

And they still frightened him.

At long last, Gil returned to the city of his birth, the city where he was a hero, acclaimed—almost godlike in his powers. They would welcome him there. They would cheer him, celebrate his deeds, soothe his wounded heart.

The goddess herself would embrace him. As she had wanted to in his youth, when he had turned his face from her.

~ o O o ~

Gil had been foolish to come back. That was his first thought when he awoke in the empty bed, head pounding, mouth dry as bone. There was nothing for him here, no job, no friends, and nothing with Esther. She saw directly into his heart, and she knew she would always hold second place there.

Second to a dead person.

Second to a dream world.

Yet hadn't she been the one to call him back? Or had that just been his madness?

Gil moaned and rolled over, searching for a glass of water on the bedside table, a cough drop, anything to moisten his parched mouth. The bathroom was too far, too unattainably far. He blinked at the light pouring through the window. Then his stomach twisted, and he staggered out of the bed after all, stumbling across the hall and onto his knees, gripping the cold porcelain as he retched into the toilet.

When he sat back an eternity later, wiping his mouth, eyes streaming with tears, he heard her behind him. "Too much wine?"

He didn't turn around. "Go away."

Her laughter tinkled, rattling against the inside of his skull like a handful of sharp-edged jacks. "Oh, Gil. Poor Gil. You see, I've changed my mind. You've convinced me; I think it can work out after all."

Now he did slowly turn his head. She stood wrapped in his robe, holding a streaming mug of coffee as she leaned against the door frame. "You might want to flush that," she added.

He just stared at her. "What do you want?"

She grinned and took a sip of the coffee. "You always were so charming when you were hung over." She leveled her eyes at him. "Last night was *incredible*. You were right. You have to tell me where you learned all that." She wiggled her hips suggestively.

Another wave of nausea rolled through Gil. He turned back to the toilet just in time.

~ o O o ~

Forgive me, Goddess, for I have sinned. I threw away your love and now I want it back.

I am sorry, Seeker. For it is too late. There are no second chances. You saw to that yourself, the first time around.

Please, Goddess. Please forgive me. I'll do anything. Anything.

~ o O o ~

Gil sat at the reception desk, smiling at the goddesses of industry as they came and went, doing their important business, buying and selling small countries as if they were trading cards. He had been lucky, so very, very lucky. Esther had found him such a good job here. He owed everything to Esther.

Not just a good job, but a good life. He had his very own room in her house, and all her pretty friends came by and permitted him to work his magic on them. Their cries of lustful pleasure filled Esther's house late into the night. And then, if she came to him after the last friend was gone, who was he to withhold his favors from her as well? She had saved his life: rescued him from his delusions, his sickness.

No matter that he was left muzzy and half-asleep all day. Receptionist wasn't a challenging job, after all.

And he was lucky to have it. So lucky.

He kept his eyes on the bank of elevators, waiting for them to open. Every time, it could be her! And even when it wasn't, he smiled anyway.

What else was he to do?

The door to the street opened, and the merest scent of cardamom floated through the lobby. Gil gasped, in the grip of a sudden powerful, soul-drenching sadness. Why? He shook his head, blinked his eyes, and reminded himself how lucky he was.

And soon enough, he was happy again.

Oh Give Me Land, Lots of Land, Under Starry Skies Above

By SHANNON PAGE *and* MARK J. FERRARI

This was the first story Mark and I wrote together. It started as a solo story; I'd been invited to the anthology Space Tramps, *edited by Jennifer Brozek, and had this great idea about a realtor stranded in space with nothing to sell. I charged into the story and ... got lost. Frustrated, I talked to Mark at length about it, and he finally said, "We've discussed collaborating; you want to write this one together?" A grateful YES was my answer, and a new writing partnership was born.* Space Tramps: Full Throttle Space Tales Volume 5 *came out in 2011.*

I shouldered my pack and moved on again, still trying to look like I belonged to someone. Someone important and frightening and powerful.

Who was I fooling?

I'd gone through lots of training before leaving Earth. I'd passed the psych tests with high scores for adaptability, calm demeanor, and flexible attitude. I'd watched virteos about all the possible dangers and side effects and unexpecteds… except for one: being marooned on Longhorn 6 with no backup, no office, no Principal Broker, and nothing to sell.

Selling was what I had left Earth to do. Selling land, specifically, and structural space, and development tech. I was a real estate broker, trained by Old Rehaus himself. I'd been on my way to help our brokerage develop Astoria Corporation's recently settled planet Greenleaf 43, not to be a stranded vagrant on some space station thousands of light years from nowhere.

Old Rehaus was dead now. I'd been lucky not to perish with him and the rest of the brokerage when our FTL carrier, *Fleetness*, had somehow come apart upon re-entry into system space. Only one small portion of the vessel survived, limping to its end on this unthinkably isolated pit stop.

Ecoballs like Longhorn 6 are designed to feel like planets. But no matter how big and round it is, how much "wide open space" they've designed, a space station is a space station. You're breathing canned air, hoofing it down tin corridors, and looking up at a "sky" with no sun.

Most problematic for me, there was no private property here. Not to own, not to buy, not to sell.

I'd spent most of the trip from Earth in Rest, a light trance state that makes time pass dreamy-fast. It's far healthier and quicker to get over once one is planet-side than Sleep, where you're put under entirely. It's more expensive too, but being alert for that initial wave of eager buyers had seemed worth the cost to me. I'd imagined those first few turns around Greenleaf's Monopoly board would set up the rest of my career there. Now there would be no Monopoly board—but Rest had saved my life. My colleagues had all decided to economize, Sleeping elsewhere on the ship, to their misfortune.

I still didn't know exactly what had happened to *Fleetness*. The Longhorn goons who'd rescued us hadn't said. They'd just brought us down here and dumped us into some huge processing bay.

The station's populace seemed watchful and grim, their dress code inspired by the collision of a circus, thrift store, and military surplus outlet. Their expressions and body language conveyed mute hopelessness. Not the kind of customer I'd been trained to work with. I had no idea how to act here, much less what to do.

Confused and fog-headed, I had obediently taken my place at the end of a long line at first, just grateful to be alive. Soon, however, I began to wonder if I'd have been better off atomized into vacuum along with the rest of my agency. Most of the women ahead of me were being sent elsewhere by rough-looking male handlers with a steady stream of lewd remarks and leering gestures. Soldiers pulled away the larger, fitter men, while older folks and children were sent through a smaller, shabbier exit. As my turn approached, a sudden wave of prickly instinct made me duck from line while none of our handlers was looking.

Longhorn 6 was a busy, crowded place. It was easy to merge with nearby streams of human traffic and just keep going.

$$\sim \text{o O o} \sim$$

Two days later, I walked down yet another tin corridor, trying to look stern and busy as my eyes flicked about, searching for threats or clues. I'd slept only once, in a deserted construction zone under a pile of refuse, and eaten nothing but the chips and bottled water distributed free of charge at scattered "refreshment stations" sponsored by Longhorn 6's corporate owner, Galactic Enterprises—Astoria's only serious rival in the interstellar real estate business.

If Galactic's patronage translated into any kind of cogent social organization or business model on Longhorn 6, however, it was still entirely opaque to me. The place just seemed one endless, rundown, hostile zoo. I knew there must be some system of registration and assignment, but it was clearly unavailable to anyone who hadn't been processed, and I still didn't trust this place or want to be inducted into any of it. I just wanted to get off of Longhorn 6 and back into a world I understood. I needed honest dirt under my feet, real air in the atmosphere. A desk, colleagues, rules I understood, superiors I knew how to please, and a big old-fashioned data-dump of listings. I'd just have asked someone to help me leave, but I had a growing fear that no one here would do that.

I needed to get hold of Astoria, before someone who mattered figured out I wasn't right, and started making my decisions for me.

But how?

~ o O o ~

I collapsed onto a bench in a sort of park on the fourteenth level of the portside residential zone. The greenery was obviously fake, but at least they'd made an effort to provide some restful space. I pulled out a sheaf of papers I'd collected from various recycling bins. Gathered together, I'd hoped they would look enough like a bundle of work orders to fool the casual observer. People were much scarcer here at this hour than they were elsewhere on the station, which was why I'd come. But whenever someone passed, I frowned down at the papers as if I were a harried admin, stealing a quick break on a quiet bench.

I must have dozed off, because the man's words startled me awake.

"What?" I dropped the papers, which fluttered to the ground at my feet.

"I said, interesting work you've got there." He glanced at the papers. The one nearest my foot was obviously a food wrapper. I had no memory of picking it up, and couldn't hide my blush. "You steal the food too, or just the wrapper?"

"How... What makes you think...?" My mouth went dry as I studied his wry expression, trying to suss out how much trouble I was in. He had an assured air that belied his relative youth. He wasn't uniformed, so not enforcement personnel, I hoped. Brown eyes, heavy eyelids, slender shoulders. Cute, if I weren't so terrified.

"Don't sweat it," he said, smiling. "But if you're gonna play these games, be more convincing. Looks bad for the rest of us." He reached into a dark green satchel and pulled out a bundle of papers, tugged the top two sheets off and handed them to me. "Like this."

My hand trembled as I took them. They seemed to be complex schematics with a few inked notes in the margins, arrows pointing to a box in the middle. "Um... thank you," I said. "What are these?"

He laughed. "Just meaningless doodles, but who's to know? Better than what you've got." He bent down to pluck the food wrapper from my pile. His hand brushed mine as he straightened and his expression changed. "How long have you been off-planet?"

"I… How did you know?"

"Your skin. You've lived in real air, and recently too." His eyes narrowed. "You're from *Fleetness*."

Well, this was bound to happen. If I understood him, he was not entirely legitimate either. "What of it?" I said, trying to sound tough.

He glanced around, as if afraid of being seen, then took a step away.

I stood up and put my hand on his arm, babbling almost involuntarily. "Take me with you—help me. You're right: I have no clue—"

He brushed off my hand, looking around more anxiously, though there was no one in the little park to overhear us.

"You weren't processed," he rasped, backing toward the exit corridor.

I followed him, clutching my sheaf of papers and my pack. Everything I owned in the world… any world. "No, I wasn't. I don't belong here."

He laughed, mirthlessly, still moving away. "You don't exist here. And we never met." He turned and ran down the corridor as if I were an imminent hull breach.

I tried to follow him, but he was very good at disappearing. I felt more like a misplaced realtor than ever.

Giving up, I stepped into a personal refresher. As the door hissed shut behind me, I sat down on the closed lid of the commode and rested my head in my hands, fighting off the urge to cry. Crying would accomplish nothing. I had to think.

I had panicked. Stupid. Was he already reporting me to someone? No. "You don't exist," he'd said. "We never met." So why had he approached me? He'd known that I was faking something, and yet had come to—what? Critique my performance? He'd had false papers too… but if he wasn't legit either, why should it have scared him that I was not?

Was my unprocessed status a crime to make even crooks here tremble?

What a terrifying thought.

Would turning myself in now help, or was I already beyond reprieve?

He had mentioned "the rest of us." Was there some larger group that, at least initially, he'd imagined I might belong to? Should I try to find them? Would they treat me any differently than he had?

The commode station gave a warning chime. A small plasma display above the handle invited me to apply for extra minutes by inserting a credit chip in the door. Too bad for me.

Wiping my eyes on the square of rough paper provided, I let myself out of the booth and stepped up to the hand-washing station, thinking to splash some water on my face.

"Follow me at a distance," said a tense but instantly familiar voice from the other side of the thin plio-flex wall above my sink. "Don't stop, and don't speak to anyone until I say to. Lose track of me, and you're on your own. Got it?"

I nodded, then realized he couldn't see me either. "Yes."

"Exit left," the voice commanded quietly.

I started down the ramp to my left and saw him, already fifteen feet away, walking off into the crowd at a calm but businesslike pace. I headed after him.

His route twisted and doubled back repeatedly, passing through crowded public hubs one moment and deserted service corridors the next. I soon stopped trying to make sense of our path. This endless maze without north, south, day or night befuddled me.

Eventually he paused in a narrow, under-street service tube to listen at a closed door. I stood some twenty feet behind him, trying to breathe quietly in the gloom.

Seeming satisfied, he slipped a key into the door's card slot, and it slid open. He finally turned to look at me and said, "What's your name?"

"Mara Sandstrom."

"Come with me, Mara," he said. "And behave."

Wondering what that meant, I followed him through the door into a larger tunnel, blinking and squinting under the light of massive arc fixtures clearly intended for use in much larger spaces. Work stations with ever-shifting data displays cluttered the chamber. The tech here was beat up but sophisticated. Intestinal tangles of heavy pipe and conduit jostled with the gadgetry for space against the tunnel walls, as if someone had tried to jam a whole traffic control hub into a sewer intersection.

People sat at some of the terminals, hard to make out in the glare. I wondered how anyone could see to work in here. Some turned as we came in, but gave us no more than a glance before turning back to their work.

"Stand there," my guide instructed, waving me toward a niche between two unmanned stations as far out of everyone's way as possible in such a crowded space. "Just wait."

I nodded.

My host walked to a second door in the tunnel's side some ways off, pressed his ear to it as well, then entered, closing it behind him. At first, I heard nothing but the sibilant whispers and whirrings of the tech around me, doing whatever it was there to do. Then drifts of animated conversation became audible. A moment later, the yelling started. Everyone turned to look at the door, and then at me with new interest before returning to their tasks as if they wanted nothing more to do with it.

As I began to sweat, the door crashed open against the metal struts around it, making the tunnel boom like a giant bell. A tall, muscular woman with dark, short-cropped hair wearing drab fatigues and a tight tank top strode through, heading straight for me with clenched lips and an angry glare. I managed to hold my ground and keep my mouth shut as she stopped abruptly, pointing at me as if I were a dog who had just peed on the kitchen floor.

"Sit there!" she said, pointing toward the terminal chair left of me. The man who'd done this to me ambled through the door behind her with his hands in his pockets and an expression waffling between defiance and chagrin.

I sat. There.

"Don't move—at all—'til I get back," said the Amazon in the tank top. She started toward the door we had come in by, then turned back and added, "If you so much as scratch your soft white ass before I return," she pointed at my betrayer, "he's going to kill you. If he fails to obey that order, I'll kill him."

To this day, I don't know what possessed me to find my voice at that of all moments. "Am I allowed to speak?"

Two leonine strides put her right in front of me, where she leaned down and said, "Feel free, tiny-tits." She bent even farther, planting her own very aggressive breasts practically in my face. "Just make sure your lips don't move." She straightened, pointing a cocked-gun gesture at my head, then turned and left the chamber like a gust of wind.

None of the terminal jockeys had so much as turned a head through this performance. Even now, they went on working as if nothing had happened. I turned to the man at fault with a look intended to convey ire, but which I suspect communicated nothing but terror.

"She didn't mean it," he said, "about your lips."

"What the hell have you done to me?" I demanded.

"Saved your soft white ass, most likely," he said with infuriating nonchalance. "That's why she's so mad. I've convinced her to do something stupid... I think. We'll know soon enough."

"Something stupid like what, exactly?" I asked, recovering from the rigid dread she'd left me in.

"Like convincing Adam Jones not to sell you straight off to the Cold Ones for sidestepping his authority the other day. Maybe even convincing him to let you join our little band of merry men despite not being vetted first by his boys. I could have been killed too, you know. Just for talking to you. Lexa might still do it, let alone Adam. I hope you're at least a little grateful."

"I'd be even more grateful," I sighed, daring to rub my eyes as well as move my lips, "if you'd fill some of the bigger gaps in all of that before she comes back."

"Gaps?" But then he smiled and said, "Okay. In here, though."

"She told me not to move..." One of the terminal jockeys snickered. Feeling foolish, I stood and followed the man into the room his boss lady had come from.

~ o O o ~

As the door shut behind us, I looked around a chamber that seemed part office, part break room, part bunk space. A cluttered desk abutted the left-hand wall, next to a low and shabby couch; a rickety chair and a cooler took up one corner, and a large purple exercise ball sat in the middle of the floor.

Just seeing the bunk's rumpled blanket and thin pillow made my body ache for rest. What I would not have done for a soft, safe space to sleep…

The man sat in the chair and waved me toward the couch, which I sank into wearily. "You got a name?" I asked.

"Robbin."

I nodded, my old training coming back: act confident even if you're not; take the offensive; ask questions; conceal surprise. I sat forward against the couch's undertow. "Who was the charming lady? Lexa, did you say?"

Robbin laughed, a little grimly. "Lexa, yeah. Queen of our resource." He waved a hand around the bleak room. "Master of all this."

"What kind of resource are we talking about?" I asked, wondering if it were something I was qualified to sell.

"Procurement mostly," he replied. "That's our focus. If you need anything you can't get on Longhorn 6, you come to us."

His answer baffled me. "Procurement? How is that a resource?"

He looked blank, then suddenly amused. "That's just what we call our… service guilds here. Resource is a name, not a commodity. There are all kinds. Lexa's resource provides procurement services. Adam's provides immigration services. He decides which resource newcomers get assigned to. Running off without his say-so was a bad idea. He's more or less the top of the food chain around here." He wagged a finger at me. "Not good to piss him off."

"But… doesn't Galactic issue work assignments here?"

"Oh, well, sure, officially." He shrugged. "But who cares? Galactic's little soldiers may stamp their forms and send all the required guff off to their distant corporate bosses, but they take their real orders from Adam or whoever he assigns them to, just like everybody else." Robbin leaned forward soberly. "The first and most important thing to understand now, Mara, is that 'official' channels are empty theater here. Everything on Longhorn 6 is run by the resources. You work with them, you'll thrive. Try getting all 'official' and you'll lose—badly. Got that?"

"I guess so," I said. "And these Cold Ones Adam Jones was going to sell me to; what are they? The beer resource?"

Robbin didn't smile. If anything, he looked even graver. Before he could answer, though, the door opened and Lexa strode back in.

I tensed, fearing she'd shoot me for moving. But she just tossed a leg over the exercise ball and planted herself on top of it.

"It's fixed," she said, ostensibly to Robbin but watching me. She grabbed two small flex-balls from the desk, and began to squeeze them absently. "Adam's added her to this month's invoice."

"Good," Robbin said, a bit uncertainly.

"Yeah. There's a price. But nothing we can't handle." Her grip on the flex-balls seemed to tighten. "So you're Mara, right?"

I nodded.

"From the *Fleetness*. Their roster lists you as a realtor?"

I nodded again.

"Well, here's the deal, take it or leave it. This tub's got no real estate, and you know nothing about how things function, which means a giant suck on our training and protection before you're of any use. Fronting you the necessary identity and credits to get started will cost us too. We'll do it, but I'll have sole authority to determine the balance of your debt—with interest—at any time. No appeal or recourse. I alone determine how your time is spent, including sleep. We protect you from competing resources, give you bunk, board, and training 'til you have a use here. In return, you work quickly to become a productive member of our resource, with whatever that entails. We don't have much room on Longhorn 6. You may have to share a bunk." Her eyes danced with amusement, though she didn't smile. "At least 'til we relocate. You in?"

Alarms were screaming in my brain. *Share a bunk? With whom?* I thought of those other women from *Fleetness*—some as young as twelve—herded off by rough, leering men. *No recourse or appeal? How much interest, and of what kind? All that front room tech hadn't looked like a comfort services operation. But still...*

"Robbin says you do procurement," I said. "What exactly do you procure?"

"Whatever's wanted," she replied. "If it's here, we get our hands on it. If it's not, we find out where it is and how to get it here. Affordably," she added, with a wry look that implied some second meaning.

"Do you procure women?" I asked, seeing no point in delicacy.

She snorted, then laughed. "Whores? You think *that's* what we want you for? You ain't got the tits for it, sweetness, or the spine. That's Chanele's resource anyway." She turned to Robbin. "How do you *find* these stray creatures? Tell her something about life, okay? I've got too much to do." She hoisted herself smoothly off the exercise ball and over to the desk, where she riffled through a pile of papers.

"Mara," Robbin said. "She's giving you a better deal than anyone else here will. I'd take it. Quickly. You owe her already just for saving you from Adam."

My mind continued to race. Take it or leave it, she'd said. In sales of property, personal or real, oral contracts aren't valid. Nor is any agreement made under duress. This could not possibly be legally binding. If I could get hold of Astoria, I could leave without breach. My license would remain clean. Meanwhile, I did need help with basic survival. I didn't have a choice. We all knew that.

"I agree to your terms."

Lexa smiled and came to shake my hand. Her grip was very strong.

~ o O o ~

I learned fast. I had to.

Three days later, I was packing up non-essentials in the resource mess in preparation for our relocation, when one of our terminal jockeys, a red-haired woman named Avini, came in and handed me a packet.

Inside I found a key card, skin chip, and bag of stick-on sensors identifying me as one Linda Margress, recently transferred from Longhorn 4 after unspecified conflict with her supervisor. That rankled me. I'd always gotten along perfectly with my superiors.

"Lexa can help you install that," Avini said, pointing to the skin chip.

"Thanks." I shuddered to think of Lexa near my skin for any reason. It seemed clear by now that the shared bunk she'd threatened was likely her own. Happily, that threat had not been followed up on... yet.

Avini rummaged through the cooler for a drink. "Can't wait for our new digs," she said, glancing at my half-filled boxes. "We got really lucky this time. Or smart." She smirked mysteriously. "Lexa's very resourceful."

"So I've gathered," I said. "I've been wondering, though. If Galactic owns all the space here, who decides how things are allocated?"

"Oh, turf's the biggest game in town," Avini said, opening her beverage. "With more newbies all the time, space keeps getting tighter, so everybody's always scrambling to trade up. There'd have been a Turf resource here ages ago, but no one's willing to hand one group sole authority over something that important."

"I can imagine," I replied. So real estate wasn't bought or sold per se here... but they were still negotiating deals for structured space—something I knew lots about. Suddenly, I could imagine being much more useful than Lexa supposed.

~ o O o ~

As moving day approached, our preparations grew increasingly frenetic. My new identity as Linda Margress enabled Lexa to start sending me on errands elsewhere in the station. I was terrified at first of screwing up and being exposed, but the tech was good. "Linda" passed through doors unchallenged, and I'd learned enough by then inside Lexa's warren to make better sense of what I encountered outside it. Soon I was walking Longhorn 6's corridors with the confidence of a native.

Robbin was a godsend in those first weeks, constantly appearing at my side to answer questions I hadn't known to ask yet, or to help with tasks Lexa had fired at me without sufficient explanation. I quickly came to appreciate and even trust him, but he was so attractive, not to mention so far above me in the pecking order, that I never suspected he might regard me as more than just another of the needy strays he loved to save.

I was often asked to carry messages to members of the Food Services resource with whom we were about to swap locations—a trade down for them. They liked to complain about that, and I took care to be a sympathetic listener, which made them even more forthcoming about the larger 'space-trading game' on Longhorn 6. I learned tons about who had or was or would be trading which space with whom, and why. As my grasp of which attributes and locations were commonly preferred or avoided increased, I began to see how such preferences might be manipulated even more effectively, and to suspect that Procurement could do better than Food Services' slightly larger but still cramped offering.

I had learned that the Transportation resource was looking not to move but to expand into new equipment and storage space. The Entertainment resource had a very spacious but unneeded warehouse they were tired of maintaining, but Transportation wasn't happy with its location. They wanted something closer to... Procurement's sector, as it happened. A few discreet inquiries convinced me that, with some trifling modifications, Entertainment's warehouse would make luxuriously spacious headquarters for us, if anyone looked beyond the building's current label to see that.

Leery of attracting any more of Lexa's attention, I dropped a few casual remarks about all this to Robbin instead. Two days later our resource was celebrating the announcement that we'd be moving not to Food Service's squalid nest down in the maintenance sector, but into Entertainment's even bigger building three decks up, smack in the station's dining and theater hub. Lexa had convinced Transportation to cover rental on Entertainment's warehouse, but move their excess storage and equipment into our better suited labyrinth of tunnels instead, free of further charge, allowing Food Services, who'd only been strong-armed by Lexa into trading down at all, to stay right where they were. Win, win, win. Everyone agreed that Lexa's cleverness seemed boundless.

Lexa, unfortunately, knew very well whose cleverness lay behind this sudden windfall. Robbin had been scrupulous about giving me credit for the idea. My *reward* was promotion to a desk job in the new hive, right in Lexa's grandly expanded office. I sat all day now at a small terminal to one side of Lexa's desk, where we could consult each other more readily about any other innovative opportunities I might come up with. And about the flatness of my chest and ass, and the cute way I always flinched when Lexa came to look over my shoulder. There were no rules in resource-land about sexual harassment in the workplace, and I soon realized that Lexa expressed interest, even admiration, through taunting and disparagement. My boyish figure might not have suited a whore, but Lexa didn't seem to mind it much.

My yearning to get off of Longhorn 6 altogether grew steadily. I floated the subject once with Robbin, whose disapproval was instantly palpable. Procurement hadn't taken me in and trained me, he admonished, just to send me off again with best wishes and a sandwich for the journey. I had debts to resolve before I went anywhere. I didn't air the topic again, but they vigilantly denied me any access to off-station communications after that.

I had an even bigger problem here, however, than mere loathing of the predatory Lexa. I simply wasn't formatted for a life of petty criminality. Ironically, it was the very act of recognizing another, much larger "innovative opportunity" for Lexa's resource that brought this fact home to me.

My interest in untapped approaches to Longhorn 6's quasi-real-estate game was now encouraged. Lexa began engineering chance opportunities for me to chat with folks from any resource I wished. She even lured the infamous Adam Jones to her office one evening on some other pretext, just so I could listen in while she salted their conversation with passing queries about his own thoughts on space around the station. He was an older gentleman who, in striking contrast to everyone else I'd seen here, looked and dressed more like a corporate board member than an underworld boss. Interest in the acquisition of place in this inherently spaceless canister was virtually bottomless, as his talk made clear. The upper echelon of underworld bosses here controlled ample wealth to purchase entire prefectures on lots of nice planets. Yet all that wealth was just being endlessly recycled on this dingy interstellar truck stop.

I was baffled by such short-sightedness until I recognized a subtle but important difference between myself and others here. Nearly everyone on Longhorn 6—maybe even its extraneous corporate functionaries—had been compelled to come as punishment for something, or been driven here only after exhausting all better options. The very idea of "elsewhere" must have seemed void to them even before arrival. The struggle just to survive here, much less bend this insular network of Darwinian ambitions and imperatives to one's own advantage, was so consuming that perhaps even those who won the game were too shaped by it to retain awareness of any world beyond.

I, however, had not come needing to stand or die here, and thus still thought to look outside the cage we shared. That simple inclination, I realized in a dizzying flash, might constitute a kind of super-power here, if used cleverly.

$$\sim \; \text{o} \; \text{O} \; \text{o} \; \sim$$

That night I fished Procurement's own extensive data banks, then reduced my findings to a single, easily comprehensible page. Next morning, I walked into Lexa's office and asked her to join me at my terminal.

She raised a brow in surprise, and came to lean, too closely as usual, over my shoulder. This time I didn't flinch, and I could tell she noticed.

"What's this, then?" she asked.

"The top list shows price ranges for extensive real-estate holdings on several desirable planets, all of which were available for purchase just prior to my departure from Earth. The middle list contains my conservative guesses at the likely net worth of Longhorn 6's most prosperous resource bosses, including yourself."

"That's any of your business why?" she asked; then, before I could respond, she snorted, "Ridiculously conservative, actually."

"I didn't have access to sufficient data to be more accurate. This longer list down here contains my much more educated estimates of probable return over just five years on any of the investments listed above."

Lexa leaned even harder into my shoulder to scan the bottom list with increasing interest, shoving her breasts against my back. "Impressive, but why should I care about real estate stuck halfway across the galaxy?" she asked, breathing the question into my ear.

"Why shouldn't you care?" I replied, shrugging her off as I stood and turned to face her squarely. "That seems a better question."

She just stared, trying, it seemed, to make sense of my answer, or perhaps of my behavior in general.

"This resource keeps meticulous track of every item on every cargo manifest, and every passenger or crew member aboard any vessel traveling within 40,000 light years of this station," I said. "That's how we locate what we wish to 'procure'. The planetary assets I've listed here are all far closer than that. Why ignore them?"

She just seemed startled by my denseness. "There are lots of ways to steer a slice of cargo from its intended route. We can lure an entire ship here, if needed. But how am I supposed to finesse some big chunk of Elysium 17 over to Longhorn 6? If anybody here wanted to purchase planetary real estate, he'd go there to enjoy it. I bring items *here* for people who need to have them *here*."

"Money moves independently of the land that generates it, Lexa. Money's easier to move than any other item in the universe. You of all people know that. Does no one here want to move the kind of money I've listed here as well?"

Lexa grew uncharacteristically silent for the second time in five minutes. I could see gears grinding into reverse behind her eyes.

"Every person on that list could nearly double their hoard within ten years," I said into her silence, "just by going to see a decent realtor."

"There... are no realtors here," she said, half gaping as my point finally pierced her shield of entrenched assumptions.

"There's *one*," I said. "This is what I'm trained to do, Lexa. Remotely, if necessary. Interested in an untapped market for something more lucrative than the occasional case of luxophore vials or taze-guns? Something for the more discriminating customer?"

"Well, well, well," she murmured, gazing inward now.

I had never seen her so off balance, and I grabbed the opportunity. "I know where and how to look for bargains. I can recognize a trap and scam the scammers in this market. I understand the language, the games, the miles of documentation involved, the legal and financial knots and how to cut them. I just need you to start tilling the soil here while I get on the net and troll around."

"Well, well, fucking well," she said, grinning at something other than my tits and ass for once.

$$\sim o \; O \; o \sim$$

Lexa wasted no time. By the following morning, Procurement's unlikely rising star had an office of her own. Our discriminating customers would, of course, need to feel that they could take me seriously. I even found the nerve to suggest that turning down the sexual brinksmanship a little might crank up my productivity even further. To my quiet amazement, Lexa had just nodded with a wry look of—was that actual respect—or just pragmatic avarice?

Most importantly, my new office contained a terminal with access to unrestricted communications. I could hardly manage complex, mega-real estate transactions, after all, without engaging in research and communication beyond Longhorn 6. My plan seemed to be working even better than I'd hoped.

As my fortunes rose, Robbin's "supportiveness" increased. I finally got the picture when he came by one afternoon to ask if I'd have a drink with him at the Blue Muse: a pricey eatery I'd heard about, but never dared to enter, given the debt I was already incurring just by breathing here under Lexa's sponsorship. When I reminded him of my strapped condition, he just looked surprised and said the drinks would be on him, of course. Though he also assured me that, given my amazing progress, I'd surely be settled up with Lexa in record time.

The Lemon Drops we ordered must have cost him dearly in their frosty flutes of real glass. They contained at least a squeeze of real lemon; I found a seed in one of mine. Ignited by the liquor, his charm grew almost incandescent, and I was very flattered—still incredulous, in fact, that a guy this cute would even notice me. A few weeks earlier, I'd probably have lunged at the extra shelter his affection might lend me. But as pretty as he was, and as helpful as he'd been, he was a creature of this place which I now hoped to leave soon. I owed him, yes, but I could not pretend to love him. I laughed at his witticisms, and expressed my gratitude for his many kindnesses, but continued to pretend I didn't understand how much more he wanted.

~ o O o ~

Certain that Lexa would carefully monitor my off-station communications, I was perfectly behaved for several weeks. My pursuit of investment opportunities was real and relentless. I even sent a few short missives to Robbin about how exciting it was to have serious work again, and how invested I felt in my future here, hoping that Lexa would see them.

Not until our first big transaction was in motion did I dare hope Lexa might have grown distracted and complacent enough for me to make an attempt at summoning rescue. Having found a credible real estate opportunity in which Astoria was involved, I sent them a complex contractual proposal with an encrypted link to my brief S.O.S. embedded in the yards of fine print at its end. I felt sure their legal sniffers would find it quickly enough, but hoped Lexa would never even read that far. Fine print, after all, was what I was here to spare her.

More than a week passed before Lexa called me to her office to discuss one of our recent proposals. When I arrived she asked me to close the door and come look at something on her desk display. I walked to her side and looked down:

From Broker Mara Sandstrom, urgent. *Fleetness* destroyed on entry into Longhorn space; unknown number of survivors held on

Longhorn 6. Send rescue. Security here doubtful. Respond to this alias only.

There wasn't even time to blanch before Lexa's backhand struck me hard enough to rattle teeth. I staggered back, holding my burning cheek and staring at her through watering eyes.

"Traitorous bitch!" she snarled. "How dare you betray me—Robbin—all of us this way, after what we've done for you?"

"How is wanting off this place betrayal?" I demanded. "I can do this work for you from anywhere, but I'll never belong here. That must be as obvious to you as it is to me. Why should you care if I manage your new empire from some place with a real sky?"

"Not just traitorous, but stupid after all," she spat in disgust. "Did you really think anyone here would let someone who knows all you do about this place just flee into the arms of some off-station corporate authority? Hasn't it occurred to you, Ms. Smartypants, what an exposure threat you'd be? If Adam were to discover this little stunt of yours, he'd have you iced yesterday." She shook her head, almost wearily. "Galactic closes its eyes to what goes on here because we make it worth its while to do so. Astoria would have no such motivation. Don't you get that?"

I did now. My stomach was a cold, hard knot of fear. They'd never let me go, however much debt I paid off. They might not even let me live now.

"If you had succeeded at this," Lexa growled, "I would have been held responsible—by anyone here with something to lose—and that's *everyone*! I'd have been fodder for the Cold Ones, and this whole resource would have been stripped of respect or leverage, and reorganized if not dismantled."

I glanced back miserably at the message still on her screen.

"Yes," she said. "That needs fixing. *Now*."

"How?" I asked, no longer able to meet her gaze.

"I don't know or care, but you have three hours to convince me that Astoria has been persuaded to disregard your idiotic message, or I'll march you to the Cold Ones myself." One look at her hard expression told me this threat wasn't empty.

~ o O o ~

Back in my office, I tried to compose some credible reversal of my appeal, but there was nothing I could say to Astoria now that would not arouse even greater suspicion. I still had no precise idea of who the Cold Ones were, or what they'd do to me, but with only three hours left before finding out, there was nothing to lose by trying something even more desperate.

I'd heard more than once about a Galactic enforcement official here, a Major Samuel Fisk, whom everyone resented or admired for refusing to be bought. Local lore held him as the only corporate functionary on Longhorn 6 wholly loyal to Galactic. It seemed time I met him.

~ o O o ~

As I hurried to find him, I kept looking over my shoulder, fearful of being overtaken by some henchman of Lexa's, but I saw nobody following. When I arrived at Major Fisk's unassuming complex, claiming urgent need to see him, I was ushered straight into his spartan office.

"How may I help you, miss…?" he asked, awaiting my name.

"Mara Sandstrom," I said, breathlessly. "I'm told you are the only fully trustworthy man on Longhorn 6. Is that true?" Confident of my shrewdly honed "realtor's ability" to read people, I knew I'd be able to parse his response for genuineness if I took him by surprise.

He looked nonplussed. "I pride myself on thinking so. My loyalties are to no one but Galactic, if that is what you mean."

He did seem sincere. I nodded. "Good. I need your help. I was brought here from the *Fleetness*." This drew a startled expression. "Before I could be processed, I was coerced into the service of… a criminal organization here."

"I am well aware of the resources," he said, "and I am in none of their pockets, if that's what you're worried about."

"Yes," I said, deeply relieved. "I have just escaped from one of them after being threatened with execution. I've contacted my previous employer—"

"Astoria Corporation, I assume?" he interjected. At my surprised pause, he spread his hands and said, "You arrived aboard the *Fleetness*…"

"Of course." Hoping my attachment to a rival company would not dispose him against me, I continued. "I believe Astoria may come to retrieve me, if I live that long. Can you protect me until then?"

"I'm glad you came to me," he said reassuringly. "I do know people who can help you. I'll escort you to them personally."

"I would be so grateful," I said.

He touched his desk display, and a functionary entered. After instructing the man to notify my prospective protectors of our imminent arrival, he turned back to me and said, "Shall we go?"

"I don't know how to thank you."

"No need for thanks," he said. "This is what I'm here for."

~ o O o ~

Neither the furtive route we traveled, nor the dark, deserted service tunnel to which he led me aroused my suspicion. We were here to hide me. Of course it would be done secretively, far from prying eyes. Not until the two forbidding men who met us there grabbed hold of me and clapped my arms into restraints did I understand I'd been betrayed.

"Who are you?" I demanded of my captors, tugging at my bonds to no avail.

"The Cold Ones," one of them replied, with the hint of a smirk. "You haven't guessed?"

"Liar!" I shouted at Fisk, my heart sinking. "Who owns you? Lexa?"

"I am owned by no one here but my employer, Galactic Enterprises."

"Then why?"

"Has no one told you who commissioned the sabotage of your vessel?" he asked. "In all this time? I'm surprised to find so much discretion here."

"Sabotage?" I asked, feeling lightheaded. "Who would want—?"

"My employer did not want yours to gain a foothold on Greenleaf 43." He shrugged apologetically. "Business at this scale requires unpleasant

things of us all. Gentlemen," he said, nodding at my captors. Then he turned
and walked away as if I were a bundle of celluboard left for the recyclers.

~ o O o ~

My captors neither spoke again, nor exhibited any perverse pleasure in
their work, but their grip never wavered until I was locked into an unfur-
nished, corrugated metal holding cell not far from where I'd been delivered.
I was soon visited there by a new if equally laconic man who handed me
a drab paper jumpsuit and demanded my clothes and few possessions in
exchange. I was not allowed privacy, but he kept his hands to himself, showing no sign of prurient interest while I changed. When I'd finished, he gave
me a bottle of water and some refreshment stand chips, then turned to go.

"How will I be killed?" I asked as he reached for the door.

"Killed?" he said over his shoulder.

"That's what you do, isn't it?" I said, trying to sound brave for some
reason. More reflexive realtor training, I suppose.

"We let people think so." He turned back to face me. "But in fact, little
of what you've been told about us is true."

"I've been told nothing," I said in frustration. "People keep mentioning
you guys like you're the ultimate nightmare, but they never tell me what you
do. You're a resource, I take it?"

He nodded. "A sort of Waste Disposal resource. We dispose of those
who prove too useless to merit the space and air they consume here, or too
troublesome to those in power. We let the general populace imagine what
they will, of course, because that scares them more effectively than anything
else, but we don't really salvage organs here, or hoard gold teeth. There's not
even any killing, unless we're left no choice. That's up to you, of course."

"Then how do you—?"

"You'll know soon enough," he said, turning away again. "Let your current troubles suffice, Ms. Sandstrom, and rest while you can." He passed
through the door, which locked behind him.

I sat down against the wall, seeking some comfortable position on the metal floor, and pondered the long list of mistakes that had landed me here. No wonder Lexa hadn't prevented my flight. She'd known there really wasn't any place for me to run. Now I was to be "disposed of", without being killed?

"This one?" said a voice outside my door.

"Yes, sir. She's in there."

My cell door clicked open once again, and a man I recognized walked in, looking as dapper and respectable as ever.

"Why, Mr. Jones," I said, beyond surprise by now. "I don't suppose you've come to rescue me."

"I rarely offer second chances, Ms. Sandstrom. Never third ones." He closed the door and leaned against the jamb. "What a lot of trouble you have been."

"So what brings a man of your importance here?" I asked.

"I sometimes check on my employees' work, especially when such important guests are involved."

"Your employees? You run this resource too?"

"No one outside our membership is allowed to know that, but yes, I oversee both immigration and emigration here. You slipped past me in one direction, but I really couldn't let it happen twice. It's quite crucial to us all that you be thoroughly misplaced before Astoria's rescue mission arrives."

"They're coming then?" I asked, with less enthusiasm than I might have felt if I had still hoped to be around for their arrival.

"Oh yes," Jones said. "They've been quite stealthy about it, but they're on their way, and with a military escort." He shook his head. "Accidents won't be viable this time, I'm afraid. We must let them dock, and seem quite as appalled as anyone to find you've disappeared. Rest assured, however, that we shall leave no stone unturned in our attempt to discover your abductors. Examples will be made of… well, all kinds of people by the time we're finished finding out what happened to you."

"And what is going to happen to me?"

"As you may know, Ms. Sandstrom, our corporate leaders here on Longhorn 6 abhor waste of any kind. Merely killing even very undesirable people results in nothing but expense without profit. On the other hand, there are numerous corporate clients out there desperate to reduce the excessive expense, labyrinthine regulatory burden, and endless documentation associated with any *legitimate* labor force. In places like Longhorn 6, Galactic Enterprises has found a way to address these problems quite profitably, by hiring people like me to harvest useless, unproductive individuals and convert them into an astonishingly valuable commodity. As I believe you have been told, Ms. Sandstrom, we're not here to kill you. We are here to offer you a brand new, immensely more productive life on Steele 17, a lovely planet in the—"

"I know very well where Steele 17 is!" I gasped, shooting to my feet. "It's a strip-mine in the Chlorite system! You're selling me into slavery?"

"No, Ms. Sandstrom. Galactic will be doing that. I am just a humble middle man conveying self-selected candidates like yourself for their consideration." He stood away from the wall, and put his hand to the door. "I did give you a second chance, my dear. And for a while I was almost glad I had. What a shame." He shook his head like a disappointed father. "Perhaps they'll need a realtor on Steele 17 as badly as we did."

He left me then, gaping in dismay. I had wanted off of Longhorn 6—but not this way.

~ o O o ~

Eventually exhaustion prevailed and I slept on my cell floor. Sometime later, a hand on my shoulder nudged me awake. Robbin bent over me, a finger to his lips.

"Come. Quietly," he whispered. "We've only got a minute."

Seemed like I was always following this man. I climbed stiffly to my feet. Whatever he meant to do with me now could hardly be worse than slavery on Steele 17.

I followed him into the corridor and found the two men who'd brought me here sprawled face down on the floor. I looked back up at Robbin in astonishment, but he shook his head and waved me urgently past them. He seemed to know where he was going, stopping only to peer around corners or listen at doors before proceeding. We finally stopped at a floor hatch, where Robbin took something from his pocket, shoved it against a key slot, then pushed the hatch door open and waved me through ahead of him. We climbed down into a poorly illuminated crawl space, through which we hurried in a crouch.

The cramped passage snaked on endlessly. Twice we had to freeze and hold our breaths as running footsteps passed above us. By the time Robbin helped me up into some blessedly taller service corridor, I had an awful crick in my neck.

"Where are we going?" I finally dared to whisper.

He just waved me after him around two more corners to a room lined with wall-lockers full of grimy coveralls and jumbled tools.

"Put this on," said Robbin, handing me a set of coveralls before pulling on his own. Then he rummaged around and produced two welding helmets. "Don't forget to tuck your hair inside," he said, handing me one before donning his.

"What are we doing?" I asked again. "Did Lexa send you?"

"Lexa won't be sending me anywhere but back to the Cold Ones, after this."

I stopped fiddling with my helmet and looked up in surprise. "You did this behind her back?"

"There was some other way?" His voice was muffled by the helmet, but his tone was unambiguously grim. "Astoria's headed here to get you," he said. "ETA five days. Lexa's spitting sparks about it."

"I know," I said. "Adam Jones told me."

Robbin's faceplate snapped around toward me. "How would you have talked to Jones?"

"He came to my cell. He's the Cold Ones' boss."

"No shit!" Robbin exclaimed. "That's info worth a fortune."

"How did you find out where I was?" I asked.

"Called in a lot of favors," he said. "You're not the first stray I've helped, you know. It pays to make friends—even here."

"So, if you're at odds with Lexa, where are we going?"

"I'm not sure yet," he admitted. "I was lucky just to find out where you were before they killed you. Haven't had a chance to think much further. But there are places we can hide until your ship comes in."

"Then what?" I asked. "For you, I mean? Where will you go?"

"With you, of course. I've just crossed Lexa badly, and cold-cocked two Cold Ones. Can't very well stay here now—not breathing anyway."

I shut my eyes, thankful that the helmet hid my face. How would he feel, I wondered, when he learned that even after this, I still didn't love him? "Actually, they weren't going to kill me," I said, half-apologetically.

"Oh, really?" he asked skeptically. "I've never heard of anyone returning from delivery to the Cold Ones."

"They don't," I said. "Adam turns them over to Galactic, who sells them to corporate interests looking for free, unregulated labor. I was slated for sale to Steele 17."

Robbin simply stared at me.

"None of you knew this? Really?" I asked.

"But the stories," Robbin said, sounding stunned. "Everyone's heard—"

"—what everyone else assumes or invents," I finished for him. "The Cold Ones just let you all believe yourselves."

"'Til they're so scary, we don't even want to think about them, much less snoop. It's the perfect curtain." Robbin shook his head. "If people here knew that Adam was selling even the worst of us to Galactic, they'd riot. He'll want us dead now even more than Lexa does. We'd better keep moving." He grabbed a hand torch off the bench beside us and handed it to me. "Just act like you can't wait to weld something."

$$\sim \text{o } \mathbf{O} \text{ o} \sim$$

For three days we snuck from hidey-hole to hidey-hole. Robbin seemed intimately familiar with every service hatch and ventilation shaft on Longhorn 6. He was an accomplished thief as well. We ate better on the run than I had ever eaten at the resource—and for free.

Early on our fourth day, Robbin found us a small, unoccupied living module where we could sit in plush inflatable chairs before a simulated roaring fire on the virteo screen.

"Why do you help people like me?" I asked him. "What's in it for you?"

"There's an ancient myth from Earth about a bandit king named Robbin Hat," he said, sheepishly. "Ever hear it?"

I shook my head.

"My father did," he said. "He loved to tell it to me when I was little. He named me after Robbin Hat, who stole from the rich and gave to the poor." Robbin shrugged. "My dad tried to be that kind of thief, I think. I guess I've always wanted to be too." He stretched out lazily, wiggling his bare toes before the virteo fire as if it were actually warm.

He had never seemed more charming to me than he did at that moment. "Robbin," I said, "I've been thinking about what Adam and Galactic have been doing here, and if we tell Astoria—"

The sound of a keycard in the door brought us both to our feet. We whirled around to find ourselves staring at the barrel of a snub-nosed scrap gun—the kind used by people who don't mind a mess.

"What a cozy place," Lexa said to Robbin, her face a mask of cold fury. "Your realtor find this for you?"

Robbin just looked blank, then dropped his gaze. "How'd you find us?"

"If your network was better than mine," she said contemptuously, "you'd have been my boss, and I'd have been your toady." She glanced at me with even greater disdain. "Her I saw coming, Robbin, but I never thought you'd stab me in the back. You know what Adam thinks of me by now. I've gone from trusted confidante to laughing stock."

"Adam's always thought you were as clueless as everybody else here," I said, recklessly. "He as good as told me so when he dropped by my cell to see how well his Cold Ones were doing their job the other day." Taunting her was suicidal, but Robbin had said that our new information about Adam was worth a fortune. I hoped she'd think so too.

"What crap are you barfing up now?" she growled.

"Adam is the Cold Ones' boss," I said. "Or hadn't he mentioned that? He uses them to harvest slave labor here on Longhorn 6, for Galactic to sell off on other planets. That's what really happens to the people they 'dispose of', but I'm sure Adam's already shared that with you too. He says it's very profitable. Does he kick back any of that wealth to trusted confidantes like you?"

"What an inventive mind you've got in that pretty head," said Lexa. "I almost hate to blow it off."

"It's true!" Robbin insisted. "Jones is in Galactic's pocket, and I'll bet slave labor's not the only way he's sold us out to them. How do you think he's held so much power for so long? He plays both ends."

"Why should I believe you either?" Lexa snapped, pointing her gun back at him.

"Adam said he would be making examples of a lot of people after Astoria comes," I pressed. "Scapegoats to explain my disappearance. How much you wanna bet that you'll be one of them?"

"Shut your fucking mouth!" she yelled, her gun on me again. But I could tell we had her, and began to talk as fast as—well, a realtor.

"Galactic sabotaged the *Fleetness*."

"What?" Lexa blurted.

I looked her in the eye. "If you don't believe me, ask Major Fisk. I think he arranged it personally." Lexa's jaw went slack, and I decided it was time to bet everything. "Galactic and Astoria are quietly at war, Lexa, and Astoria's been losing. Can you imagine what they'd give for what we know about Galactic? They could destroy their biggest rival overnight. Forget Procurement. Astoria could give us rule of this entire station!"

"Or I could kill you both and let Astoria hand everything to me," she said.

"Your testimony is just secondhand hearsay," I told her. "I'm the only direct or credible witness, and Astoria won't pay for what won't hold up in court."

"None of that'll matter anyway after Adam fingers you for Mara's kidnap, Lexa," Robbin interjected. "Incriminating you discredits your testimony and saves his neck. You can't think he won't see that. I'd be pissed at us too, Lexa, but come on."

"It doesn't matter how we do this," Lexa said. "Adam will—"

"Adam will go down in flames with his partner, Galactic," I cut in. "Help us hide for one more day, get us onto that ship alive tomorrow, and let Astoria set you up for life. Or shoot that thing and go back to your trusted confidante for a pat on the head. That's the deal. Take it or leave it."

~ o O o ~

The rest, as they say, is history. Lexa held up her part of the bargain easily enough. Jones was so sure of her that he never thought to look for us under her skirts. Rumor has it he was last seen shortly after Lexa got us aboard Astoria's transport, screaming away from Longhorn 6 in a small private craft. His Cold Ones have vanished into legend here as well.

Galactic Enterprises is history too. And, as expected, Astoria has rewarded us lavishly enough to make even Lexa blush.

It's been six months now, and I'm finally getting used to my new routine here. Robbin is my second-in-command. Lexa… Well, Lexa works for us. She's our top enforcer now; number-three dog in Longhorn 6's food chain, and damned well paid for what she does. Not all she might have hoped for, but considering that I knew enough to have her clapped in chains for life if I had chosen to share her history with Astoria too, I think she's content.

Am I bummed to find myself still stuck out here on Longhorn 6? Not so much. I live in the former Station Master's palace now, and spend my days administering Astoria's new construction project. Longhorn 6 already orbited a star. It just had no planets, so Astoria has decided to build a very nice one. I can see the work progressing from my window, without even getting out of bed. And when it's done and ready for settlement, its first on-site brokerage will be mine.

Robbin is still trying to convince me to be his Maid Marianne, but I haven't decided. One way or another, he'll be fine.

And so will I.

The Hippie Monster
of Eel River

The submission guidelines for Close Encounters of the Urban Kind *called for "when urban legends meet alien encounters." Thankfully, it also said that the urban legends could be invented by the author. I ran with that, setting this story twenty years after my novel* Eel River, *the events forgotten and mythologized, ready to terrify a new generation.* Close Encounters *was published by Apex in 2010.*

Krystle leaned over the bathroom countertop, the fake-wood-grain surface pressing against her hipbone as she got as close to the mirror as possible. She paused, holding the liquid eyeliner a fraction of an inch from her eye, waiting for the tremor to stop. Probably she should have done this first. Another example of *planning ahead*, as her mother loved to go on and on about.

Planning ahead. Krystle planned ahead *just fine*, thank you very much.

She willed her hand to be still, and it finally obeyed, at least long enough for her to draw thick black lines around both eyes. It quivered a bit at the end of the left eye, but the mascara would hide the raggedness.

"Christina? Are you almost done in there?" Her mother's voice was accompanied by a sharp rapping. The thin wood of the bathroom door bowed inward with the force of the old woman's fist.

"Krystle," the girl muttered, and then more loudly, "Jeeeezus! Can't I have some *privacy* in my own *bathroom*?"

"If you had your own bathroom, maybe you could!" After one final pound, her mother moved off down the shag-carpeted hallway.

"Jeeee-zus," Krystle said again, relishing the sound of it, and the feeling of the sibilants on her tongue. She put the eyeliner down and moved on to the blush, painting a reasonable approximation of a healthy glow into the hollows of her cheeks. Then three coats of mascara, some dark lip liner surrounding peach gloss lipstick, a spritz of White Diamonds, and she was good to go.

She scooped all the makeup into the top drawer and turned to leave, then spotted her hand mirror still resting on the closed seat of the toilet. "Right: clean up after yourself, Krystle," she said, bending down. The sight of the scraps of dust at the corner of the mirror called to her. One more little snort, and then she'd be off. Trent wouldn't be here for another ten minutes at least.

Pulling the paper bindle from the coin pocket at the front of her Levi's, Krystle carefully unfolded it, measured out less than a quarter of what she had left, and nudged it onto the mirror with the razor blade. Then she squatted next to the toilet, tap-tap-tapping the powder ever finer before arranging it in two short lines. Next came the dollar bill, rolled tight to make a straw. She'd done it through a fifty one time. Her dream was to use a hundred-dollar bill, but nobody had ever managed to pull together that much cash at once.

Some day.

Leaning over the mirror, Krystle snorted the speed: right nostril first, then left. After scooting the dollar around to make sure no residue was wasted, she unrolled and folded it and shoved it back in her pocket, then went to the sink. She wet her fingertips, lifted them to her nose, and inhaled the drops of water with a sharp sniff. Then she stood there a moment, waiting for the drip.

Ahhh.

The tangy cash-scented stinging burn of the drug as it touched the back of her throat made her smile. *This is what it's all about.*

Sniffling, she stuck the mirror in the drawer with her makeup and unlocked the bathroom door.

~ o O o ~

Trent drove them out beyond the valley, over the hill to the Eel River, not far from Clayton's. He parked just below the bridge, next to Russ's battered red F150 pickup; another truck pulled in behind him, blocking them in.

Krystle did not care. It was the first weekend of summer: the biggest-ass party in a season of big-ass parties, and she and Trent would be here till dawn.

She could already hear the laughter and smell the cigarette smoke down by the river as she started to open her door and sidle out into the night. "Hang on," Trent said, pulling out a bindle of his own. He favored glossy dark magazine paper, usually *Sports Illustrated*. Krystle preferred snowy-white printer paper: pure and simple. Clayton would package it any way you liked; that was what was great about him. He understood his customers.

Anyway, Krystle would not turn down Trent's speed, no matter how it was packaged. She let go of the door handle and turned to face her boyfriend.

He measured a couple of generous lumps out onto the scrap of steel he used for a traveling mirror, then coaxed them into four lines with the side of his driver's license. Krystle almost offered him her razor blade, tucked behind her bindle in her jeans, but he was doing fine. He liked to be the big man, the man with the truck, the man with the drugs.

Her man.

It was all right with her. When he offered up the mirror and his own rolled-up bill (a five—big man indeed), she leaned in and snorted them up expertly. "Thanks, dude."

"My pleasure." He took his own lines, then stuck the mirror in the glove box without even wiping it down.

Everyone was different.

"Yow," Krystle said as the harsh powder sat on her nasal passages. She'd go dip her fingers in the river to get the drip she craved. Plus, you were supposed to rinse out your nose every time. If you didn't, you'd get a deviated septum, like all those coke users in the eighties.

Her heart racing, she got down from the truck and headed for the water, greeting friends and strangers as she went. Well, no one was a stranger really, not in this small town; she could name every kid on the rocky shore if she took the time. But they weren't *important*. Only her friends were *important*. And rinsing her nose, that was too. Krystle felt nine feet tall and powerful and thin and strong and *rocking* solid hot as she strode to the river's edge, but her nose twitched and *damn* she needed to get some water in there right now damn it!

"Careful of the Hippie Monster," Trent called out as he joined a few guys gathered around the keg—John, and Russ, and a big hairy dude everyone called the Ogre. The guys all laughed, and Krystle rolled her eyes.

"Yeah, right." They thought they were so funny. Get a little beer in them and they thought they were even funnier.

Besides, the Hippie Monster had been further down the river. And it was years ago. And everyone said it was just a wild animal, plus some kind of cult, with a bunch of idiots OD'ing on hallucinogens.

Which only went to prove what an urban legend it was. You couldn't OD on hallucinogens. You could have a bad trip, sure; but you only overdosed on heroin or PCP or stuff like that.

The river water had a muddy, green-algae-like scent to it, but it cleaned her nostrils and gave her the drip she needed just fine. Suddenly thirsty, Krystle went in search of a beer.

She did not have to look far.

~ o O o ~

Clayton was supposed to come down the hill about midnight and hang out, someone said. With his long greasy blonde hair and filthy blue jeans,

Krystle always thought he didn't exactly fit in with the high school crowd. That, plus being super old, like forty or something. But she would be happy to see him. He was one of the few adults who treated the kids like equals.

And sold them speed, of course.

He cooked it up in a shed behind his cabin. It was totally reinforced and triple-insulated to keep the smell inside, and to not burn down the forest. His entire complex—shed, cabin, lean-to garage, and a whole collection of dead cars—was protected by a tall fence with razor-wire on top and a couple of big scary dogs.

Krystle remembered the first time she'd been included on a trip to Clayton's. That was when she was with Jeff; before Trent. She'd been so excited that she got to go, to see where it came from. To meet the guy himself—an outlaw! It felt dangerous and cool and important.

The reality was a bit bleaker than that, but she'd still felt special sitting on the countertop in his kitchen, sipping from the drink they'd given her—amaretto and milk. It was too sweet and kind of gross, and alcohol had never really been her thing anyway. Plus, the lights were too bright inside. She'd stared down into the drink as Jeff and Clayton did their business (this was before she'd started buying her own stash), watching the ice cubes melt into the milk, making little rivers of clear liquid.

Krystle sniffed again, the memory making her queasy. She took a sip of her beer, then set the plastic cup down on a rock. Not thirsty any more.

What she was now was energized, totally, pure blasting focused WIRED energized oh my god. Her legs needed to *move*, her arms wanted to pump and bring air into her body, sweet fresh oxygen. She hadn't really needed that last line... Oh well, it would wear off eventually. Faster, if she walked a bit.

She could go up to the road, but then she'd have to walk through the party again, all the laughing guys. And someone would want to *talk* to her, and she just fucking couldn't handle that right now, okay? She could walk up to Clayton's; but she didn't like his dogs, and if he wasn't expecting company, that could be bad. But she had to go somewhere, do something.

Her heart was racing, beating way too fast. She wasn't scared—this had totally happened before, she knew what to do—but it was super annoying, and if she had to *talk* to someone it would be even *more* annoying, and did there always have to be someone around asking questions, did you always have to *explain* shit to everyone?

Krystle started walking down the flat, rocky beach, away from the party. She picked her way slowly at first so that she would look like she was just strolling, so Trent wouldn't think she was mad and follow her, or want to fuck in the bushes or something. But her wired-up muscles strained and yearned against her pace. She was walking like a robot, she knew it, but couldn't stop. It was dark out, probably nobody noticed.

She got to the bend in the river, where the beach narrowed. Now she was out of sight of the party—of anyone who wasn't right down by the water's edge, anyway. She could walk faster here, and she did.

Damn, it felt good.

Krystle strode on, and the night air filled her lungs, and her legs burst with energy and speed—well, ha-ha, speed as in going-fast, but speed as in the drug too, of course! Which is why it was called that, she knew that, but it was funny, sometimes she forgot. It was speed because it made your heart go fast and your thoughts go fast and your muscles go fast. And your stomach too: speed was the best thing for dieting, like, ever. Speed had taken Krystle's plump, curvy early-teen body and winnowed it down to the lean, strong, gorgeous thing she was today.

God, she loved speed.

The beach narrowed more as the sounds of the party faded behind her. Soon she'd have to turn back; the trees grew all the way down to the river's edge, dipping their branches into the water. But she didn't want to go back, she wasn't ready. The party seemed like a stupid thing. Why had she wanted to come, after all? She hated these people, everyone. Same old same old. Why did she have to live in this stupid town anyway? Why couldn't she ever get *out*?

She could walk back and forth on this part of the beach. But that seemed even stupider than the party. And someone would see.

Krystle got to the low branches on the water and peered around them.

The beach picked up just past them in another long, open stretch. She pushed at the branches, but the trees were too thick and wouldn't move, wouldn't let her through. She'd have to go into the water.

She stood back, hands on her hips, and thought about it. Then she bent down and took off her high-heeled sandals.

The water was shallow here, and much colder than she'd expected. When she swam in the Eel River, it was usually later in the summer; this felt like snow-melt. She gasped as it touched her ankles, and slipped a little on the slimy algae that grew on the rocks. Reaching out with the hand that wasn't holding her sandals, she steadied herself on a thick branch, but it swayed at her touch.

"Fuck!" she yelled, only barely managing to keep her balance. If she fell in, she'd get her stash wet, and ruin it. It would dissolve in the river. It was only about fifteen bucks worth, but still. Not like she was a millionaire or anything.

With a colossal effort, Krystle kept from immersing herself. When she was certain she had her footing, she stepped forward, moving around the protruding branches.

The icy water lapped at her calves as it wicked up her jeans, approaching her knees. It felt like it was only about a foot deep at the deepest part, but damn, it was cold.

Then she'd gotten to the edge of the branches; now she was past, and there was the rest of the beach. Krystle picked up her pace and scrambled up towards the bank. Her foot slipped again on a big flat slick rock; she nearly tumbled up onto the shore, shivering and dripping.

"Fuck," she said again, softer this time.

Her heart was still pounding, but this time with anxiety. She had come *this close* to falling in and losing her stash. And getting all wet, and looking like a dork.

Not only that, but she would have to go back through the water to get back! Stupid, stupid!

"I'll go up to the road," she told herself. She realized she was on the crazy hippie beach now; they would have a path to the road, even if nobody had lived here for years. Then she could walk back to the party.

Right. Cool.

Satisfied, Krystle started walking down the beach, looking for the path. It was sandier on this side of the trees, and a bit steeper. And damn, it was dark. She wished she had a flashlight, but who took a flashlight to a party? Only dorks, she was sure.

But how hard could it be to find a path?

Once she got to the road, it would be fine. Of course there weren't any streetlights out here, twenty miles down a country dirt road, but her eyes would adjust to the starlight and the way would be open enough for her to find her way back. The noise of the party would guide her. There was only one road, anyway.

But damn, it was dark.

Suddenly, Krystle was very, very ready to get back. A crawling panic seized her and she half-ran up to the top of the beach, where the forest encroached hard and thick. Where was their stupid path? There had to be one. It would be overgrown, but it would have to be there, sort of, anyway. But she found nothing. She pushed and clawed at the branches and they clawed her back, scratching her face. "Fuck!"

Then one part of the forest seemed less thick than the rest, and she could see a bit of sandy ground under it, she thought. Or at least a lighter patch. Krystle pushed into it, shoving the branches aside and sliding her skinny body into the opening. But three steps in, it had closed up again. She turned all the way around: nowhere to go.

Whimpering, she slipped back out and stood on the beach once more. Her whole body was shaking, and her heart was slamming away, must be a hundred beats a minute.

Krystle turned around and looked at the water. She would have to go back through it.

After she rested. As much as her body was racing, she was also exhausted, she realized. She sat down on the cold sand and tried to catch her breath, to still her heart. *Just slow down,* she thought, soothing herself. *Slow down.*

That's when she noticed the bottom of the river glowing.

It was a low, steady green iridescence, pulsating slightly. The light made a sort of broken shimmering on the surface of the water, but it was also changing in its depths, she could see that.

"What the fuck?" Krystle leaned forward, too frightened to get up and have a closer look; too fascinated to leave it be.

Besides, she couldn't run away. Where would she go?

Her heart rate doubled, it seemed, and ached in her chest.

What *was* it? "Algae," she whispered aloud. It had to be; some sort of weird glowy green algae thing, reflecting the moon back or something. The rocks were slippery enough.

But there was no moon tonight, and the damn thing was getting brighter.

When the shape broke the surface of the water, Krystle fell backwards on the sand, her eyes rolling and her mouth gaping open.

$$\sim \, o \, O \, o \, \sim$$

Long have we waited, and far we have reached.

It was a dream. It had to be a dream. She was not seeing a total space alien thing coming out of the water. She was *not*.

Trust the words of your heart, and carry our message.

The only words of her heart were that it was going to fucking burst from beating so fast. She was lying on the freezing cold sand on a moonless night, staring up at the stars, but also seeing an *alien*. A monster. Coming out of the water. Impossible.

There is another way. Your path is faulty. The path of everyone on this planet is faulty. We have come to share our wisdom.

The Hippie Monster! That had to be it. Krystle struggled to move her limbs, to turn her head, to get up, but it was as though she was bound with a thousand tiny ropes. She could not budge. Also, she was still seeing the stars at the same time as she was seeing the long, narrow, big-headed, big-eyed alien, like right from a movie. In the water.

We choose the shape that makes sense to you. To make it clear, to make our origins clear. Do not fear. It is merely an image. Listen to the message.

Then it all became blurry, and still she could not move. Krystle felt cold, but her body would not shiver. Her mind roamed the stars, seeing visions that were not possible—extra dimensions, twisted shapes, creatures that bent and soared around others, a long line of bubbles that popped and soothed. And a strong sense of peace and joy grew in her—slowly at first, and then more rapidly, as her mind and body opened up to the concept.

It was better than any drug ever. Better than mushrooms, more visual than acid, more euphoric than coke. It was true. It was real. The Hippie Monster wasn't a monster at all. It was an alien, a creature from another planet, and it was using her to take a message to the rest of humanity.

A message of peace, and harmony. A new way of being. Hope and love, and an end to faulty pleasure-seeking behaviors that only harmed. Instead, a pure, true joy: a promise of hope to humanity, from the stars.

All she had to do was carry this simple message.

Krystle started to laugh, there on the beach; joy sprung from her frozen lips, echoed through the trees, across the river. "Yes," she whispered. "Yes! I will."

~ o O o ~

When she came to herself again, she was lying on her side. Sand stuck to the corner of her mouth where she had drooled; she sat up and wiped it off.

"Holy fuck," she said, staring down at the water, heart still pounding. Now there was no more green glow, no more alien.

But it had happened. And now she understood everything. The thing—whatever it was—it had been here for decades. Trapped, moored to the land, to the river. It had tried to use the hippies to get the word out, to save humanity and its own self; but they had failed, for some reason.

Now the thing told her it was all up to her.

"No," she whispered. There was no way.

The very thought of it sent a sharp, acidic stab of fear through her chest. "No..." She scrambled to her feet, backing away from the water until she bumped into the trees, almost tripping over a tangled root. Turning, her breath escaped her as she saw the trail leading upwards, suddenly as clear as if it had landing lights. She ran up it with a gasp of relief as her wet sandals touched the groomed surface of the dirt road, still a bit washboarded from last winter's rains, but much easier than the beach.

Nearly running back to the party, Krystle noticed lights up the hill at Clayton's place. If what the alien said was true, he would have to go; drugs were forbidden. In fact, the whole party was no good, according to the monster. Teenagers shouldn't be drinking beer late at night down by the river. They should be spreading the word.

Anyone who wasn't already completely corrupted, that was.

But what was she supposed to do? She was only a girl. A skinny, weak girl.

It was much faster getting back; within a few minutes, she was picking her way through the parked cars, heading for the noise below. Russ's truck was rocking gently and the windows were fogged up. Krystle frowned.

That was bad too.

So much to do! So much to solve. How could she carry this burden?

Her fingers went to her pocket, where the tiny razor blade rested behind the bindle. It was small, but it was sharp...

The bindle sang to her, though. The sweet, sweet call of speed. Such strength.

Krystle straightened her shoulders and walked towards the laughter.

"*There* you are," Trent said, slipping an arm around her and planting a beery kiss on the side of her face. "What happened to you?"

She stood trembling in his embrace, staring up at him even as he turned to talk to Trish. Exposing his neck, his jugular. Everyone was so fragile; she couldn't believe she'd never noticed this. Her fingers twitched on her pocket, rubbing, caressing. Trent's hand slipped casually to cup her ass.

It felt good. Right. Sexy, and solid. Safe.

Too bad it was all a lie.

"Nothing," she said, dropping her hand, then leaning up to return his kiss. "Nothing."

She shrunk away from him after a minute. Coming down was hard. She'd never hallucinated on speed before, but apparently there was a first time for everything. Krystle yearned for the comfortable familiarity of her own stuff. She didn't like Trent's. It tasted too much like magazine paper. And it was way too rushy. Clayton must have mixed the batch wrong.

That stuff was crazy.

It would all be okay later, after she got her head back together. It would. And then they'd fuck in the bushes, or on the front seat of his truck, like Russ and Lisa were doing. Because this was the biggest-ass party of a summer of big-ass parties, and it had to be done up right.

"I need a beer," she said, slipping out from under her boyfriend's arm and heading for the keg.

But she hadn't even gotten halfway to the river before she saw the glowing green, shimmering across the water. Almost like it was winking up at her.

"No," she whispered again, as she sank to her knees. "No, oh please no, don't make me…"

The glimmer of green caught the light of a distant star and echoed in Krystle's head as though that had been its purpose from the very start. From the beginning of it all, a million billion light years away across the universe.

And she whispered, "No."

Bone Island

By SHANNON PAGE *and* JAY LAKE

Despite all the yoga I do, my back often hurts. Figuring it was the human condition (getting older and all), I didn't worry much about it, till finally one day my chiropractor suggested I get some x-rays. Turns out I have a couple of congenitally fused vertebrae at the bottom of my spine… and something called a "bone island" in my left hip. Which of course I mentioned to Jay, whereupon he said, "That's a great story title!" Thus, "Bone Island." It was published in Interzone in 2009.

It's not what you think. The chalk-white hills give our place its name, rising cleanly from the cold blue water of the bight. Not anything more nefarious or other-worldly. That's what we tell the tourists, anyway. Hiding in plain sight.

Although, if you think about it, what is chalk? Or limestone, or what have you—nothing more than the bones of billions of long-dead sea creatures.

So maybe it's not such a bad name after all. Bone Island. My terrible home.

~ o O o ~

Sara Maarinen set her mind against me from the moment she arrived on the island. I could say that I don't know why, and there is truth in that, although of course everything is always more complicated than it seems.

I can explain.

First I have to tell you about the cottage in the tall weeds that grow like Circe's loom-weavings amid the rocks and heather of the lower meadows. The cottage that is said to contain the long-dead spirits of Bone Island, along with some of the bones of our ancestors.

There, see, I have misled you already. The bones, they are there. They jut up from the earth of the cottage's garden, pushing rotted boards from broken coffins before them. They are restless in their repose.

A woman used to live there. She could have been my grandmother. Hell, she could have been Eve's grandmother, she was so old. Those weeds were her herbs once. That cottage was her home, a single wisp of blue smoke spiraling ever upward like a lost soul seeking heaven. She delivered babies and physicked sick milch-cows and knew where to dig for the best water, and so people called her a witch.

The Bone Island Witch, of course, though that sounds mostly like something you'd see in a tourist brochure.

But what is a witch? You might ask the same question about a doctor or a preacher. Someone with a little special knowledge and the good of the world lodged in some corner of their heart will always seem like a threat to many. (At least, that's what we tell the tourists.)

But the witch died, as even the oldest women do. There is no ultimate reward for outliving your contemporaries. She was buried not amid the restless bones of her own yard (for she truly *was* a witch) but just outside the rusted iron fence around the Moravian Church Cemetery at the edge of the Commons. The cemetery for respect, outside the fence Just In Case.

It was the Bone Island Witch whose empty, pointed shoes Sara Maarinen came to fill.

It was she who set in motion everything that went wrong afterwards, when the restless bones danced and the white beaches ran with red.

~ o O o ~

Sara came from the mainland. She showed up one fine morning with a lawyer and a real estate agent and a briefcase full of official papers demonstrating beyond the shadow of a doubt that she owned the cottage. It had been left to her by an elderly maiden aunt—not our witch, no, although those fancy papers traced a lineage back to her in some complicated and ultimately inarguable way. They were French papers, festooned with bright golden seals and official stamps and pale blue ribbons. French bureaucracy is the most serious kind.

Even so, she brought the lawyer for additional seriousness. And she brought the real estate agent because she planned to sell the cottage at once.

That was, of course, before she saw it.

I know all this because I'd made it my business to keep an eye on the unquiet place these past few years.

I also know all this because Bone Island is small and everyone understands everyone else's least privacies, in the way of good inbred communities the world over.

But mostly I know all this because when the bones walked anew and the blackest crows came to haunt the cottage walls, Sara herself took me in her arms and set in motion the end of the story. The story I will now set down in these pages. The story that may save you, if you heed it true. Because although your details surely differ from ours, the magic underneath holds from Bone Island to Cape Town to the tip of Greenland, and everywhere in between.

~ o O o ~

"Don't you be listening to her," Grant Archerson said. He stood before me, tiny beads of sweat forming along his jaw, just below the scar.

I looked away, gave a wink to Janey Iverson instead, out without her little one this fine evening, then took a long drink of my ale, swallowing and wiping my mouth with the back of a hand before answering Grant. "Why not?"

Grant eyed the frosty glass on the bar, measuring the size of my appetite, my greed. My thirst. If he only knew. "She's not right, that's all." He
shrugged, as if to say, *Isn't it obvious?*

But what is obvious? That a raven-haired woman from across the sea
should bring trouble? Of course she would, and she wouldn't be the first.
Trouble we knew, trouble we had aplenty on Bone Island. You might almost
say we looked for it.

I opened my mouth to say so, but Grant's eyes flicked to the door
behind me even as I felt the cool night air on my back. It would be her, of
course. Grant shook his head and turned away.

I wiped the smile from my face before I turned around. The words died
in my throat as I gazed upon Christina.

"I thought so," she said. Without moving her head, she somehow took
in the entire room and dismissed it. I saw the shiver of a stranger tucked at
a corner table. "Come on now—home with you."

I wanted to apologize, to explain. Not to Christina. To the rest of them.

~ o O o ~

There are many creation stories, and all of them are wrong. Who could
know the mind of Goddess, after all? Her dreams encompass more than the
sum of human thought. The merest blink of Her eye is aeons in the passing.
Her thoughts are slow tsunamis which ripple through the world invisible
and destructive as a plague.

In some of those stories, a god or the son of a god is slain. His bones
become mountains, his skin becomes the land, his blood becomes the rivers
and oceans. This is true enough in its way, as anyone who has ever known
the lore of a Corn King can attest. Blood on the plow is the oldest sacra-
ment of civilization, once bounds were first measured and the land settled
in harness. The queen picked her husband, lay with him before her cheering
subjects, then split his skull with a mattock or a hoe or an obsidian knife
that his newly-royal blood might bless the land.

So it is with the world. Those many creation stories are wrong, but they all carry truth like the germ waiting in an old pauper's grave. There are bones in the world, greater and deeper than even the thunder lizards of times long before. Bone Island is almost the last such outcropping, a place where once angels feasted on the corpse of a god.

Imagine if you will a place where every speck of soil, the walls of every well, the foundation of every home, is infused with a magic older than the line of monkeys from which we are descended. Time is nothing to Goddess, and everything. She is ancient of days and new as a baby's blue eye all at once. How can her power be less, which we drink and breathe and eat every day?

Still, from time to time some leave the island, or a local brings back a husband from a farther-away place. We thought Sara Maarinen was the grandchild of such a marriage, an outcross. Her grandmother had taken something from the heart of Bone Island which in the end drew Sara home.

~ o O o ~

The boat put in at the barnacle-encrusted dock on an eerily calm Tuesday in the month of July. A trim figure with stridently raven hair stood in the bow, leaning forward and putting a hand to her forehead, as if posing. She needn't have bothered. We'd all be watching, oh yes we would.

She wore serious city clothes, all in black except for a vivid fuchsia scarf, and foolish high-heeled shoes. She carried a bag made from the skins of exotic rodents, filled with new-world magic: a telephone that needed no wires, a calendar made without paper.

We were not impressed. Bone Island keeps its secret ways, but not from ignorance. From choice. Besides, the tricksy little batteries in those things have a way of failing here between the limitless ocean and the ancient land.

The press of Christina's fingers was still strong upon my left shoulder. There would be bruises there later, like the tattoos of scattered grapes. She'd done a reading, and drawn from me in the process. Not magic, this, not in the new-world sense of wizards and sparkles and spells from Under the Hill.

Just a way of listening to the world, more carefully than most would

credit. It can be done anywhere—our limestone and talc hills are no more
a requirement than the black dresses or the mouse blood. In other days,
corpse-tallow candles were used to open the reading sight, but one can do
it with a Bic lighter.

Someone to draw on, to draw down on, was part of it as well.

"She comes, Cary," Christina had said. Her touch was warm to the edge
of painful. The bones in my shoulder ached. "The cottage cries, the soil
churns."

The soil always churns, I thought. By ant or plow or restless spirit, it
never stops. All I said was, "Yes," in the voiceless whisper which usually
pleased her most.

"Scatter salt beneath her feet." Christina's free hand darted like a blue-
bottle wasp, pressed a soft bag into my grip. Because it couldn't be just any
salt. She'd released me then, and I'd slumped forward as I always do at those
moments.

At the dock I spread my burden. Salt by the sea would seem as point-
less as taking blood to the butcher's, but everything has a purpose. Old
Kennewick sailing the boat on its twice daily trip across the bight would
know better than to step out before this woman in urban black.

Even if he hadn't seen the grainy sparkle drifting from my hand, he'd
understand what my presence meant. As for the salt itself, let her track the
stuff far and wide. Some magics are so simple as to be nothing but good
sense.

I stepped forward and extended a hand to help her out of the boat.

"Welcome to Bone Island, Mistress…?"

Sara Maarinen—for I already knew her name full well—stared at my
fingers as if they were scabbed over. She set her mouth and accepted my
help, coming up onto the dock. "I am Ms. Maarinen," she told me, as if
announcing foreign royalty.

I flashed her my pub grin, the one that usually got me a kiss at least, if
not free beer and undivided female attention. "And I suppose I'm not. Cary
Palka, at your service."

"I don't believe I know any Palkas," she said with a tone that could have frosted pumpkins. She turned back to Kennewick. "Have this boy take my bags to the White Rock Inn."

Old Kennewick tugged on his hat brim like an idiot parody of some pastoral peasant. As she turned away I saw venom on his face. Not for me, but for Sara Maarinen. I nodded, rolling my eyes in a way which everyone around here knew meant "Christina".

He began to laugh, an emphysemal wheezing fit to compete with the crying of the circling gulls. And then he pushed off from the dock almost before I could grab the blessed suitcases.

～ o O o ～

She took the best room in the White Rock, of course, even though it meant shoving aside Dorothy Iverson's cousin Sheila, here for her annual month-long visit. I know she would have taken it anyway, even if it hadn't had a direct view of the cottage; she was just that sort of person. And she organized Gertrude to bring her room service breakfast—coffee, biscuits, and blood sausage on a tidy little tray. So maybe she knew her own island power already. Certainly she was accustomed to getting her way, without question.

Her lawyer and real estate agent, newly arrived on the biweekly mail plane, had to make do with lesser rooms.

They got started right quick the next day, at the crack of noon, when a freshly bathed Sara descended the creaking staircase of the White Rock with a black leather briefcase under her arm and a swath of papers in her hand. *Look at Her Highness*, I thought, seeing her. *Hot water brought to her room too!* I smiled at Gertrude, who aimed a slap at my sore shoulder I had to dance to avoid.

"Don't you be grinning at things you don't understand, boy," she hissed.

"Oh, I think I understand this just fine, Gertie," I said, then darted for the back door. It was time to feed the ducks. And even if it wasn't, I was going to do it anyway.

Outside, the howling fog-wind hit me in the face like a drunk's well-aimed fist. I growled back into the teeth of it, pushing forward even as it threatened to slam me against the building. Ah, summer on Bone Island. The yews flung fat droplets on my head as I passed by them, squinting. I couldn't even see the pond, though it was scarcely twenty steps from the inn's back door. But I could hear the ducks chortling to their peeping young as they paddled about in the wind-whipped cress. They finally saw me and converged at the muddy bank.

I reached into the pocket of my greatcoat and pulled out the bag of salt. "Well, now, what is this?" I asked aloud. The ducks looked back at me. "For certain this was all scattered yesterday, and yet here it is anew?"

The ducks made no answer. It was not cracked corn and yardberry seeds, and that was all they knew.

$$\sim \text{o } \mathbf{O} \text{ o} \sim$$

There's magic and there's magic. Any fool can dream of spells wrestled from ancient, smoking grimoires, but the truth of that is near enough to nothing but dreams and legends. Things people want to believe, because the details seem so right. Plenty of stagecraft to support their opinions, until some folk confuse those opinions with facts. Noisy magic is rare, but not impossible.

The magic of salt and stone, of seeing and saying, of water and wind— that's the magic which can be found in the world by an observant child. Watch a cat at a sun-drenched winter window for a long, quiet while. Eventually you may catch Tabby with frost on her paws, save without ever first hearing the creak of the door.

That second, the quiet magic, is what was held tight-clutched by the Bone Island Witch, may the pennies never leave her eyes. Others of us too, Christina most of all, have the knowing. It's a magic which will never show a purple sparkle, wouldn't be caught dead in a silver moon hanging chainwise around a pretty little neck. Quiet magic is everywhere but improbable.

That magic made the salt which I spread by the dock. Noisy magic returned it to my pocket, rude as a fart at a funeral and twice as distressing.

We already knew Sara Maarinen was trouble. We just hadn't known what kind of trouble. Leaving the ducks to their querulous displeasures, I headed through the fog for Christina's home, above the boarded windows of the old Leister Mercantile.

~ o O o ~

Pressing through the familiar weather, it came to me that maybe this fog-wind wasn't quite so ordinary as I'd thought. This was summer, which was ever a cold, cold season on Bone Island, but the sun wasn't even a pale glower above. If not for the clocks in the sitting room of the White Rock, I'd have had no notion whether the world was in dusk, dawn or in between.

Had Sara Maarinen called the weather to her? She had the law on her side, a shield of papers and agentry as impenetrable as any stopping web. Even the oldest gammer with her leather clogs and milky eye-of-wisdom couldn't do better than a city lawyer.

The new woman didn't need to call the wind. But it had come, perhaps of its own accord. Maybe it followed her, punished her, threatened to thrust her back from whence she came. Or it could have been the old Witch, complaining from her mossy grave outside the churchyard.

How would I know, anyway? I didn't have the power of a reading. I was just a human battery. In times before, I would have been a sacrifice atop one of the old bluestones on the high bluffs to the north. Now I was Christina's sweetling, giving of myself, but well supplied with ale and bed favors in exchange for my continued services.

It wasn't ale or bed favors I was wanting today, though. It was knowing how the salt had jumped back into the bag, and how the bag had jumped back into the pocket of my greatcoat. Sure as the cemetery gates creak, it wasn't the majesty of the law which had done this.

Christina would be furious, but she'd be smart enough not to blame me for the business. Probably. I shivered as the mercantile loomed out of the driving fog. The side stairs were slippery as ever, but my feet knew them well.

Up to her well-decorated door, and knocked three short raps—*tak, tak, tak*—as was our arrangement. I stood as the wind buffeted me, amusing myself with leaning into it, letting the steady push of its force hold me suspended over the railing. The wind, in turn, amused itself with letting up every so often, threatening to throw me to the muddy track below. We fought to a standoff, and Christina had not come to the door.

Tak, tak, tak. And silence, save the howling gale about me.

Most peculiar.

I did not dare put my ear to her door or my eye to her keyhole. The memory still stung from the last time I'd taken such unwonted liberties. Instead, I rapped once more, then gave a heavy sigh and took my thirsty body back down the reeking stairs.

Sara Maarinen herself was before me as I took the final step. I had not seen her coming, and you may well believe I had been looking. She was much on my mind, and then she was clutching the raw woolen collar of my coat and pulling, pulling. She drew my reluctant ear to her lipsticked mouth and whispered, "You'll not find what you need up there, young Palka. Though it may amuse you to tumble in her bed, she is no gift for you."

I reached for my easy pub grin, but it slipped from my grasp even as I drew away from Sara's hiss. "I… You don't…" Words failed me.

"My cottage," she said. "I am told you hold the key. You will take me there now."

I looked up and down the street, but no one ventured out into the howl and the whine that poured down from the angry skies. No, this I would have to do on my own.

It had ever been so, since Grandfather had given me the Palka legacy.

Sara Maarinen let go of my coat and spun around, marching down the street without a glance behind her. As I followed, I noted the sparkle of salt at her heels.

~ o O o ~

Grandfather had been generally accounted a difficult man. Famously so, in fact, and this on an island renowned for difficult people. Our folk were stubborn as the Irish, thick as the Norwegians, and slow-tempered as any vengeful moneylender of old. Bone Island had feuds which dated back before the Christ came to our shores, rooted in such trivial causes as pig-thievery and fence-hopping.

We are a proud people, and we are proudest of the fossils carried in the bedrock of our pride.

Yet even among these folk, who could turn a single misspoken word into the slow-burning sport of a seasons-long quarrel, Grandfather Palka had been another kind of man entirely. He must have been young once, for no one is born into their later age, but by the time I came along to know him, there wasn't a soul to testify to whatever wit or charm or grace had sustained him through his younger years, two wives and three mistresses.

My grandfather was an iron bastard with flinty eyes and bones which might just as well have been quarried out of the island itself. He didn't have either kind of magic, just the cynical wisdom of an old man in a hardscrabble place.

It was he who took me out into the raddled hawthorn copse that filled the ravine behind the Palka farm. It was he who showed me the cave hidden behind the brambles that lined the stand of trees. It was he who took me within, to the broken altar and the old stone axe with stains as deep as time.

"Cary," he'd said. "Time was, the business of living got done here."

Grandfather wasn't much for talking, either, beyond "pass the salt." That alone was very nearly a lecture. When he went on after a long slow breath, I was amazed. "Our name means 'priest' in the old tongue. It also means 'keeper.'"

He looked at me sidelong, those gray eyes sparkling like the sea beneath a storm front.

I nodded to show I was serious, that I was listening, that I wasn't scared. All lies, of course, but a hard man of five decades can see through even the lies of a barely teen-aged boy, as I was then.

"Got no duties now except memory. The witches took the business from us long ago." His fingers brushed the ax, its crude handle perhaps generations old, yet still surely renewed time and again across the span of Bone Island's history until the original was only a memory of a memory. "And we let them keep it," he added. "You won't be wanting it back."

After a while in which the wind whickered at the shallow cave mouth and the reek of salt almost overcame me, I asked the question which seemed obvious to me. "Sir, what is it I am to remember?"

"Why there is still blood on this ax after a dozen dozen generations," he said slowly. "What it is that brings the midwinter sun to the sky and spring crops from the soil." He looked at me again, the ax forgotten now. "And that you, a Palka, are always going to be alone, until you can give the duty to a son or nephew or grandson."

Alone, that was me, following Sara Maarinen to the witch's cottage. The garden was turned as if freshly plowed, though I knew better. The windy fog had lifted a bit, so the feral orchards behind the house could be spied in silhouette like a line of acromegalic soldiers on sentry duty.

The Palka legacy was a flinty old ax and a hole in the ground, and I had neither of them now. Only the memory of something I didn't understand, and the stirring certainty that whatever had baffled Christina's magic and worried everyone here on the island was tied into the that old, old business the witches had taken from one of my grandfather's grandfathers, back when the sun was redder and the ice lay on the ocean so the wolves could cross the bight.

"You know it's mine," Sara Maarinen said. She had stopped all a-sudden on the path and now stood facing me, her fingers pressing into the bruises Christina had left behind.

She understood too much, this woman with the noisy magic.

"No, I don't know that," I told her, and wondered how the hell those words had found their way out of my mouth. Clearly I was on my own way to being famously difficult. Or possibly famously dead, if my stirring intuition was not simply spinning nightmares out of no cloth at all.

Where *was* Christina?

Sara smiled, at long last. She let my shoulder go and tossed her raven-colored hair over her shoulder, in a gesture I would have understood utterly coming from an island girl in the pub: from Janey Iverson out and about without her daughter, or Ruth Wilder, before she'd taken up with Connor Makepeace. But from Sara, it only served to shrink my manhood— what of it still remained as I shivered through this frigid wind from off the sea. "You know it's mine," she repeated, and then all I could do was follow her again.

$$\sim \text{ o } \text{O} \text{ o } \sim$$

Of course she was a witch, descended from the witches. I'd been fooling myself before, pretending doubt. We all had, and a poor showing on us to have done so, but so we did. In our defense, the witches' line had thinned and faltered, strained through the outcrossed blood from the mainland folk, till the best anyone who still had the touch could do was call a few crows to her side, and then only if they felt like it. (The crows, that is.) The old one, buried outside the churchyard fence, had been the last true witch. Too many of us secretly thought this a good thing.

There were some who could, as Christina did, see things that weren't there, at least not yet. It's a small magic, but there were a few times in my life when I'd have not turned it down.

Such as the moment we arrived at the front door of the Bone Island Witch's cottage. I'd have given any number of brimming pints of fresh ale to know what I'd find within, without having to open the door first, with this terrible woman hovering at my shoulder.

Sara gave me that chilly grin again, the one that had unmanned me on the path. "Let me in, Palka."

I stood on the stoop in the blowing, grime-gray fog, trying not to shake. My hands clung to the insides of my greatcoat pockets like Gracie Fenniman had to the bones of her tug after it broke up on Deacon's Rock last winter. My arms would not obey the command of my brain. I was certain that Sara Maarinen was going to commit foul magic on me if I did not move, but still I stood.

Then I felt her move a step closer to me, and the moment was shattered. I hauled out the skeleton key and shoved it into the lock. Something crusty and white fell out and fluttered to the ground—not salt, not this time. Something worse. And it was jammed in the lock, so I had to wrestle the key. But there was no turning back now. Sara's breath was thick and greedy in my ear as she leaned in, watching the key in the hole. I smelled her breakfast of blood sausage and pork-fat-laden biscuits, and had to swallow my rising gorge with an effort.

The key slipped, and finally turned.

The door eased open as if it had not been shut up these long lonely years.

~ o O o ~

I'd first met Christina shortly after Grandfather had shown me the duty. I mean, I'd always known her. Everybody on Bone Island knows everybody else, or at the least we're aware of each other. She'd been a senior in our tiny school when I first started, impossibly tall and old, practically an adult. When I was biking down chalky paths to risk a cliff-top header into the ocean, she'd been doing whatever young adults do on an island with fewer than a dozen retail businesses.

I've seen TV. I know on the mainland kids get jobs at the mall or join the army or live in huge apartments in New York City with a dozen of their friends. Some of them even go to college. Some of *us* even go to college. We're not ignorant.

Not Christina. Whatever she did in those years was invisible to me, though of course later on I realized she was finding the quiet magic.

When Grandfather showed me the duty, I was fourteen. Scruffy beard which wouldn't fool anybody but the boy in the mirror, narrow shoulders stuck up high in a pretense of manly pride, saved from my own social ineptitude only by a ready smile and the curious kindnesses of a small place where everyone understands one another's faults and loves them anyway.

When a slender twenty-five-year-old Christina stopped me on the town's one paved street—cobbles, not macadam, for we have far more rocks than tar in this place—of course I paid attention to her. She was pretty. I was young. She was a woman. I was convinced I was a man already.

"You're a Palka," she said.

I stared at her: I knew she knew that. "The Palka, really." Mother and Father were already gone, and Grandfather, well, he was old. That's how I saw it then, when in effect the entire universe had only been created a decade and a half earlier at the moment of my birth.

"The Palka." Something in her smile made my groin twitch. I squirmed on my bike saddle. Christina continued: "Come see me sometime. I live over the mercantile."

My God, I thought. *I have a date.* With a real woman. With *breasts* and everything.

"Um, yeah, sure." I was so cool. I even flipped my hair.

The smile changed, and I felt very small then. The wind changed with it, bringing the salt-and-rot smell off the harbor, and when I glanced away for a moment to take the sting from my eyes, she was gone.

I don't suppose I need to tell you what happened when I went up to her place. No wild fantasies, no sexual initiations. She wanted to talk about see-ings and blood and the old families of Bone Island. Beautiful and dangerous as Christina was, it was like talking to Grandfather.

What I didn't understand until later was that the sex would come when I opened myself up to her seeings. And when it did come, it wasn't anything like I'd hoped it would be. But by then it was much too late.

The old witches, they didn't need boys like me. They carried it all within themselves, the noisy power.

The duty, it belonged to me, if only I could understand it. It was all connected, like a trapline beneath the leaves.

With that thought, I realized the brass knob beneath my hand was as cold as Sara Maarinen's bloody breath on my neck.

"Go on, boy," she said, eerily gentle. "Or are you afraid?"

"Ma'am," I said fervently, "I am always afraid."

With the lock unleashed, the door pulled at my hand as if the haints within tugged on it in their eager, unquiet rest. I let the knob go and the door fell open as I blinked my eyes in disbelief.

Inside, it was just as we had left it. The chairs were neatly set around the polished oaken table, the small bed was made up, and the air was fresh with a faint scent of pine, as though Gertie had come down with her needle-broom and swept up ten minutes ago.

Strangest of all, of course, was the bright sunlight that slanted through the small back window.

I stood in the doorway, staring at the golden light. It couldn't be.

"Well?" Sara Maarinen hissed.

"I…" My voice died in my throat. I tried to step back, to look at the sky behind me, back in the real world. It was as grey and sopping as ever. The fog was roaring up from the bight again, loping along on its big senseless panther feet.

Sara laid her cold silver eyes on me. "You what, Palka?"

I swallowed a hard lump in my throat and tore my gaze away from the impossible window. "Nothing." I led her into the cottage. *Her* cottage, according to mainland law and the magic of paperwork.

She pushed past me, her city clothes making little silken whispery sounds as she went by. Straight for the diadem that Grandfather had hammered into the far wall she went, and when she got there, she put her thin white hands on it so eagerly it made me quiver. I watched her, unable to do anything else. After a minute I realized she was speaking, or crooning, but low, under her breath. I couldn't make out any words. Maybe she was just humming at it as she caressed the evil thing.

All the while she ignored the sunlit window, so I did too. At least, I did not speak of it. I remained in the doorway, waiting for my next instructions.

That was when Christina showed up.

~ o O o ~

Back when my parents had first died, Grant Archerson spent some time taking an interest in me. Avuncular, I think the word is—like an old uncle. Nothing creepy. Here on Bone Island, all the real weirdoes seem to be women.

Nothing magical, either. I mean, I talk about it all the time, I think about it all the time, but really, most people here are just people. Maybe they know a bit more about what some things mean than mainlanders. The one fencepost with a shadow stretching the wrong way round at dusk. Why the swallows fly just *that* way over the Moravian Church steeple. When not to knock on the witch's cottage door.

That's not magic. That's situational awareness.

And Grant was about as unmagical as a wooden spoon.

What he was, was the guy who ran the Tossed Pot, one of two bars on Bone Island. The other was the Scupper, down by the Fishing Pier, and mostly the working sailors drank there, along with anyone come in working a boat who wasn't local. Nice enough place, if you like everything to smell and taste like fried fish (or fried fisherman), but the conversation lags quickly once you talk about anything that doesn't involve a hull on open water.

The Tossed Pot, on the other hand, was the sort of bar that tourists dream of discovering. Which pretty much all of the ones we get do, since it's also the only public restaurant on the island besides the dining room of the White Rock. There's a dozen places to eat easy enough, if you drop by with a loaf of bread and a pound of butter for the table, but only one with a signboard and a menu and beer taps. Inside looks like the club room of another age, faded Imperial ambitions and war mementos brought home by men who fought under the tropical sun in woolen uniforms and puttees.

Which was total bullshit, of course. Grant bought that stuff up from catalogs, and swapped out the decor two or three times a year. A sort of hobby.

But he was also a hell of a nice guy, who kept track of what happened to the kids young and old. You wanted to ask about Dolly Paternoster's daughter, drop by the Pot and chat up Grant. Dolly slept under a mossy granite headstone now, but Margot wrote Grant a postcard every few months. The little kids, too.

So when Father fell out of Old Kennewick's boat trying to save a crate of Mark Fenniman's chickens in a rising storm, Grant knew before I did. A week later Mother disappeared down at Bishop's Head looking for the body on the tide. Or maybe she went for a swim to join him. I've never known, and Christina never said. But Grant probably knows, and he came looking for me even before Granddaddy found out.

For a while I lived half at the Tossed Pot and half at the Palka farm. I was too young to drink, even by Bone Island standards, and Grant had enough situational awareness to see where I was headed in life—college wasn't in the script, he knew that—so he gently sent me back to the farm until I outgrew it as all farm children do.

But still, if I had a father on this place, a father of the heart, it was Grant Archerson. I don't think he liked my bedwandering ways, and he never thought much of how I let Christina use me, but he still cared enough to keep tabs on me, and speak up from time to time.

Right now I was wishing mightily I'd listened to him, earlier on or just now. Being caught between Christina and Sara Maarinen was like being ground between two stones.

"*What* are you doing?" Christina asked, with that look in her eye and the barbed wire edge in her voice.

I turned to see what Sara Maarinen would say to this when Christina grabbed me right on the sore part of my shoulder.

It was me she was talking to.

Sara looked up anyway, and I swear by all the old gods and tiny fishes, she smiled.

I stood between the two women, staring from one fine-featured face to the other. Only then did I see their strong resemblance. Of course, Sara's city-cut hair and fancy clothes were as much of a distraction as Christina's tangled locks and honest island woolens, but that was no excuse for my not noticing it before.

"Well, Palka? Are you going to answer her?" Sara's voice slashed into my dumb reverie. What did it matter if they were kin? The whole island was kin, if you counted back far enough.

I shook my head and gave Christina my sweetest smile, but she could read the terror on my face as though it were scrawled there in charcoal. Her eyes bored into me, and then she shook her head ever so slightly.

Behind me, Sara's laugh flowed into the room. It was as false as the sunlight from the far window, but it rang sweet. "I guess the cat's got his tongue," she said, now leaning against the wall so that her upper back touched the diadem. "He said he wanted to welcome me to the cottage, so I took him up on it. And such a charming little place it is!" She spread her arms as if showing off the place to prospective tenants.

Christina gave a low hiss as I struggled to find my voice. It was a lie, a foul and terrible lie! And where had Christina been? I could say nothing. Christina still held my bruised shoulder. I thought she'd draw blood.

"I don't know your full game yet, witchdaughter, but this is not yours." Christina's grip tightened as she spoke. I didn't know if she was referring to the cottage or to me, but Sara's eyes widened nonetheless. "You would do well to board that ferry and hie yourself back where you came from before harm is done here."

Sara's expression did not change. "You know I cannot do that." Her voice was a lesson in cool, calm, and collected. Of course, *her* shoulder wasn't being wrenched from her body.

"Don't tell me what I do and do not know." Christina almost whispered the last words.

The cottage darkened in that moment, as the window behind Sara began to admit the reality of the day outside. I missed the sunlight, even if it was tricksy magic. And in the next moment, I was being hauled up the street to the apartment above the mercantile.

~ o O o ~

"What the hell was that?" I asked as we mounted the steps in the fog.

"Not out here." Christina's voice was chopped, as if she struggled against panic.

There are no secrets on an island this small. What she thought to keep hidden was beyond me. Everyone who'd seen Sara Maarinen—old

Kennewick, Grant Archerson, Gertie, the loungers at the White Rock—
knew some version of the truth already. Words chased one another through
my head in a sort of summoning: witchdaughters, bloodkin, mirror-twins,
changelings. Children of the bone.

I thought of the Palka duty, the stained ax in its dank hole, and said
nothing more.

We pushed into the apartment. It was a witchy enough place, of course,
hung with travel posters of Bavarian castles and the Golden Gate Bridge,
a shelf of chipped china horses along one wall, orchids struggling on the
windowsill for sufficient sunlight. No purple silks or tinkling charms for
Christina. Quiet magic.

But she was unquiet now. "What possessed you?"

"'Possessed' is such an ugly term." She stiffened, and I wondered why
we were fighting when by rights we should be plotting. "The salt failed,
Christina. Then *she* took me in hand, demanded I let her in. I could not
refuse her, any more than I can refuse you." And for much the same reasons,
I did not add. "Who is she to you?"

"No one." Christina whirled away from me, striding across her cracked
floorboards like an army on the march. The mercantile had closed when I
was a small boy, but I imagined the drumming of her heels echoing among
the shrouded shelves and dusty cobwebs down below. She turned back,
tangled hair flying and eyes flashing.

All I could think was of the way her body bent like a storm-tossed sea
as we made love, the same swirling hair, the same wild look on her face.

"No!" she shouted, for of course my own witch knew what was in my
thoughts.

"Sara Maarinen called sunlight through the cottage windows," I said
quietly, pitching my voice down to draw Christina from the perch of her
anger, for of course her familiar knew her witchy ways. "Driftglass off the
ocean, melted and recast with the blood of gulls and gravedust in the forms."
My voice had the cadence of lessoning, for such I recited. "Frames made
from shipwreck wood. Those windows are *mirrors* that reflect power. She is
the Bone Island witch come again."

Christina looked stricken. "No…"

"And she is your sister." I already knew the color of Sara Maarinen's nipples, the flavor of her as I set my mouth between her thighs, for she would be like Christina in all things save the nature of her power. Noisy magic and quiet magic, two halves of the same shell, split to be parceled lest they unite too great.

I wondered exactly what it was that the Palka ax had been meant to split.

Christina advanced on me, rage still in her eyes. Her hands trembled as she lifted them toward me. I don't know if she meant to strike me down or seize me for another sacrifice, but instead she pulled me into a rib-jarring embrace.

Her breath was warm in my ear, and my body surged as it always did to the scent of her. "She was never meant to be here, Cary. I am afraid."

I held my witch as she cried a while, something she had never done in my memory, and wondered what my place in all this would be.

~ o O o ~

Here on Bone Island we have recipes for many things we never make. Literal recipes, in some cases. Most children over the age of six know how to make kraken stew, despite the fact that no kraken has been seen here or anywhere else since time out of legend. Likewise mermaid sausage, which had always struck me as a delightfully perverse idea.

So it was with the witch's cottage. There was only one cottage, and it survived despite a lack of maintenance or improvement, unitary and needing no replacement. But still many of us knew how to measure a foundation course for a new witch's cottage, and what (or whom) to bury beneath the hearthstone, and how the windowglass should be cast, and the facing of the doors.

I'd long thought such knowledge must have uses beyond winter tale telling and providing fodder for the seaside games of children. Even when I was little, it intrigued me to comprehend the proper use of goat entrails.

Mainland children were not so lucky, I knew, removed from the purpose of their rituals so that a charm against the plague was nothing more than a dancing game.

On Bone Island, when we said a charm against the plague, we knew damned well what the ring around the rosie was.

But we didn't have the plague. And we only had one witch, who died when I was still quite young, and who had never sought her own replacement. It was like the failing of a line of queens, now succeeded by the minor nobility like Christina.

Except Sara Maarinen was a princess. And if she was a princess, so was Christina. And *that* meant that there were secrets on this island, secrets which no one had ever let me into, at the least.

Christina sat in the old wicker rocker, dribbling salt into her claret, then drinking it anyway as a patch of struggling sunlight advanced across the floor at her feet. I watched her a while, and began to feel a mighty need to go talk to Grandfather. He'd not spared a word for me since I'd taken up with Christina, even when we'd crossed paths, he on his way to the Moravian Church of a Saturday night and me on mine back to the pub.

But now I needed him. The duty needed me.

The thought came unbidden to my mind: A hive can have only one queen.

I found my greatcoat, tucked a few necessary things in the pocket, draped a shawl over Christina's shivering shoulders, then let myself out. The river of her power was but a seep now, as she journeyed through some country of imagination and regret.

It was time for me to seek the past as well.

~ o O o ~

'Duty' is such an unlovely word. It implies a burden, a chore, something laid upon one's unwilling shoulders. Duty doesn't sound pretty, but more like a soiling of something best left clean. Onerous and filthy.

I want to say that the Palka duty belies its name, but I've told enough untruths in my life, and I shan't be lying any longer. This tale is my first solemn attempt at honesty—everything honest and needful, that is, not the sweet half-truths that island girls and tourists alike are pleased to hear, after the ale has run freely for a few hours and the music has started up once more.

As I walked up the main street for the fourth time this day, I passed the pub, heard the laughter inside, and was sore tempted. The sun—well, no, don't let me lie again. The sun I hadn't seen much of these many months, beyond the witch's false-playing cottage window. The daylight, let me say instead, was beginning to fade, as in warmer climes the sun slips beyond the horizon and good honest folks gather their children home and prepare the evening meal.

I wanted an ale, or stronger drink. And I wanted it badly. My feet drew themselves of their own accord back to the doorway so resolutely passed a moment ago. I could smell the beer, and Archerson's honeysuckle wine, and the straw on the floor, and even a bit of manure tramped in on someone's careless bootheel. My hand was raised to the handle. It was warm in there, and heads would turn as I entered, faces would open in greeting, sweet bottoms would scoot over on benches to make room for me. I could see it all. I heard Janey Iverson's sweet laughter, and my hand gripped the doorknob.

I dropped it and turned away abruptly, closing my eyes against my inner vision. No more lies also meant no more delays, no more avoiding my task. My burden.

My duty.

The road turned at the edge of the main street and climbed a little rise, where it then dwindled to a path that skulked drunkard through the windward trees. Bent and miserly, these poor remnants of someone's foolish idea about greening up the place still held their own against the howling sea wind, though they creaked and groaned with the effort, and dropped ice water down the back of my greatcoat. At least they kept the worst of the wind off the leeward farms, Grandfather's included.

Poor things.

The Palka would keep his place out here, though, and I would have to seek him out at his own hearth. That much I understood.

The last few trees were huddled together, as if to prevent one another from flying off the island altogether. The path narrowed so, I had to turn sideways to squeeze between them. Every time I did this, I wondered how stout Gertie managed, when she came for Grandfather's washing and other weekly necessaries.

And then I was through, and Grandfather's ancient house stood before me, vanishing into the mist and reappearing like an uneasy ghost.

It struck me in that moment how much he and the Bone Island Witch were alike. She too was old, alone but not lonely, unfriendly but not friendless, living in a building which seemed to be endlessly recreated without ever coming down or being built back up again.

But where her cottage had an air of ancient spells about it, screaming "magic" like a set right out of some Hollywood location scout's fever dream, Grandfather's screamed "farm". The toolsheds, the rusting plows inverted like broken riflestocks over soldiers' graves, the ancient cart overgrown with brambles, the goat pens, the straggling orchards along the lee of the chalk-white spinal ridge which erupted from the thin soil just to the east of the steading.

It was a farm which grew nothing but small boys fed on duty, tended and harvested by the old men they would become.

This was the one entrance on Bone Island I would never have to rap my knuckles against. Grandfather might have adopted a silent, passionless disdain for me, but I was still family. The only family left without a tiny little flower farm six feet above their heads.

My fingers stopped gently against the grain of the door. These planks had been rough sawn from driftwood, smoothed down by generations of wind, rain and callused hands. Beneath my touch was the quietest magic of all, earth and plow and family. That magic had left its veneer like a water stain.

Family, did it all come down to that?

I walked inside.

"Grandfather?"

The great room—for this was a real farmhouse—smelled of old ashes and stale tea. Comfortable furniture bulked unused as it had in the years since the last of the Palka women died, shadows of a merrier past with four feet and faded upholstery. There was no fire set, only a cold, burned down log. The long table which had once seated a dozen had a meal set, abandoned now.

Grandfather never walked away from a mess.

On the edge of panic, I whirled. His sweater and boots were not in their accustomed place by the door.

He had walked out, then. In an unaccountable hurry, leaving the fire unlaid and a dirty plate on the table. I checked. The eggs were old, at least a day.

Where?

But I already knew where.

Back outside into the howling fog, up through the struggling orchard, and along the oldest path this island boasted.

'Palka' meant priest. Our duty was only memory now, but Grandfather was surely at prayer, remembering whatever it was the ancient ax whispered to him in the long, dark winter nights that filled this island's soul like matted cobwebs.

That's what I told myself, anyway, hoping against hope that there was nothing darker afoot. The bag of salt back in my greatcoat pocket loomed large in my imagination. A day ago, Sara Maarinen was landing on Bone Island. A day ago, Grandfather saw or heard or felt something which made him push back from his eggs and walk away.

A day ago, I was coming to understand, my world had ended, and whatever had been made in its place was unknown to me. Truth, painful and incomplete, but far better than a lie over beer and sausages with a girl pressing up against each arm.

~ o O o ~

My feet were heavy within my boots as I made my way to the haw-thorn-choked ravine, and the cave within. Every step took me closer to the end—my doom and my duty both. And what would come after? Somehow, I always thought I'd have more time.

I heard Grandfather before I saw him. His words were strange to my ears. At first I thought he was speaking some ancient tongue, a long-forgot-ten language of our forebears on the island. Then I heard chanting—could it be? It made no sense. Grandfather's prayers were ever the most basic, plain-spoken. From his mouth to God's ear, and no messing around with pretty poetry.

Only when I stepped through the dim light leaking from the mouth of the cave did I see him, and realize that he was laughing It was a bitter, defeated laugh, filled with the pain of centuries, handed down from Palka to Palka, stored in the freshly-bloodied ax.

"Grandfather!" I rushed to him where he was crouched on the floor, cradling the ax as if it were a stillborn infant.

The Palka continued with the terrible sound, heedless of me by his side, shaking his head as the unholy mirth poured from him. Tears leaked from the corners of his eyes, streaming salty down his wrinkled face. He clung to the ax, even as the blood oozed from its sharp blade, staining his dungarees and pooling on the floor of the cave.

"What happened?" I shook his arm, hard. Anything to get him to stop the awful, mad laughter.

He finally noticed me, turning a bleary blue eye to my face. He was far past reason, but he saw me all the same.

"It's too late." Grandfather rocked back and forth on the floor, the ax shifting in his grasp. I wondered if the blood was his, hoping against hope that I wasn't seeing the end of him, that this was all a bizarre mistake.

"Too late for what?" I asked, though I knew full well. But he had to say it. He had to be the one to finish passing the duty on to me, end my youth with a sharp-edged whimper.

He had to be the one to hand me the blooded ax.

As for everyone else who might have played a part this day—well, their restless bones already danced beneath the soil.

"You must…" He stared at me. Tears poured, sweat beaded on his fore-head, though it was well near freezing in the dank cave. "You must…" He couldn't bring himself to say it.

Instead, he held the ax out to me.

Hands trembled as someone I used to be reached out for the time-worn haft, polished by generations of bitter, callused palms. That person stood in the half-light of the cave, surrounded by the press of pale bone-rock, breath flooded with the meaty, sharp scent of blood which had run from nowhere to nowhere, stopping here along the way to pool at his feet. Dust motes spiraled in the damp wind eddying from outside, each indi-vidual speck of white gleaming fairy-bright as it danced its moment in the foggy glare from without, like the souls of men rising up from a ship's shattered bones.

That person's shoulder ached, where a witch had pressed him too close. That person's back twitched, from walking before another witch so danger-ous and angry. That person's fingers closed on the wooden handle, grip-ping despite the blood and the walnut-wrinkled knuckles of another, older person still caught in the spell of the duty.

Spell it was, woven around an ancient blade forged and reforged just as soil, air and water become grain which becomes a cow which becomes beef which becomes a man which becomes shit which becomes soil, air and water once more. Never changing, ever different, the truth hidden in half a dozen forms but always the same.

Open any grave and you will find worms. Open any skull and you will find demons. Touch this ax, person who I used to be, and you will find—

~ o O o ~

Inside every girl born are all the children she will ever carry. A female infant has ovaries, tiny and poorly developed, but they are there, and filled with eggs. So it is with the world as a whole, each potential future encysted within the shapes and bounds of the present. Just as the eggs flow from a woman on a river of blood, so do the futures flow from the world on a river of blood.

Once wasp-minded people of modest stature lived beneath the hollow hills behind giant doors of stone, worshipping a copper-crowned woman and gods so old and strange that the stories retold around midsummer fires could not help but come out twisted as a witch's soup ladle.

Once people who went below with them to drink their mead and lie with their women did not come back until their children's children slept beneath the churchyard soil, and people called them elfshot and sleep-woken and bound them over to the sea for the coldest judgment.

Once the world voiced magic on the very wind, and the changing of the leaves foretold the patterns of the winter snow and where the wolf would hunt by the bitter moon.

Once a girl was born, her parentage irrelevant to her fate, in that the oldest doors slipped a crack so that spiders scuttled out, bearing among their number a bodiless shadow which roamed this forlorn relic of creation until it found that girl, and using a magic known only to those who bore swords of thorn and shields of beaten copper, split her from herself.

The ax told me these things, and many more secrets besides, when it remade me between one breath and the next there in the cave above my sobbing Grandfather. I reached down to stroke the blood from his eyes, and dropped my greatcoat over him to shelter him against the chillier fog of evening which can lay a glissade of ice over everything in its path, then I turned once more into the last of the day.

Only one thing the ax had failed to tell me: how a blade might unite what had so long ago been torn asunder.

Only one thing the ax had lied to me about: parentage is never irrelevant to fate.

Walking like an older man, I passed the footprints of a callow, careless youth along the orchard path leading back to my farm. A person whistled tunelessly, swinging a bloody ax to gauge its heft, though neither he nor I expected to use it as a weapon in that most obvious of ways, even at this late moment. Naïve? Perhaps. Even so, on we went.

If tiny shapes buzzed through the fog along my progress, I did not take note of them. Some things it is best not to see until you have the power to loose and to bind them.

~ o O o ~

I was back on the main street before I knew I had passed through the whispering, weeping trees that hugged the path. My mind touched lightly on my body, holding it only enough to guide my boots where they needed to go. I came back to myself on the stone steps of the cottage. My knuckles were already rapping on the door, the ax held firm in my grip.

The door flew open, though by no one's living hand. Sara Maarinen and my Christina stood at the far end of the small room. They faced each other, a pace apart, locked in some terrible binding of fear and hatred and power and… love?

Neither head turned; they kept staring into each other's eyes. Damp air filled the cottage even as the power crackled between them. It grabbed me in its salty embrace, pawed through my heart and mind and soul, gripped my manhood, squeezed my guts till they threatened to explode.

I stood there. I held the ax.

A sound came from the two witchlings, high and keening, a whine or song or scream, echoing through the small room. My head pounded with it, and my own voice joined theirs, against my will—leaping from my lungs unbidden, uncontrollable.

I lifted the ax. I held it high, and pointed its sharp edge at the space between Sara and Christina.

My shoulder throbbed, and my arms almost threw the ax down, but I held it steady.

Sara Maarinen broke the gaze first. She turned a face of death to me, her mouth twisted into an ugly, grinning rictus. Released, Christina fell to the floor, her eyes rolling back in her head.

"Cary Palka," Sara said, in an entirely normal voice. "Put that silly thing down and come here." She reached out her arms as if to embrace me.

"No," I said, even as I lowered the ax. My right foot moved a step forward. The wound in my shoulder turned and twisted, beyond pain—it was as if a sharp spiny creature had found a home in there, but was now threatening to decamp, erupting right through my skin. I moaned, and my left foot joined my right. "No!"

Christina lay unconscious on the floor. One leg splayed out toward the middle of the room, where it was touched by a ray of sunlight from the impossible window.

I had to get her out of that light. I knew it—I didn't know why, or how, but that light could not continue to touch her. It was the key, even more than my ax.

I took another step forward, this time towards Christina. But that was also towards Sara.

"Excellent," Sara Maarinen said. Her death-mask smile widened. The keening howl had not stopped, though none of our voices were adding to it. It whipped through the room. I blinked my eyes, wanting to stop up my ears, but I could not loose my grip on the ax.

Another step.

Sara raised her arms higher, reaching to me, pulling me further in even as she took a step backwards. Away? No—she was moving to the tidy bed. The bed that was bathed in the same sunlight that was stealing Christina's soul away, bit by bit.

"That's right, come to me." Now Sara's voice was soft and crooning, but it froze my heart all the same. And yet to her I went. I could do no less than to obey. Her blood had the owning of mine, as it always had.

My unwilling body eased into her arms as she leaned back, taking us both onto the narrow bed in a terrible parody of lovers. I still held the ax, making me slow and awkward. Sara pushed at my arm, still grinning, trying to nudge the bloody thing aside. She wouldn't put her thin hands on it. "Come, sweet, put that down and touch me. Touch me everywhere."

My fingers would not let go, though my mind screamed out to do as she bid. She was danger, and magic, and desire, and fear all at once. The sunlight was warm on my back, and it made the blood sparkle and glow.

Sara pushed my arm again, as she leaned up and kissed my face, the hollow of my throat, just as Christina did.

Christina!

I moaned, low and soft, as I tried to turn my head to see my witch. Sara took my face between her hands and brought it back to her mouth, kissing me hard. My lips opened to hers as I let her in, let her taste my essence, my echoing traces of whatever magic I possessed that had made Christina seek me out in the first place. Sara ate it up, writhing and rolling beneath me.

I grew hard, wanting her, even as I was desperate to flee. My body, no longer unwilling, played traitor to me, craving something far greater than it should have to endure.

My fingers loosened on the ax, just a bit. I gripped it again, swallowing a curse, and struggled anew to pull away from Sara Maarinen.

She wrapped strong legs around mine and dragged my hips down, matching my groin to hers. Fully dressed we were, but intertwined more intimately than most lovers ever achieve, as she enticed every bit of my will and soul out through my mouth and breath and pores and into her hungry body.

"You are mine," she whispered, then set her mouth to mine once more.

I felt both drained and invigorated by her touch, her kiss. The ax slipped an inch as my fingers sought to travel familiar pathways, the landscape of Christina's body, Sara's body... I grabbed it tighter once more. I would not let go of it, I would not! All would be lost.

Sara twisted and purred underneath me, inflaming me further. Her movements brought us both out of the sun for a moment. The icy air on my back was a tonic; in the moment of clarity, I heard Grandfather's quavering voice: "The duty! Do it!"

Sara hissed as I pulled away from her, stronger this time. My knuckles were white where I held the ax. I staggered to my feet and danced away from Sara's claw-like hands. "No!" she screamed.

On the floor at my feet, Christina stirred. I could feel her weakness, her loss of power. I reached down with my free hand and moved her leg out of the sunlight, then was forced to jump back as Sara leapt for me.

Everyone was screaming, though none of us were. What was that sound? My ears rang from it. I darted away from Sara, but she was fast, and came for me again.

Then I saw the diadem, and I knew.

I fended Sara off once more, stepped around Christina's prone body, and raised the dripping ax high over my head.

Grandfather, why did you do this? He had nailed the awful thing there in the first place, all those years back. He had thought that would put paid to it, to its terrible magic: fastening it to this dead cottage amid the tall weeds and dancing bones. No such luck.

Sara saw what I was doing, and the shrill wailing grew even louder. "No!" she shouted, over the din.

I brought the ax down hard, meaning to smash the awful object in two. The blade bounced off it, sending droplets of blood flying. Some fell on Christina, who moaned and stirred again. I could smell the blood burning into her sweet flesh, where her leg was exposed.

I raised the ax and smashed again. Once more, the diadem resisted both the force of the magic and my own youthful strength, but I did knock it from the wall. It fell clanging to the floor, then rolled across the room, coming to a stop at the front door.

Sara lunged for it, but stopped short.

In the open doorway stood a tiny child, Janey Iverson's poppet, not quite two years old, and of indeterminate parentage, as they say. Not mine, I was pretty sure. She was an adorable thing, saucer-wide blue eyes framed by a halo of wild golden curls, and cheeks so fat and rosy even a ruined witch's familiar like me couldn't resist pinching them.

Little Laureen picked up the diadem and placed it atop those curls.

Sara screamed. Christina awoke and joined her witchsister in screaming.

I stared at the child.

Janey appeared behind her, snatching the youngling up and hefting her into strong mother's arms. "There you are! You gave me an awful fright!" Without a glance inside the cottage, she marched down the front path and back into the street.

Laureen stared solemnly back at me, clutching at her mother's plump shoulder. I watched those unblinking blue eyes and thought, *She does look like me.*

I realized something more, too, in that moment, though I didn't want to admit it. There was more wisdom, more magic in that two-year-old face than in any witch, foreign-born or locally grown.

A sound brought me back to myself—or, rather, the absence of sound. The high wailing, keening noise had vanished with the diadem on the poppet's head. I turned around to face Sara and Christina, to finish what I had started.

The cottage was empty.

I let the air slide out of my lungs as I leaned against the front wall. They were both gone, as if they'd never been there in the first place. The only evidence that anyone had passed through the room was the mussed bed, and the splintered hole in the back wall where I'd hacked away the diadem. Even the sunlit window was shadow-dark.

That's when I realized the ax was gone as well. Even the droplets of blood had vanished.

I ran to the tangled yard, shouting, "Christina! Christina!" After a bit of wild flailing, I called for Sara as well. But they were both gone, and a part of me knew it. Knew it the moment the terrible artifact had touched those golden curls.

I stumbled on something in the weeds and fell to the ground. Something hard, jutting out of the soil. I reached back for it—a stick, a rock? My fingers found it and pulled. It was a bone, thick and ancient.

Cursing, I dropped it and scrambled to my feet, but my boots found another bone at once. They were pushing outward from the very ground, rising to the surface. The whole yard was filled with them—and beyond the yard, all the way down the slope to the beach.

And here was the blood, all the blood that had vanished from the cottage, and then some—gallons, tubs of blood, running in thick rivulets down the sand, pouring into the boiling bight, crashing back against the shore in pink foamy bubbles, then rolling out again. Blood, muddying the sand, dripping from the trees, spattering my shirt and hands and face. Fat wasps with the faces of raddled women flew amid the droplets, shrieking curses in the language of stock and stone. Two women fought on the beach, barely visible in the blood and fog, alike as twins, familiar as lovers.

Crows screamed overhead, and I answered them, running wildly. I needed to retrieve my ax. I hadn't fulfilled the duty.

"You have," came a quiet voice at the back of my mind. Grandfather? But no one was there. I stopped my wild running and clung to the trunk of a tree, letting the blood pour over me, sink into the sand, slip into the sea.

"You have," I heard again.

A heavy rain started just then, as if the fog-laden clouds had finally given up their burden, all at once.

I fell to my knees, put my face in my hands, and wept.

$$\sim \text{ o } O \text{ o } \sim$$

"Damned peculiar weather we're having," Grant Archerson remarked to the room at large. He let his eyes rest on me a moment longer than necessary. "Damned peculiar."

Sunlight streamed in through the filthy windowpanes of the Tossed Pot, highlighting the thick layers of dust that rested everywhere on the kitschy decor. No sense tidying up, when the light was always so gloomy, Grant always maintained. Except for three days now, the golden sun had blessed Bone Island with its sweet charms, bringing housewives out to sweep their porches, an extra boatload of tourists from the mainland, and a foul temper from Grant.

No one had mentioned Sara Maarinen. It was as if she had never existed. Christina… Well, her presence was everywhere, like a friend half-seen passing a street corner at night. I imagined the ax, bloody and snug in a chalky grave between two women twined tight as any sacrifice at the foot of a standing stone. Noisy magic and quiet magic, united once more. Had the entirety of Bone Island become the witch's window?

No matter. Sunlight would pass, and people still went about the business of living no matter who was bleeding in the back alley. I shrugged and rested a hand on Janey Iverson's warm knee. "Might have to buy a short-sleeved shirt if this keeps up."

Laureen played at our feet, the diadem still nestled in her curls. Something flashed in the child's bright blue eyes from time to time, then passed again like clouds before the sun. There was a witch line, and a line of keepers. Always had been. Always would be. Who was to say they couldn't be the same line?

Janey, who was cousin to Christina's mother, smiled at me and laid her head on my shoulder. "Can't get her to take that silly thing off, even for bed," she murmured.

I just nodded, then looked to Grant. "Another ale?"

Home

*This story was commissioned for the coolest anthology idea—stories that grew from a single musical album (*Scenes from the Second Storey*) from an obscure band (*The God Machine*). Each story would be one song, and would carry that song's title; beyond that, we were given free rein. The song I was given was "Home".*

The assignment arrived when I was deeply concerned with home. My life was in total upheaval—divorce, leaving my home state and a career and pretty much everything—and I didn't know what was ahead of me. So I bought the album, listened to it over and over again (it is marvelous, actually), and wrote this. The anthology was published by Morrigan Books in 2013.

I keep having real estate dreams. Night dreams, I mean; everyone in this golden state of mine has unattainable fantasies. I'm a lifelong Californian, so dreaming of Victorians, Craftsman bungalows, sweet little Edwardians, even an Eichler or a Marina style—this is all to be expected.

These dreams, though, they're unusual. Peculiar.

Disturbing, even.

They weren't always like this. I've always dreamt of homes—houses where I've actually lived during the awake side of my life; mansions and palaces I saw in movies or read about in books; or dwellings from nowhere but the gelid depths of my overactive imagination.

For a long time after my first marriage crashed and burned, I dreamt repeatedly of finding new rooms, entire new floors, wings even, in my house. My therapist loved those dreams. "It's your consciousness, your creativity! New paths, new directions, new areas of your mind are opening up!"

Well, okay, I thought; *whatever, fine.* I just figured it meant I wanted more space, that I was sick and tired of living in tiny cramped apartments with too much hand-me-down shit: sagging love seats and blenders that barely worked and painted particle board bookcases and unmatched glassware, cracked and pitted with hard use. And the apartments themselves: mildew everywhere, peeling paint on the high ceilings, stained and warped hardwood floors, a general odor of decay and neglect underneath the reek of burnt grease from our inept experiments in cookery, curtains made from bedsheets or Indian tapestries. Who wouldn't want to find a fresh start, a whole new floor, rooms opening into more rooms, light and air and color and loveliness?

By the time my second marriage foundered on the shoals of quiet despair, I had the lovely house with all the extra rooms, and the light and the color and all that, but it didn't feel like home. It wasn't where I was safe or comfortable or welcome… welcome to be me, at any rate. I promise you it didn't start out this way, but by the end, I was living a role. Playing the part of someone else entirely.

Well, it wasn't my home. That much is clear, now. At some level, I must have always known.

So here I am. Just me and the orchids in yet another rented apartment, dreaming of home.

~ o O o ~

Home is where the whisky is.

Home is where you cry alone.

Home is where the temperature is up to you.

Home is where there's fresh flowers. Or not. Home is where the dreams are.

Home is where you can find me.

I'm not sure it's a coincidence that "home" and "hope" differ by only one little letter, only a few ticks apart in the great alphabet. There is so much hope involved in setting up a new home with a new lover, mate, husband. Love and joy and excitement and the absolute certainty that this is now *it*, and will be *it*, for the rest of your silly lives. Every salad bowl purchased, every rug laid down, every piece of art hung on the walls… tangible expressions of desperate, pathetic, wretched hope.

Even the brand of toothpaste. He uses Colgate, and you're a Crest person born and bred? Someone will compromise, you will agree, a change will be made, your journey toward soul-mate-ness takes another creamy, minty-fresh step! Pearly white smiles of hope!

Ah me.

But I promised to tell you about the dreams, and how mine are different. I know you don't want to hear another tale of dreams. Dreams are boring, dreams are a cop-out, they are a story that does not make sense. The first serious piece of fiction I wrote, I cheated the ending with the classic "And then she woke up."

Forgive me. I was only eleven. I know better now.

I wish I could wake up.

In the classic, happy real estate dream, I am walking through my house when I find a door I haven't noticed before. Opening it, revealing the new room beyond, I immediately rejoice and begin making plans for moving furniture in here, settling, incorporating this space into the house.

In the newer, unhappy real estate dreams, my discoveries are darker. I haven't noticed that half the roof is missing, or that the floors droop or sag, or that there's an eight-lane freeway just outside the window, cutting the yard in two. It's a good thing I'm not seeing that therapist any more. She would be very worried about me.

If we spent our time talking about dreams, that is. Unlikely, I have to say. I have much greater issues now.

~ o O o ~

I was cooking my dinner—red beans and rice from a mix, to which I added an Italian sausage saved from the week before, plus some frozen shrimp and frozen peas dropped in right at the end—fantastic stuff, and makes leftovers for days. Rinsing the shrimp, I looked up and noticed great billows of white, acrid smoke pouring out of the window of the apartment building directly behind mine. You'll forgive me if I admit that my first thought was for my own home, such as it is; but I quickly ran outside to investigate, grabbing my phone along the way.

Good thing, I suppose; I was already dialing 911 as I heard the screams. Flames licked upward, bruising the wood of the outer walls and crackling the paint. Now the smoke was black. An ugly smell of burnt hair was every-where, along with something darker underneath. The sirens came quickly—a fire station is only half a block from here—but I couldn't tell if the scream-ing stopped due to rescue or tragedy.

After the firemen shooed me away, I went back inside and finished my cooking, saving my own meal from becoming a catastrophe. What else could I do? In the modern world, there is no role for the helpful bystander. We are only in the way, once qualified help arrives.

Somehow worse, though, in a big city like this there's no gossip, no dissemination of information, no way to know what happened. No one to ask. I don't even know the woman who lives across the hall from me, though on a hot night when we both have our back doors open, I can see that her kitchen has much newer appliances than mine and a really nice tile countertop, a foil to my chipped Formica.

No matter, I thought. *I won't be here long.*

Tell me about your first home. Walk me through it, every square inch of it. What did each room mean to you? Were any rooms forbidden?

Tell me about the first home you loved.

Tell me about the first home you made love in.

Tell me about the first home you were left behind in.

Or kicked out of.

Or just left.

Someone died in that kitchen fire. I know they did. In the night I could still hear her screams, though when I got up to look out the window she fell silent.

She was in my dreams.

I know that's impossible. But she was there.

She wanders from room to room in a huge house and she's screaming and wailing and *burning burning burning* and her hair bursts into flames and her clothes have long burnt away so her skin crackles and blackens and her eyeballs melt and pour down her ruined face and the uniquely disturbing smell gets up my nostrils and still she cannot stop screaming, screaming.

The house begins to haunt my days. Or maybe it's the lack of sleep. Or the heartbreak. The death of hope. God, how I wanted this one to be different. Or at least tolerable. But in the end, I realize that I am peculiarly unsuited for love. Destined to be alone, fundamentally, forever. Destined to not find my home, my promised land, my resting point.

It's the house of my dreams, but not the happy dreams, oh no. Still it is huge, with convoluted, twisting turning hallways and passages, and way too many rooms. She roams them, wailing—yet she is me and I am her and—oh, I see I am telling this all wrong. Let me start over.

It is a large house, but not very attractive, in fact rather plain. Many people have lived here over the decades since it was first built; very few have called it home. It is not spooky or scary or particularly dark or forbidding; it's just, well, unloved. And in an awkward part of town—not really city, not really country.

Then the city encroaches more seriously, and the large old house gets carved up into large comfortable apartments.

After a time, the apartments get further divided into smaller apartments, and another building is built in what used to be the yard. It is increasingly expensive to live here, space is at a premium. Soon, the house is in the city itself; the small awkwardly shaped apartments rent for thousands of dollars a month, and are tarted up with painted woodwork and bright linoleum that quickly cracks and fades.

This is when she comes. This is when she cooks that fatal dinner. This is when she breaks down the barriers that divide what was once a home, whole and intact. This is what she roams after death.

And only I can hear her.

Home is where the ghosts are.

Home is where your mother is.

Home is emotionally and politically fraught: hometown team. Home base. Home port. Home on the range. Homeboy. Homebody. Homemaker.

Homely. Home schooling. Homemade. Department of Homeland Security. Home is a lie.

~ o O o ~

She stands before me, a blackened skeleton in the darkness, barely visible. The night wind howls through her hollow bones; her teeth chatter, her ribs bump against themselves like a handful of dice thrown across an oak table.

"You're taking me home," she whispers.

"I have nothing to do with this," I answer, although my lips do not move. Am I awake or asleep? Which is more real—the angry remains of this foolish woman taken before her time because of a miscalculation in the kitchen, or the tattered shreds of my own wasted life?

"To the promised land." Her empty eyes stare past me. I'm too exhausted to even be terrified.

"Please go." But there is no energy behind my words.

~ o O o ~

I think part of the trouble may be that I was raised by wolves. I mean, not literally, not entirely; it's probably safer to say that I raised myself. My parents—young, over-educated, optimistic, perhaps foolish—fell prey to the predominant narratives of the Age of Aquarius, and experimented with every, well, experimental form of home and community and family before giving up on one another to settle down into entirely traditional marriages. But during my childhood there were many homes, shifting partnerships, an assortment of configurations that were called "family" and deemed perfect and right and the be-all, end-all answer. All before I was ten years old.

Soon enough, I learned how to make my own peanut butter and raw honey sandwiches on cracked wheat bread, how to amuse myself without the benefit of television or playmates, how to find my own way to the little rural school in the morning. Such innocent days. Today if you see a spooky blonde seven-year-old girl in Goodwill clothes walking down a country road all alone, no adult around for miles and miles, you think there's trouble.

Although, I suppose that was true even then, wasn't it?

Shopping list:
- Bananas
- Milk
- Strawberries
- Toilet brush
- Power drill with hole saw bit
- Pistachio ice cream
- Laundry soap (and quarters for the machines)

The air stank of the fire for days, until the fog blew in from the coast and blanketed everything in a soup of damp, sodden air. Then it just smelled like mold. As per usual.

Should have bought some cleanser to go along with that toilet brush.

I became afraid of my bed, afraid of going to sleep. Which was foolish at best, and dangerous at worst: the hallucinations only increase with the hours awake. But I just couldn't stand it. She stalked my nights far worse than my days, and I did not want to see her. I stole catnaps, sneaking into the dream world in five- and ten-minute snippets, dashing back out again before I'd get caught.

"I should just move out," I said aloud to myself in the kitchen as I stared at the marred building behind mine, struggling to keep my weary eyes open.

Speaking of hallucinations. Well, there she was. I'm on the third floor, so I knew it couldn't be real, but there she was, peering back through my window. "He's taking me home," she said, without sound, though I heard her.

"Yeah, yeah, to the promised land."

She nodded, her bony, broken and burnt face eager, lighting up with excitement.

I was even more exhausted, but this time, the terror found me. I took a Vicodin left over from my last emergency room visit, washing it down with a healthy slug of Bushmill's. Then I threw myself at my bed, pulling the covers over my head as though I was a child in a fairy tale. As if that would help.

~ o O o ~

What does she want from me? I couldn't have saved her. I'm the one who called 911, for crying out loud. I did the best I could. They sent us away, they sent us all away. I'm not the one who burned up my own stupid kitchen.

~ o O o ~

The lawyer said I could have a lot more money, and for a lot longer, but I would have to do a whole bunch of specific things. It was too hard to remember them all. I wrote it all down in the meeting, or at least I thought I did, but when I looked at my notes they were a jumbled, crazy mess. The scribbles of a madwoman. She was costing me $300 an hour, the lawyer was; I was trying to focus so hard, so goddamn hard, and I had to pee so badly, but I didn't want to take any of my precious time to go pee—how much would two minutes of peeing cost? Five dollars a minute—that's a ten-dollar pee! That's three lunches!—so I just held it, but in retrospect, that was probably foolish. Probably I lost more than two minutes to the distraction of having to pee so bad.

I knew she counted her minutes very carefully, though. As we were walking out and shaking hands and doing those nice social things that normal people do, I looked at my watch and said, "Oh, man, no wonder I'm hungry for lunch! It's one-thirty!"

"One-twenty," she'd said, smiling.

~ o O o ~

The things I have to do:
- Don't get married again. *Duh.*
- Find the quit-claim deed. *Hmm.*
- Stop talking to him. *Who is she kidding?*
- Don't sign anything. *Okay.*
- I don't remember the rest.

~ o O o ~

What was I supposed to do here? Who would ever imagine that a spooky little hippie child who wore used clothes and ate government surplus cheese would grow up to be the kind of woman who would fight over real estate worth hundreds of thousands of dollars? The tiniest slip-up on my part could cost me thousands of lunches! Terrifying.

He said the house was never mine. I agreed with him there—I could never leave my books on the coffee table or an unwashed dish in the sink—but I still thought he was wrong, so far as the money goes. That's what lawyers are for, everyone says.

To my mind, lawyers are for making money for their own selves, but I knew it wasn't helpful for me to point this out.

"Cross my heart and hope to die."

"You're already dead." *And you have no heart*, I wanted to add, but that was cruel. She must have known. If I could see right through the blackened bones of her chest, surely she was aware of that.

"Jesus made him do it."

She followed me into the living room, bones clacking and thumping, the smells of fire and mold warring with one another, clinging to her in a foul miasma. I ignored her, but she wouldn't stop.

"Jesus made him do it."

"He did not." I didn't look at her. "Go away, stop bothering me. I can't help you."

"You don't understand." Her death-scent increased its assault on my nostrils; she must have moved closer. I felt as though if I touched her, I would die too. I willed her to vanish. I could almost hear her breathing, pungent air filling nonexistent lungs, then rattling back out again through an empty, bony throat.

Finally I turned to her with what I hoped was a bored expression. I knew my eyes were wide with fear—I couldn't help that.

But now she was gone. Just the odor lingered.

The purple orchid on the top shelf in the window caught my eye. I went over and brought it down for a closer look. Its leaves were dark, oily; drooping, almost. "What's the matter, baby?" I crooned as I brushed a gentle finger across the biggest leaf. It came away smeared with a moist, sooty funk.

I didn't even have to lift my finger to my nose. I knew what it would smell like.

~ o O o ~

Inventory (items to be retrieved later, when I have room for them):
The rest of my books.
Christmas box.
Wedding dress.
Camping gear (who gets the tent???)
Bicycle, helmet, pump, etc.
Snakey.

~ o O o ~

I don't return the lawyer's calls.
I don't return *his* call, or the weird emails.
I don't go to the PO Box and check my snail mail. Then I stop checking

any of my email.

I stay in the apartment for a few days, as motionless as possible. When I don't move around so much, she seems to stay away. I slowly sink into a state of mind where I'm not really awake and not really asleep: I'm safe! This is the answer. Hiding in my own head.

When I realize I am literally picking lint out of my belly button, I know I have to stop this.

~ o O o ~

Actually, lint is the wrong word for it. I don't know who ever came up with that. It's more like grime, some peculiar body emission. And with a deliciously awful reek—nothing in the world smells quite like that stuff you dig out of your belly button.

It comes out easier if it's a bit wet.

But if you're going to use saliva, it's better to start there, rather than after your finger has been poking around a while. Trust me.

~ o O o ~

I fired the lawyer yesterday. It isn't about the money, I finally realized that. I don't care—*he* can have it all, if it means that much to him. If I bought a house with the dirty, begrudged spoils of that dead marriage, then it would be tainted, fouled with bad intent, with betrayal, with ill wishes. It would not be a home.

It would not be *my* home.

"Now you understand," she says, smiling her grinning-skull teeth.

She stands before me, more decrepit than ever. It won't be long before she cannot manifest at all. I don't have much time.

I lift my t-shirt over my head and let it fall to the floor. Opening my arms, I welcome her into a bare-skin embrace.

She cocks her head, as if puzzled for a moment, then moves toward me. The smell of her isn't so awful any more. I'm getting used to it, I guess.

Everything in here is already so coated with the stuff, I could hardly help doing so. The orchids are dying, their leaves starving for oxygen, smothered by the greasy soot, the tiny bits and pieces of her life that flew through the air and became part of me.

My life.

My home.

"You're taking me home," I whisper as she steps into my arms. I pull her close, cracking her blackened bones, shattering them. Jagged edges press into my skin as she begins to fall to pieces. They draw blood, lots and lots of blood, nourishing her even as it pours, floods, drains away from me. Soon I will be gone, no more in this world—I'll find my home, my real home. The pain will stop.

She cries, a high keening sound melding with the wind that rushes through the gaps and spaces that make up what's left of her.

I cry, matching her breath for breath, as the pain gathers and grows, as the air fills with smoke and the reek of burnt hair, burnt flesh, burnt blood.

~ o O o ~

It wasn't supposed to be like this.

I'm still here, wandering from room to room, crying, looking for help. Trying to reach somebody, anybody. I find a new door and open it, but it isn't an undiscovered room this time, it's just more of the same—the Formica kitchen, the dark living room. Again and again.

The roof is gone, and the eight-lane highway now comes right through the house, and the fire is back, and she's here too and dying again, and nobody will come to save her in time, and nobody will come to save *me* in time—and it just goes on and on and on like this, around and around, an endless circle of dread and pain and sorrow and mournful heartbreak and failure and more pain, always more pain.

I wish I could wake up.

I know I won't.

This is home.

If This Were a Romance...

By SHANNON PAGE and JAY LAKE

"Love and Rockets!" came the anthology call. So naturally the eighties band came to mind, and I started a story called "The Word That Would Best Describe This Feeling." Of course, the editors were looking for romance in space, not old goth rock. As with most of my collaborative stories, Jay's contributions improved the story considerably, and it acquired a new title (though my first line remained). Love and Rockets *was published by DAW in 2010.*

*H*aunted, Loren thought. *The man haunts me.*

Not that there was anything sane or rational or even halfway intelligent that she could do about it. Of course not. Furthermore, she wasn't even sure he knew what he was doing.

It was just that he appeared... everywhere. She'd be walking down a narrow steel service gallery embedded in the Hullframe 280 gardens, wrench in hand, sent to adjust the timing on the mildew pumps—and there he would be. Squeezing past her, his arm brushing hers as his eyes scanned ahead to the great towering falls of greenery that made up the bulk of Ship's biological resources.

Or it would be end of shift and she would have stopped off for a ration of slivovitz in Frame Zero, the generic little bar on Deck 47 near her bunk bay, and he'd be in there, huddled at a small table talking to some officer she didn't recognize. Not that Crew spent much time down here in work gang country.

Or what happened today. She was all the way across Ship's circumference, a full one-eighty from her usual workshift site, at the coreward edge of the habitable area where the passageways began running to anoxic atmospheres and the bulkheads carried exotic gas warnings in a multitude of languages and symbols, running an errand for her gang boss. Even the grav plates were wonky there—Loren had to watch every step, as the bad patches tended to accumulate a lot more dust. And she was lost; the numbers seemed scattered over here, half the hatches not even marked; the passageways didn't follow the normal patterns. They bulged and shifted around to make room for the gardens hullward, but still, why did it have to be *this* complicated?

Loren hefted the carryall of excess He-3 cartridges around to her other hip and sighed. Heavy: too heavy. She should have brought a waist pack, but she didn't think she'd be carrying them so long. "Blasted things," she muttered. The corner of the carryall dug into her side; the cartridges rattled against one another. Why couldn't Gramma Francesca have sent a runner? She was a biomechanic: skilled far above this sort of makework.

And then he was there. Not a haunting at all, but just about treading on her boots as she turned a blind corner.

"Oh! I am sorry, sir." She reeled back, nearly dropping the carryall, and felt her face flush. Had he heard her?

"Citizen," he said, his voice softer and somehow higher than she'd expected. "My fault: I wasn't attending."

His accent was that of the highest echelons of senior Crew. This much, at least, she'd expected. His words, though... Far more polite than one of her class could ever expect from one of his class.

The Captain would not take as Consort any other than a man of the highest rank, after all.

"No, the fault is mine," she murmured, and struggled to reposition the carryall, ease gracefully past him, not look him in the eye, and show proper respect all at once. As several of these actions were impossible to perform simultaneously, she managed only a hesitant step forward before he spoke again.

"Citizen: your name, if you please?"

"Loren 68. Sir." With an uncharacteristic fit of compulsive honesty, she added, "Work gang Forty-Seven Charlie. Best gang in the decks, sir."

A small smile flickered across the officer's face. "Citizen Loren, do you have a pass for this area?"

She fumbled with the carryall again, then finally set it down at her feet. Holding out her left wristband, she blushed even further as she said, "Gramma Francesca gave me a thirty-minute override. But I'm lost..."

He sniffed as he examined the blinking red light on the band. "Very well." Then, taking her hand gently in his and turning it over, he tapped a code onto the tiny keypad at her wrist. The band beeped; the glow changed to green; delicious, startled shivers of craving and delight emanated up her arm from his casual touch. "There you are. Thirty more minutes. Your destination is that way." He dropped her hand—nearly painful, the loss of contact!—and pointed ahead.

"Thank you, sir, thank you!"

"Carry on." With that, he was gone, leaving her a whiff of his scent and a handful of wicked memories.

~ o O o ~

Two shots of slivovitz down that night, and still sleep would not come. *Haunted.* After an hour of this, Loren sat up in her bunk and turned on the console, then pulled up the entertainment files. Old stories, she liked; the oldest, ones that took place on Earth.

A planet she had never seen.

A planet no one she knew had ever seen.

You'd have to be nearly two centuries old to have any memories of

Earth. And, while technically possible, people of that age were vanishingly rare. At least the sort of people she knew.

The Consort probably knew Earthlings among the senior Crew...

"Stop it," she whispered, and continued searching through her files.

A Regency romance: a tale of love and unattainability. A man of the highest station, one who is betrothed to a woman of his caste. A simple girl, humble, shy, making her way through the edges of someone else's fairy tale. An accidental encounter, and then another; a brush of the arm; a casual exchange... Loren laughed at herself, but reread the story anyway, savoring every word.

When she was finished, she wanted to weep.

Of course, everything was backwards, just all wrong, here in the real world. Nothing like the stories. For it to be a true romance, the Consort should have offered to carry the carryall today, not sent Loren on her way with a sharp word.

And she should be a stolen child of the aristocracy—a princess in disguise, or hidden, through some astonishing mix-up of fortune. Awaiting discovery of her rightful place... and the hand of her prince.

But no. Loren was already in her rightful place, and lucky to have it. Her workshift was not onerous, her teammates were decent and engaging, and Gramma Francesca was a benevolent work gang boss. She'd heard stories, knew how it could be.

So why did she feel as though her life was being wasted, one unendurable sliver at a time?

~ o O o ~

Gram Keith, the overboss of the Deck 48 work gangs and convenor of all the decks from 45 to 52 in the three hundred series hullframes, had called a general meeting. "Hurry, Citizens, hurry!" Gramma Francesca marched down the bunking passageway, rapping on hatches with her wand, sending tiny jolts of Direction into everyone's right-hand wristbands. "We're starting in five minutes!"

Loren tumbled out of bed and yanked on the suit she'd worn yester-day—no time to turn it in for a clean one—then splashed her face with water from the tiny sink at the foot of her bunk. She dried her hands on her hair, smoothing it down and tucking the excess into the suit's collar. To much of a rush to find a ponytail holder either... a small act of rebellion, or merely independence, keeping her hair long. It was also a colossal pain in the ass, when it came to close work in the deep machinery where the grav plates were variable and the snag hazards multiplied.

No matter. She wasn't going to cut it.

Her head pounding from the slivovitz, or perhaps just the lack of sleep, she grabbed a handful of Pain-Free from the passageway bin on her way out, chewing the chalky tablets as she hurried along with her bunkmates to the ramp leading to the next deck.

"Late night?" Garen had fallen into step alongside Loren. Now he struggled to keep up with her long stride. She wasn't going to make it any easier on him, either.

"Why do you ask, Citizen?"

He nodded at her hand, but it was empty now. So he'd been watching her. As usual.

"You have dust at the corner of your mouth," he said, after a pause that was just a bit too long.

She wiped with the back of her hand, but found nothing. Who did he think he was fooling? "Thanks," she said, giving him a look that said just the opposite.

He sat next to her in the meeting. After she ignored several of his whis-pered remarks, he fell silent.

Which allowed her to pay attention to Gram Keith, of course. As they were supposed to. Unfortunate that things should be so dull, but such was life.

The bulk of the meeting was to go over the reordered workshift assign-ments. Loren listened carefully until her own number was mentioned. No changes there. Good.

She was woolgathering again, letting her mind drift to... well, to hauntings, truth be told. Tall, slender, pale men appearing at the unexpected ends of passageways, empty service bays, a gentle brush on the inside of a wrist, all accidental—when she heard a sharp inbreath next to her.

"What?" she whispered to Garen.

The young man was bright-eyed, his face flushed. "I'm transferred, to your unit. Effective immediately."

Loren stared at him, her heart lurching. Not *him*. "But you don't know anything about biomechanics."

"I'll be support. It's a way up, a way in. You know I've always wanted to do that kind of work."

Then they both jumped as Gramma Francesca sent a small jolt of Control to their wristbands. **Quiet** came through the line, the order emanating through Loren's brain as if it was a thought of her own. Her mouth closed automatically and her attention returned to the announcements.

~ o O o ~

If this were a romance, Garen would be a prince, fallen from his high station, unrecognizable in humble garb, manure on his shoes and a painful shyness masking his nobility. Loren would be yearning for the unattainable lord, all the while not seeing the even more fantastic man so close to hand.

No: that would only be true if Garen were the hero of the romance. Not Loren.

No: it could still be true, if Garen were not truly, utterly, miserably horrible. And if the Consort were not so unbelievably, thrillingly desirable.

It could be no kind of romance that had Garen anywhere in it.

Loren turned in her bunk once more, fussing at the covers. The thin blanket seemed too skimpy at times, and all too much at other times.

Not the blanket's fault, of course.

And was Garen really so horrible? Truly?

Yes, he was a pest; yes, he was manipulative and sneaky and weak-chinned and had an odd way of cocking his head when he was thinking… but did that make him impossible?

Well, yes, it did. Garen was impossible. Loren knew that much, at least, from the romances: if you have to talk yourself into a man, you don't want him.

Finally giving up, Loren sat up and dialed another entertainment, a period virteo this time with glittering eye candy and wonderful set pieces. But even that failed to distract. Her mind kept returning to its hauntings... interspersed with terrifying images of spending every day with Garen, now that he had somehow maneuvered the transfer. The eager boy asking her endless questions, inserting himself into her every conversation, even— shudder—somehow arranging that she should be the one to train him.

Oh, of *course* he would do that. He probably already had! She should apply for a change of workshift immediately. She would talk to Gramma Francesca first thing at lights-up. Anything—she'd transfer to anything. Even to an Outside work gang... though "dangerous" barely began to describe Outside work. Ship sailed through hard space, radiation sleeting across Her skin like scalpels waiting to sculpt an unlucky Citizen's cells into monstrous assassins of the body.

The story on the screen before her played on; Loren barely watched. Partway through, a figure caught her eye, and she gasped. Did a double take, then ran the transmission back to see it again.

It couldn't be.

An actor in the ancient drama... he looked just like the Consort. Tall and slender and pale...

No. It wasn't him, of course; the dramas were made in the entertainment division, and actors were chosen from the general Citizenry, men and women and inters just like Loren. And Garen.

General Citizens did not become Consorts to the Captain.

Still, she looked at the scene several times before letting the drama run forward again. The tall actor had a minor role to play: cousin to the penniless heroine. He only appeared in one other scene, and in that one, he was clearly not the Consort.

Of course he wasn't.

Because her life was not a romance. And the Consort was not for her.

And if she didn't choose to bond with Garen, or someone else like him, someone actually *available* to her, Loren would spend her life alone. She would not be able to apply for an upgrade to dual quarters; she would not be given celebratory rations of slivovitz every fourth cycle; she would not get to put on the white armband that signified pair-bonding and sometimes provided curfew waivers as well as sundry other benefits.

She would not have anyone to talk to, late at night, when the chattering in her brain refused to die down.

She would not ever understand what love felt like.

Yet if the Consort was not for her, then why did he keep showing up, dangling himself in her line of vision, appearing everywhere she happened to be? Haunting her? Ship was enormous—tens of thousands of Citizens, many hundreds of the upper echelon. Loren had never seen the Captain or any of the senior Crew in the flesh. Only the Consort. Again and again. What were the odds of that?

He was doing it somehow. He was sending her a message. He was powerful: he could do so with very little trouble. But he couldn't do so openly. Not a man in his position. She was supposed to understand.

Even in the entertainments she somehow chose to watch: why had those particular ones become available to her? Especially the one with the actor who looked just like the Consort?

Of course Loren's life was a romance—it had to be. And of course she was the heroine of it. Except she had understood it all wrong. She was not a classical heroine: rather, she was the hero. He was the captive, betrothed to the Captain, no doubt against his will. If she would not take charge, if she would not rescue him, then who would?

By the time the entertainment ended, Loren had made her decision.

~ o O o ~

She rose before lights-up and collected a clean suit from the rack at the end of the passageway, then stole back to her bunkroom and washed her entire body using the tiny sink. Likely nobody would be in the communal 'freshers at this hour; even so, she didn't want to take a chance at being seen. At being asked questions.

Instead of braiding her long hair or tucking it away as usual, Loren left it loose, brushing the strands out with her fingers. In the romances, the heroine had a hairbrush, with a silver handle and boar's hair bristles. Here aboard Ship, in transit for generations, heroines had to make do without. There were no boars, nor silver, to start with. And with standard-issue jumpsuits and heavy black boots, when she really should be wearing gossamer gowns and dainty golden sandals...

"Right," she whispered, easing one last tangle from her hair. "And while I'm at it, I might as well wish for a walk in the woods. And a pony."

If they had woods.

Or ponies.

Though of course, if she was the hero, she should have a sword and a suit of armor. Equally impossible. As a biomechanic, at least she could *grow* a pony.

Carrying her boots until she'd left the sleeping area, Loren made it out without waking anyone. Or so she hoped, anyway.

She didn't begin breathing easier until she'd reached the high-speed lifts at Hullframe 341, out of her range but not actually a forbidden area. Holding up her left armband to the console, she punched in the override code that Gramma Francesca most usually used to release the workers for temporary assignments. Citizens were not supposed to know these codes, but everyone did. Gang bosses were expected to change them regularly, but the hassle involved was just too much.

So long as everyone kept quiet and didn't steal too much from the stores, everything worked out just fine.

Loren hoped she wasn't knocking over the entire system right now... but if she was—so be it. She'd pay the price later, and hope the trouble would be worth it.

The high-speed lift beeped in response to her override code. Doors opened with a whoosh and a clank. The engineering part of Loren's brain noted the clank and was already diagnosing probable cause and likely repair strategies before the part that was in charge at the moment took over.

"No dice, princess," she whispered to herself as the doors closed her into the lift. "This goes well, you'll never repair another lift again."

~ o O o ~

The hullward decks were unlike anything she'd ever seen before. Loren knew how Ship was laid out; everyone had seen schematics all their lives, and with her biomechanic's engineering training, she understood better than most how the structure was held together.

The beauty of it struck her most. Wide, sweeping open spaces overhead, tied to one another by the thinnest spans of gleaming gossamer-spun titanium while their glittering crystalline panels provided a view of the stars outside. Multideck spans of bulkhead covered in what had to be merely decorative greenery. The very air scented fresh as if it had not roiled through a million lungs before hers. The long views down to coreward levels unthinkably lower, farther away, demonstrating the grand scale of Ship. Even the color scheme on bulkheads and panels and informational signage was different up here in hullward country: contrasting mauve and a deep green, a combination that somehow conveyed both comfort and majesty. Yes, it was true: Crew really did have it better than the Citizenry.

How pleasant it would be to live up here!

After a minute, Loren realized she had no idea where to go next.

The Captain dwelled at the top hullward level, along the outer hull: everyone knew that. But where? There weren't even hatches up here, much less numbered ones—assuming Loren would know what number to look for.

She had thought it would be obvious. In the virteo romances, the powerful always had red carpets, brazen trumpets, massive doorways. Nothing at all was obvious, though. Loren wandered down a long balcony, stealing glances over the elegant, too-thin rail to the unfathomable depths below, trying to figure out where the center was. The balcony ended in a set of passageways fanning out in a pattern of spokes. She hesitated, then chose the middle way and kept on. Here there were hatches, at least, but they were still not numbered, not labeled.

No signage at all. She could think of several safety code write-ups from that.

Where *was* everyone? It was quiet, too quiet. Did no one live here at all? Was the whole notion of a Captain and a Bridge just a hoax? Ship was vast, and contained multitudes. Right now, anything seemed possible.

Was the Consort a myth, too? No, he was real. A haunting, and so very, very real.

So where were all the people who should be up here?

That question was answered a moment later, when two guards rounded the corner, bored expressions on their faces.

"Citizen," the woman said, her eyes snapping into focus a moment quicker than the male guard's did.

"Ma'am," Loren answered, automatically, her hand going to cover her left wristband.

"Your pass?"

"I…" This was it: the moment she had been waiting for. All the sleepless nights, all the dreams, all the desperation of her determined flight up here. "I need to see the Consort. I have urgent business with him."

The woman guard—she had red hair, longer than Loren's, pulled back in a ponytail, and unusually pale eyes—stood a little taller and glanced at her partner. "Your *pass*, Citizen," she repeated.

The male guard nodded and still said nothing.

Loren sighed and held out her wrist. "Gramma Francesca sent me, from Deck 47, in the three hundreds. The errand is urgent, and she programmed my pass quickly—it might not be exactly right." *Of course it's not exactly right—it's not even sort of right. But it's all I've got.*

The woman took Loren's hand, turning it gently, and peered at the left wristband. It was an odd echo of the Consort's action two days ago.

And, oddly, the touch gave Loren the same shivering thrill.

In the privacy of her own mind, Loren laughed at herself. *Now any time someone gives me a new assignment or checks my status, I'm going to giggle like a schoolgirl? Oh, wonderful.*

The guard finished her inspection, frowning. She turned to her partner and began to speak quietly in coded language.

The woman was going to deny Loren. They were going to stop her, to send her back. This was her only chance, and they were going to stop her.

Loren yanked the heavy wrench out of her pocket and held it high, brandishing it over both their heads. "I know it's wrong, and I don't care. I've *got* to see the Consort! I have to!" She reached back; she'd hit the man first, and maybe the woman would run.

The female guard didn't move, didn't speak, for a long moment. Then she drew her weapon in a blur of movement and Loren's world went blank.

~ o O o ~

Loren awoke in pain—the usual pain, from a stun-blow, magnified by what must have been several applications of Control and Direction to her wristband.

She was lying on a cot in a small holding cell. Had she been sent back to Deck 47? Most likely.

Loren sat up, rubbing her face, trying to ignore the pain. Her head seared with it, and the backs of her eyes, and a stab of agony ran through her left calf muscle. "Oh...."

After a minute, the pain ebbed a bit, but still, Loren wished she had a huge handful of Pain-Free. Or a big ration of slivovitz.

Why was her calf hurting so much? Hadn't the guard hit her in the chest, as they usually did?

Loren studied the small room as her vision steadied. No manual controls on the inside of the hatch, just a keypad and a sensor. Yes: a holding cell. Too bad for her if there was a fire or a life support failure. Perhaps a bit more spacious than she'd expected, but since she had never occupied one, merely repaired the isolated airflow systems supporting them, she wasn't entirely sure.

One long table against the bulkhead, with nothing on it; a sink, with no mirror over it; a small sanitary device in the corner, with a ration of wipes beside it. The cot upon which she sat, steel frame with the usual thickness of mattress and the usual blanket. Nothing out of the ordinary, nothing she wouldn't have expected to find.

It took her a while to realize what was different about the cell. The bulkheads were painted mauve, with dark green accents.

~ o O o ~

After a time, the hatch slid open. Loren crouched on the cot, her knees drawn up, rubbing the sore calf. Her headache surged forward as her eyes snapped to the hatchway.

It was the redheaded guard, alone, and unarmed. She slipped in, then tapped the keypad. The hatch snicked shut behind her.

"What...?" Loren started, then stopped herself. This whole business had more than a whiff of danger to it. Of things that weren't allowed.

"Quiet," the guard said, unnecessarily. She sat beside Loren on the cot, perhaps just a bit too close, facing her.

From this distance, Loren could see that her pale eyes were sea-gray. It was a striking look, with the lush red hair.

Hair that was now loose and flowing over the woman's shoulders.

"Tell me why you've come here," the guard now whispered, "and I may be able to help you."

"I..." Loren stared back into the woman's eyes. God, she was beautiful. Loren had been with women before—what girl hadn't?—but it had never done anything much for her. Women together: that wasn't how the romances went, after all. "I told you. I came to see the Consort."

The woman shook her head, but a smile hovered at the corners of her mouth. "Yes, you said that. But you know and I know that your gang boss didn't send you. Look: tell, and I might be able to do something. But quickly."

Loren bit her lip, then told the woman all.

~ o O o ~

She waited in the cell. After she'd poured out her heart and soul, the woman—Sonia was her name, and it suited her, Loren thought—had nodded, then hugged her tightly. "Be strong," she whispered. "I'll be back."

The next time the hatch opened, though, it was just an orderly with a tray of food. Rations that were neither better nor worse than what she'd get in the gang mess back on Deck 47 or from the dispensers scattered throughout her part of Ship.

She ate the food, though she had little appetite. At least her aches and pains were subsiding.

A few more hours went by. Loren was wishing hard that the cell had been provided with an entertainment console when the hatch snicked open again, and Sonia entered.

The Consort was right behind her.

"Ohhh," Loren sighed, as they both stepped into the cell and closed the hatch behind them. Full of words, she was, thousands of words—and they all failed her, in this moment. The moment she'd been waiting for; the reason she'd taken this risk, risen to this level…

"Yes, this is the one," the Consort said to Sonia.

"I thought so." Sonia sat on the cot beside Loren once more, though Loren barely noticed. The Consort stood just inside the hatch, watching her with an unreadable expression. She couldn't keep her eyes off him. He was even more beautiful than she'd remembered.

"Have you told her?" he asked Sonia.

"Not yet. I wanted to be sure."

Now Loren turned to the other woman. "Told me what?"

The redheaded guard took Loren's hands, both of them, and smiled at her. Yes, the woman was lovely indeed. Was everyone so gorgeous here in the upper echelons? Even the workers? Loren shook away the thought. It didn't matter. Of course they were good-looking. That was why they were privileged, right?

"We have an exciting proposal for you."

This is it, she thought, as a thrill filled her chest, saturated her heart with joy. She had been right. The Consort was looking for escape, a way out—he had singled Loren out, chosen her—life was a romance indeed...

Even if it wasn't playing out exactly as Loren had hoped, had dreamed. It would be better if it were she and the Consort alone, if it were his hands in hers right now, not Sonia's...

But the woman was still talking. Loren had missed the first few words, but snapped to attention at the word "Outside."

"...never recruit for such missions openly," she was saying. "Too many people think they're strong enough, capable enough, for what we face out there, but they're not."

"Out... Outside?" Loren stammered. What?

"Yes." Sonia smiled even more broadly. "It's a new mission, just being formed, to map out our arrival. *In this generation!* The team will be doing planetary surveys. Exploration and mapping. High danger, high chance of injury..."

"High reward." The Consort finally spoke again. "And we think you're perfectly suited as the team's biomechanic."

Loren stared back at the man of her dreams. Her mind was both blank and racing. Thoughts, half-formed, flitted through her head and then vanished, chased by other, even crazier thoughts. Finally, she managed, "Why me? There must be hundreds of better engineering techs in and out of the bio specialties."

"But none more daring. None with your initiative." Sonia again. "Look at what you've done, all the rules you've broken, the risks you've taken."

"But not... That wasn't for going *Outside*." She didn't want to die! Were they insane? Was she going to wake up at any moment, safe in her own bunk?

The Consort laughed. "No, of course not. As Sonia said, we can't advertise for this—we'd get all sorts of fools. You couldn't have known."

"We've had our eye on you for some time," Sonia went on. "When your gang boss first reported that you routinely modified your work logs to cover the fact that you finished jobs faster than anyone else, but didn't ask to take on a new assignment, we knew you had ingenuity, and a strong sense of self-preservation."

"I..." Gramma Francesca had known about the logs? She thought she'd hidden that without a trace.

"And when we reviewed the records of what entertainments you ordered, we knew you were a dreamer, a woman with imagination." The Consort, this time.

"No one without imagination survives Outside." Sonia gazed at Loren, her face serious, pleading.

They meant it, these people. But no, there was no way.

Unless...

"What is the reward?" she asked.

Sonia beamed back at her, and the Consort smiled and took a step forward. "Name your price."

Loren looked up into his eyes. "You."

His smile fell away and his eyes narrowed. "Don't be a fool, *Citizen*." Her heart sank at the tone of the Consort's voice. "I meant credits, privileges—anything you desire that one of your station can have. Extra rations, larger quarters. Any work assignment you request upon your return."

"I don't want that." Loren felt herself filling with desperate urgency, a sense of recklessness. She had nothing left to lose. "If you've been researching me and watching me all this time, you *know* what I want. That's why you've been following me personally, isn't it? Haunting me. You *know*. And you know I won't settle for some stupid larger bunk and a dozen extra drinks per cycle. You know."

His expression was not changing as she spoke. She might as well be arguing with empty air. Beside her, Sonia looked sad, disappointed. It didn't mar the woman's loveliness any.

"Impossible," the Consort finally said.

Loren stared back at him. Up close, she could see the tiny lines at the corners of his eyes. His hair was thinning, just a bit. His suit, though made of exquisite material, fit him rather too tight around the hips, too loose around the shoulders.

He was not perfect.

He was not the hero.

"Let me go below, then," she said. "Just send me back."

"It's not that simple," the Consort began, but Sonia interrupted: "Yes, it is. We haven't told her anything that isn't general knowledge, or at least general rumor." She looked at Loren. "You can go."

Who was in charge here? Surely the Consort outranked a mere guard? But the man only nodded, and within minutes, Loren was back in the same high-speed lift she'd come up on, carrying nothing but memories and hastily-swallowed tears.

~ o O o ~

Loren slouched in Frame Zero, the small bar on Deck 47, two ration glasses of slivovitz on the table before her. The murmur of conversation surrounded her; she listened idly to it, picking up words here and there, but nothing coherent.

Nothing interesting.

Garen walked in, scanned the room, and saw her. His face broke into a broad grin as he came over to her table and sat down.

"Hi! I haven't seen you in days!"

"Yes. They've got me working over in the gardens at Hullframe 280. A big duct rupture. Got to do a bunch of reconditioning."

Garen frowned briefly, then returned to grinning. "I'd love it if you'd show me some day..."

"No can do. I can't pull you off of your own important work." Gramma Francesca had him stripping bimetallic windings from old coil drive cores. Yes, her work gang boss didn't miss a trick.

He sighed, then seemed to notice the two drinks. "Oh! For me? Thanks!"

"No." Loren reached a hand out, ready to bat his away if he reached for one. But her tone was enough. Her tone, and her next words: "I've got a date."

"Oh." An awkward pause, as color rose in his sallow, unattractive face. Then he was gone.

"I've got a date," Loren whispered under her breath. "A date with a redhead…"

Life wasn't a romance, after all. Not in the usual, traditional sense: with tall handsome knights in shining armor. But that didn't mean it had to be boring.

Mad Gus Missteps

From the 'Legends of Beer' Catalogue: Volume 17, Canto 210

By MARK J. FERRARI *and* SHANNON PAGE

Mark and I were at a party when our friend Phyl said, "Write me a story for my beer anthology! I need it next week!" I am a wine drinker; Mark, when he drinks at all, prefers sweet cocktails. Nevertheless, we set to it. The oral history transcript format (and the footnotes) were my idea; the plot, the humor, the delightful absurdity is all Mark. How Beer Saved the World was published by Sky Warrior in 2013.

The following is transcribed from an interview with extremely aged [1] German pig farmer Gustavo Dourtmundschtradel, conducted in English[2] by Roland Halifax, an oral history researcher from Bisonford University in Littleville, Iowa,[3] originally recorded on November 22nd, 1993 at Gustavo's ancestral farmhouse in the hamlet of Frauschlesundmunster.[4]

---

1 At the time of this interview, Mr. Dourtmundschtradel was 91 years old and largely confined to a wicker wheelchair. He died just two years later, having fallen, somehow, from his chair into an old well more than 500 meters from the house.

2 Mr. Dourtmundschtradel's English was quite good owing to a lifetime of extensive international travel and very active participation in American commodities markets, trading primarily in pork bellies.

3 Not to be confused with Oxford Community College in the unincorporated town of Verylittleville, Ohio—or with Deerford Vocational School in Teenytinyville, Idaho, both commonly confused with Bisonford in Littleville, Iowa.

4 Since this interview was conducted, the hamlet of Frauschlesundmunster has been leveled to accommodate an industrial bio-engineering facility and shopping complex. The Dourtmundschtradel ancestral farm now lies largely beneath the new development's seventeen-acre parking structure. Hence the value in preserving oral history.

RH: Thank you for agreeing to speak with me, Herr Dourtmundschtradel.

GD: A man of my age is of no further use with the pigs, Herr Halifax. It is good to have some other occupation—and to hope, of course, that some of my ancestral lore may be preserved… For some more appreciative audience, perhaps, than my *dummkopf*[5] son, who never believes a word I speak, and his even dimmer offspring with their video games and little music players. [*Thoughtful pause*] I must confess to fearing that the Dourtmundschtradel line is failing. Soon, our stories may be all that remains of us.

RH: Ah… Well then… What story would you like to start with?

GD: It is always best to start at the beginning, *ja*[6]? So I will tell you first, Herr Halifax, the oldest story in my family's possession. A tale of the liberation of Durn in Schkerrinwald—the place from which my line originates, too many centuries ago to count now.

RH: Can you give me even an approximate century in which to place this account?

GD: *Ach du Lieber Himmel!*[7] No, lad. My tale comes from a time before centuries had been invented. This is from the… How is it in English?… The *Jahren sehr lange Geschichten.*[8]

RH: Good heavens![9] That's quite an old story! However did you come by it?

GD: I had it from my father.

RH: And… do you know how he came by it?

GD: Had it from his father, of course—who had it from his father, and so on. I am 91 years old, Herr Halifax. The time we have is maybe short to

---

5 An uncomplimentary German term referring to someone of questionable analytic skills.

6 German term for "ya".

7 German phrase roughly translated into English as, "Akk to God in heaven!"

8 Roughly translated: "The Age of Rather Long Stories"; a very brief and obscure period between the Teutonic Age of Legends and the subsequent Time of Succinct Essays, which, in turn, ended some seven centuries prior to The Moment of Memos preceding what we now refer to as "recorded European history".

9 An English phrase roughly translated into German as "Ach du Lieber Himmel!"

waste on such trivialities, *ja*?

RH: Sorry. Do go on.

GD: Well, as you will no doubt have heard, Europe was a dark place to be living in those days. But even by such standards, the isolated village of Durn was darker than most. It had many nicknames then, all of them words for *misery* of one kind or another.

RH: I've never heard of any Durn Village.

GD: Of course not. It was gone not long after this story transpired. The meager valley to which it clung was but an inhospitable rent in the high mountains of Schkerrinwald.

RH: Where is Schkerrinwald, exactly?

GD: Gone as well—a mere century or two after Durn. The whole empire of Vorkenfast was never more than one of many tenuous experiments in kingdom-craft back then.

RH: I must confess, I've never heard of an empire named Vorkenfast either.

GD: How could you have? I would never have heard of it myself, were my people not descended from the place.[10] And yet, out of Durn, meanest village of Schkerrinwald, least kingdom of the tenuous Vorkenfast Empire, came the greatest blessing ever bestowed upon Europe.

RH: Which was…?

GD: Why, *beer*, of course![11] And my own many-times-great-grandfather was the man who first brought that golden gift into the land of Germany.

RH: I'm sorry… Did you just say… that *your* family introduced *beer* to Germany?

GD: *Ja.*[12]

RH: [*Unintelligible sounds of surprise and/or confusion.*]

GD: Before you inform me once again that you have never heard of

---

10 Subsequent research has confirmed that the village of Durn, the kingdom of Schkerrinwald, and the Vorkenfast Empire are certainly quite gone, and apparently unheard of by anyone other than Mr. Dourtmundschtradel.

11 This assertion is disputed by some scholars.

12 As is this one.

this, Herr Halifax, allow me to concede that any tangible evidence of this claim vanished with my ancient ancestors, which is why I have never elected to tell even my disappointing son of this secret handed down through so many of my forefathers. I have no doubt of the tale's veracity. Neither my father, nor any of his fathers were liars—or fools.[13] My son, alas, is the first of us for that. But I am German,[14] and my people do not so much enjoy playing the laughingstock as do those of your young country, so I have kept silent until now. You seem a pleasant fellow, wise enough to value the past more than most, but if you think my tale too improbable, let us leave it and proceed to some other.

RH: No, no! Please, Herr Dourtmundschtradel, continue. I'm quite fascinated.

GD: Very well, then…

The valley of Durn, as I was saying, had been oppressed for decades by a tyrant who styled himself Lord Augustus Stephenson of the Brown Feather;[15] a paranoid bombast who kept a small army of henchmen stabled like cattle in his heavily fortified manse upon a steep rise at the valley's southern end. This pretense of a castle squatted like a guardhouse between the village and a great waterfall that marked the valley's only navigable passage to the outside world. No one came or went from Durn without Lord Stephenson's leave, which is to say that almost no one ever came or went from Durn at all—except as prisoners or exiles.[16]

This self-styled "Lord" was universally referred to by the valley's unfortunate inhabitants as Mad Gus—never within his hearing, of course—for few

---

13 And this one.

14 This assertion is both verifiable and undisputed.

15 In conversation with Mr. Dourtmundschtradel after the recording of this interview, the interviewer learned that the "brown feather" referred to was on display in Stephenson's so-called throne room, where he made loud and frequent claims that it had been plucked by his father from the tail of a phoenix, and thus somehow proved his divine right to rule—though, to virtually all others, Dourtmundschtradel asserts, it looked an awful lot like the feather of a common owl.

16 This policy might go a long way toward explaining the dearth of any reference to Lord Augustus Stephenson or Durn Valley in the known historical record.

in Durn had not suffered frequent outrages at his unpredictable whim. Mad Gus saw punishment as a preventative measure. "Spare the rod and spoil the child" was not just his favorite Bible verse; it was the only one he knew. He liked it so well that he had it carved upon his coat of arms.[17] A week did not go by without someone's wife dragged from the house and sold to slavers in remuneration for some petty debt to Stephenson, real or imagined—or someone's home or barn torched in the middle of the night as warning against whatever wrong Mad Gus imagined was being contemplated in their hearts—or someone's child abducted and caged up at the castle until he or she grew old enough to serve Mad Gus as yet another henchman or kitchen drudge—or someone's husband beaten just for entertainment in the fields or village square by the tyrant's "peacekeepers". Neither loitering, truancy, gossip, nor public play or celebration were allowed in Durn. Only labor was tolerated there, and Mad Gus took *all* of whatever anyone's labor produced beyond the little required by them to starve through another winter without actually dying.[18]

RH: What a grim situation… Why did these people not revolt? It doesn't sound as if they had much to lose.

GD: It was the beer, Herr Halifax.

RH: The beer? I… don't quite see—

GD: The one exception to Mad Gus's insane selfishness and cruelty was the *beer*. Or so it seems, at first glance, *ja*?

RH: Ah. Right… First glance at… what, exactly?

GD: Understand, Herr Halifax, the people of Durn were allowed one male goat or cow and one female. Any kids or calves produced were confiscated just as soon as they were weaned, and taken off to grace the royal table—as was any milk not used for making cheese. Mad Gus's subjects were

---

17 If not apocryphal, this detail places the origins of Mr. Dourtmundschtradel's tale sometime after the introduction of Christianity to Europe, and thus well after The Age of Rather Long Stories—not to mention the first known invention of beer—casting potential doubt upon the rest of his tale, though Durn may conceivably have been the cradle of modern beer for that part of Europe—whatever part of Europe that was, exactly.

18 The practice described here was actually fairly common in medieval Europe, often referred to in official documents as "managing the tax base".

encouraged to make all the cheese they wished, but not allowed to eat a bite of it. Off to the castle with that too, straight from the molds. Folk kept just half a bushel of whatever produce they might eke out of the rocky soil. All the rest was seized as "tax" upon harvest and sent up to the tyrant's bulging granaries and cellars against some rainy day. *His* rainy day, of course, not theirs. But! Strangely enough, folk were allowed to keep all the hops and grain that they might wish—just as long as it was brewed straight into beer. You would expect that once the work of brewing had been done, all that beer would vanish up into the castle with the rest, *ja*? But to everyone's carefully suppressed astonishment, no! Mad Gus allowed the folk of Durn to keep their beer as well. As much as they could make and store and drink.

RH: Why?

GD: Mad Gus claimed to hate the stuff. With a passion—as one might expect of such a tyrant, *ja*? What other kind of man could hate such divine elixir? One might even surmise that this deviant abhorrence was the very cause of his degraded character. But the truth is otherwise, I think. Mad Gus was likely not so mad as that.

RH: But still… why then? It makes no sense.

GD: Does it not?

RH: Why are you smiling that way?

GD: All in good time, young man. First, you must know something about how beer came to be, for, as I said, it came to be right there in Durn. No one else had ever tried—or thought of trying—to make beer then.[19] Why would they have? Beer begins as pretty noxious stuff prior to the miracle of fermentation. Its first manufacture in Durn was just an accident—the result, in fact, of Mad Gus's own relentless greed.

It is said that some poor farmer, whose name is sadly lost to us, had tried to cheat Mad Gus out of his excessive "tax" by hiding a few scant ingredients for bread and herbal soup within his little hovel, thinking that

---

19 As Mr. Dourtmundschtradel attributes his tale to The Age of Rather Long Stories, a period by definition outside the historical record, it is impossible to ask, much less determine, whether the historical record corroborates or contests his claim that no one else had made or heard of beer prior to its creation in Durn. (See footnote 16.)

the tyrant's henchmen would not notice such a small omission. But Mad Gus had trained his men quite… *passionately*, let us say, and they were not deceived. So, when the poor man saw them ride into his yard, he poured all his illicit grain and herbs and yeast into the only hiding place at his disposal, an extremely large urn of water, unfortunately still half full, then jammed a rag into its mouth in hopes that his assailants would not look inside. They did, of course. That urn was likely the only object in the hovel worth examining. When they saw the soupy mess he'd made of his ill-gotten grain, they shoved the rag back into place and left the mess to rot. The man himself was left to rot as well, inside Mad Gus's dungeon.

Somehow, though, the hapless man survived Mad Gus's hospitality, and three months later, was released—which was not so great a favor as it may seem at first. Winter was well arrived by then. The valley was all hunkered down to starve until the spring, and the paroled farmer, already weak and hungry from his ordeal, had no one to assist him. Amidst the snowdrifts that had blown into his open hovel since they'd taken him away, he found nothing but the water urn they'd left, still containing all the food he had possessed. Without much hope, I imagine, he removed the rag and peered inside. Have you ever seen the afterbirth of fresh beer, Herr Halifax?[20]

RH: I fear I haven't.

GD: It does not smell too bad, and it gives off a certain heat in fermentation, so it was not likely frozen, which was doubtless fortunate, but it is otherwise a most unappealing sight. Still, a man starving in winter might try anything. It seems he drank some of the fizzy, clotted broth into which all that grain and yeast had composted in his absence, likely hoping it might still provide at least a trace more nutritional value than could be derived from the frozen clay of his packed-earth floor, or the weathered wooden lintel of his doorway.[21] It must not have tasted *too* badly, for it seems he drank enough of it to experience a strange and wonderful euphoria.

---

20 Mr. Dourtmundschtradel's description of the process by which this particular mixture came into being engenders some doubt as to whether the "beer" described bore much if any resemblance to the modern libation so named.

21 A sound assumption, even under scrutiny by modern investigative methods.

RH: You're not telling me that no one had ever been drunk before this, are you?

GD: Not in Durn, they hadn't. And no one ever anywhere, not from beer.[22]

RH: Good heavens.

GD: Indeed. The urn was apparently large enough to provide a bit more of the miraculous substance to share with neighbors, who, in exchange for this transcendent experience, gave him enough food to delay his death from excessive starvation for several more weeks.

RH: He still died—after all that?!

GD: Alas. It seems he did. Martyred to bring beer into the world. I am told that one could find shrines dedicated to him throughout Schkerrinwald for centuries afterward.

RH: I'm sorry, Herr Dourtmundschtradel, but I feel compelled to ask: does this story of yours get any happier?

GD: Has beer ever made *you*... happy, Herr Halifax?

RH: Well... er... I suppose it... may have... Once or twice.

GD: Then you have your answer. This is the story of beer, young man, which has not just one, but many millions of happy endings.[23]

RH: I'm not sure that's exactly what I—

GD: Returning to the point, however, they say that when Mad Gus was informed of the poor man's struggle to survive on rotted grain in spoiled water, he laughed long and loud, then ordered one of his henchmen to bring him a small flask of the substance to examine. It is further said that he found the sample so revolting, he killed the man who'd brought it to him.[24]

RH: What a monster.

GD: As I've said, what else can be expected of a man who dislikes beer?

---

22 Again: a claim impossible to test from any tale attributed to The Age of Very Long Stories, etc.

23 More rigorous analysis places this figure closer to 14.6 billion happy endings to date, though this result must be balanced against an estimated 9.375 billion unhappy endings to date. Individual results may vary.

24 This practice too was fairly common in medieval Europe, commonly referred to as "information management".

After that, it amused him to invite the rest of his subjects to drink all the rotten grain and bitter, spoiled water they wished—which is, ostensibly, how the limitations on retention of certain staples became so liberalized. "If these ungrateful subjects find my provision for them insufficient," Mad Gus is said to have announced, "then they may *drink* all the bread they want."

RH: Er… Well, all right. But it could not have taken long for him to notice that they liked the stuff. Wouldn't he have changed his mind then?

GD: Oh, they were no doubt careful to pretend dislike of this new concoction, and that they drank it purely out of dietary desperation—as may well have been the case at first. But I suspect the real reason they persisted in drinking it, and the real reason Mad Gus went on letting them, were one and the same: beer's *effect*. Left so little else to eat, they must have pinched their noses and endured this new "liquid bread" for breakfast, lunch and dinner, *ja*? No doubt they found the drunken state this left them in as… *engaging*, shall we say, as so many of us still do. But can you not see how useful Mad Gus may have found this unintended consequence as well?

RH: I'm… not sure I can. Assuming most of them were happy drunks, I'd still expect a man like that to have put a stop to it, just on principle.

GD: Think of them not as "happy", Herr Halifax, but as "pacified", for I suspect that is how Mad Gus saw them. He must have known—as you yourself have pointed out—that he was in danger should they ever decide they'd had enough. But while a people always pleasantly drunk or at least partially hung over may clearly still get angry, they are far less likely to get very motivated, much less *organized, ja*?[25]

RH: Why, that's… diabolical. Your father told you all this?

GD: The outlines, young man, the outlines… And this is where my story really starts. Or where the story starts being mine, at any rate. My family's ancestral founder was a man named Gundar Dourtmund. The *schtradel* portion of our surname was not added until many centuries later. Young

---

25 This strategy has been a staple of good governance in nearly every empire known to history, though means have varied widely from vodka in Russia and gin in Britain, to opium in China and the Middle East, to marijuana, chocolate Ding Dongs, cheeseburgers, television, and, of course, handheld video games in the US.

Gundar was technically a barley farmer in Durn, though, like all the others in that benighted valley, he lived as little more than a miserable serf. He too had lost crops, cattle, property, and family members to Mad Gus's vindictive whims. But he too subsisted largely on beer, and so had simply drifted like the others into a state of muddled resignation.

One autumn morning, as he was pulling a great cart of freshly harvested barley from his fields through the village on his way to Mad Gus's castle granaries—without benefit of any oxen, for his only animals had been stolen by Mad Gus's men the previous week[26]—he chanced to see his good friend, Horning Brock, the village innkeeper, standing outside his establishment. After more than a millennium, of course, none can say exactly what passed between them there, but one can well imagine how their conversation must have gone.

"Where are your oxen?" Brock would surely have asked.

"Where do you suppose?" Gundar probably replied.

They would likely have glanced up wearily at Mad Gus's hulking manse.

"Ah," Brock sighs. "Just so with my dear Marya."

"No!" Gundar gasps. "They took your wife?"

Brock nods sadly. "Two weeks ago. And my sweet daughter, Hester, just last Tuesday. Had you not heard?"

"Sadly, no," Gundar answers. "I've been busy in the fields with harvest for some weeks now, as you see."

"And poor Lily just last night."

"Your five-year-old?!" Gundar gasps. "Whatever have you done to piss them off so, Horning?"

"They've not told me yet," Brock answers. "They're clearly very busy at the moment, but I'm sure they'll get around to explanations just as soon as there's a lull in all this kidnapping." The two men likely turn another wistful glance up at the tyrant's fort. "At least they've left my little Kamber," Brock

---

26 Given the situation described in Durn, it does seem plausible that Gundar might have gone to such trouble in transporting his harvest to Mad Gus's granaries, desperate not to leave Gus's men any excuse to visit him at home and perhaps burn down the place while they were there.

adds, trying to seem stoic. "It's true he's only three; but he can fair well reach the stove already, if he stands upon a box. Should they come for me as well, I'm sure he'll make a fine innkeeper just as soon as he can lift more than his nose above the counter."[27]

Or, if not these words exactly, I am sure their conversation would have been something very like this. It's how things were in Durn back then.

At any rate, it is passed down that Brock invited Gundar inside to share a stein of beer; and given all the sadness both men had to process, it would have been extremely rude of Gundar to refuse him. He removed the yoke from his shoulders, and left his barley wagon in the street.

It is never a good idea to drink beer quickly, of course. There were no antacids in those days.[28] So they lingered over that first stein, as one does. It turned out that many other calamities had been suffered recently by various townsfolk, of which Gundar had heard nothing, being preoccupied with harvest. So another stein or two were had as Brock brought Gundar up to date on all of Gus's latest shenanigans.

To that point, they had been drinking a light and pleasant lager,[29] as one did then in the mornings after breakfast, but before they knew it, lunchtime had arrived, and being an hospitable man by both trade and nature, Brock could hardly have sent Gundar back to his long slog without some meal to sustain him. So he brought out a potato,[30] and poured them each a pint of

---

27 There were no laws at this time forbidding minors to serve or sell alcohol.

28 There were, of course, antacids in those days. They just hadn't been discovered yet.

29 A standard lager of medieval vintage would likely have weighed in at 4.7% alcohol.

30 This passing reference may be even more startling than Dourtmundschtradel's assertion that beer was invented in Durn--as potatoes are not thought to have been introduced to Europe from the New World until sometime around 1500BC. This apparent anachronism now has some scholars speculating that if Durn Valley was the lowly potato's actual cradle, and some of the tubers made their way to Scandinavia (which could not have been far away given the naming conventions prevalent throughout this narrative), they might well have been transported from there to North America by seafaring Nordic explorers—whom we now know visited the New World many centuries before Columbus did—where they could have flourished and spread, only to be rediscovered and brought back to Europe centuries later just in time to catalyze Ireland's great potato blight! How ironic would that be?

pale ale[31] to wash it down with. Of course, Gundar was not the sort of man to accept another fellow's largesse and then just rush off without so much as a fare-thee-well. Even peasant manners dictate that one linger after such a meal for at least the minimal pleasantries and small talk.

This courtesy occasioned another stein or two, and, it being afternoon by then, they moved to hearty oatmeal stout.[32] As the sun slanted lower through the inn's bottle-glass windows, and the air began to chill, the two men finished off their very satisfying visit with a pint or two, or five perhaps, of Brock's fine late-season porter.[33] Then Gundar stood at last, with relatively minor difficulty, and thanked Brock warmly, while insisting that he really must be off to finish his delivery.

They stumbled outside together, and soon had the barley wagon's yoke untangled from the ground and firmly settled onto Brock's stout shoulders. It took just a minute more to have it off again, and onto Gundar's shoulders. Then, with a determined heave or two, my many-times-great-grandfather was off again toward Mad Gus's hilltop granary—even by Durn's standards, quite profoundly "shitfaced", as you Americans say. Little did he know what was about to come of such a mundane visit with his friend.

RH: Herr Dourtmundschtradel, I really must congratulate you on such clarity of memory at your age.[34] How long has it been since you last heard this tale from your father?

GD: It is difficult to be certain. He told it to me many times, but the last I can recall was during a long train ride to visit one of his mistresses when I was… eight years old, perhaps. He died not long after that. Of a gunshot wound. To the back. Quite a tangle at the time…

---

31 A standard pale ale of the time would be estimated at approximately 5.2%

32 A hearty oatmeal stout of the time, estimated close to 6.4%, though batches doubtless varied widely.

33 Quality late-season porter of the day: 8.9% at the very least.

34 By this point in the narrative, any wary historian will likely have begun to question such an extraordinary volume of detailed dialogue woven through an account ostensibly one or more thousand years old. It does seem that some degree of apocryphal embellishment may reasonably be posited.

RH: My condolences, Herr Dourtmundschtradel.

GD: Thank you, Herr Halifax, but I assure you it is all ancient history to me now.

RH: Well, I must say, this tale of yours is really… very long. Perhaps I ought to change the tape before we go further.

[Tape two]

RH: All right. I think we're ready to continue. You were saying…?

GD: Yes. Well. By all accounts, Gundar was so drunk, the fact he ever even reached the granary gates is yet another sign of divinity's hand in this affair. It was near twilight when Gundar finally wheezed and wobbled to a halt within the castle courtyard. And who was he astonished and dismayed to find there waiting for him, but Mad Gus himself.

RH: Uh-oh.

GD: [*Wheezy laughter, followed by a fit of coughing.*] The brevity of which your language is so capable never ceases to astonish me, Herr Halifax. It is just so… *laughable.*[35]

But yes. Just as you say, 'Uh-oh.' From what my father handed down to me, the ensuing conversation between Mad Gus and Gundar went something more or less like this:

Mad Gus says, "You're late, you drunken sot! We've been waiting for you here all afternoon and into dinner!"

All Gundar's inebriated brain can manufacture in reply is, "Why?"

"You dare ask me *WHY?!*" Mad Gus bellows. "What an impertinent question! Are you too drunk to see who stands before you?"

"Before me?" Gundar looks around, bewildered. "I didn't mean to cut in line. If someone was here first, I'm glad to wait."

"I'm talking about *me*, Barrel Brains!" says the tyrant. "Your *ruler* stands before you—*waiting* for a wagonload of barley that should have been here before lunch!"

---

35 As any competent linguist will confirm, to translate a sneeze into German requires at least two paragraphs of text. German words and syntax are renowned for their length and complexity. Apparently, Mr. Dourtmundschtradel finds American linguistic minimalisms equally absurd.

"*You're* before me?" asks Gundar, even more confused. "But... why would you be made to wait in line... in your own courtyard? You're the ruler."

"*There is no line, you idiot!*" Mad Gus shouts. "*You're the only one in line!*"

"Then... what's the problem?" Gundar pleads.

"*YOU'RE LATE!!!*" screams the tyrant.

"For what?" whines Gundar. Even he can tell this isn't being managed well, but granary deliveries were never "by appointment". If there'd been some schedule here, he had never been informed of it... Then again, his friend Brock still hadn't been informed of why they'd kidnapped his two daughters and his wife...

"I sent men to your farm this morning for the barley," Mad Gus growls,[36] clearly struggling to regain his composure. "They were informed by a neighbor of yours—since imprisoned—that you'd already left to drag your little wagon here—where we've been *waiting* for you all damn day!"

"Waiting?" Gundar asks again. "For a cartful of barley...?"

"When you failed to show up as expected, I'd have bet my second pair of pants that you were trying to flee the valley with *my barley*! In fact, I still think that's what you tried to do. So what went wrong, *dummkopf*?"

"I wasn't trying to flee anywhere," Gundar protests. "You know the only way out of Durn leads right through here. Where else could I have gone? Up a cliff? With a cartload of barley?"

"Call me stupid one more time," says Gus, "and you can laugh it up down in my dungeons with your insolent neighbor. If you weren't trying to run away, where have you been all day? It should not have taken you two hours to get here from your pathetic little farm."

Gundar opens his mouth to say he'd just been visiting with Brock, but some lonely, semi-lucid synapse in his finally sobering mind suggests that Brock has already suffered too much at Gus's hands. Sadly, this brief window of lucidity then closes up again as quickly as it had popped open,

---

36 Alas for Gundar's considerable effort to avoid just this kind of attention.

and Gundar is so pie-eyed that he can't quite distinguish at that moment between thoughts and words—which is how the thought, *I should just have turned this Gottdamn*[37] *barley into beer,*[38] becomes so inconveniently audible.

"You should have... what?" says Mad Gus very quietly.

"What?" Gundar replies, still only half aware that he had thought aloud.

"Leave your wagon when you go, cur," Mad Gus tells him, very quietly indeed. "I will have that with the barley for your insolence."

"But... but without the cart, how am I to bring you next year's harvest?" Gundar stammers.

"Shut your bung hole, peasant," Mad Gus answers as quietly as Gundar has ever heard him speak, "and leave here. Now. Or I will have your worthless head to decorate the cart with."

Well, as you might imagine, Herr Halifax, all this distressing banter has finally cleared Gundar's mind enough to understand that it is time to run—and not back to his farm where who knew what fate might await him. Where Mad Gus was concerned, displays of quiet restraint were never known to be propitious.

RH: Very ominous indeed. But since you're here today, I must assume your ancestor survived this misstep.

GD: Indeed, for, though Gundar did not realize it, he had just induced Mad Gus to a commit an even greater misstep of his own.

Unsure that anywhere within the village would be safe for him, Gundar slept out in the forest, wrapped in his cloak against the cold. Early the next morning, he snuck back, hoping to find sanctuary underneath the inn kept by his friend Horner Brock. There was a secret second cellar there, you see, dug out just spoonfuls of dirt at a time over many years by a wide conspiracy of barroom patrons. This small space was used to hide important things or people in times of extraordinary need *if* Brock deemed it could be

---

37 Colloquial expletive.

38 Recall that villagers were permitted to forgo surrendering their grain to Mad Gus if it was surrendered instead to one of Durn's many beer distillers for immediate brewing.

done without arousing suspicion in the castle. We will never know whether Brock would have deemed Gundar's need sufficient, for he arrived to find an hysterical mob gathered in Brock's barroom.

"Gus's men have emptied all the brewing vats, and carted off the beer!" they cry when Gundar enters. "Every barrel, bottle, and bota bag in the entire village!"

"*Gott in Himmel!*"[39] Gundar exclaims, quite hungry by that hour, and having hoped to get a stein or two of breakfast there, if not even a potato to scrub it down with. "Why would they do such a thing?"

"They came last night," he is angrily informed, "claiming you'd spat into Mad Gus's face and told him no one ought to pay his grain tax anymore! He thinks we are ungrateful now!"

Gundar gapes at them in utter disbelief, then slaps his forehead.

"Can this be true, Gundar?" Brock asks him. "Were you so insane?"

"I do vaguely remember that Mad Gus and I misunderstood each other when I went to offer up my harvest," Gundar tells them. "That much is true, I think. But if I'd spat at any part of him, would I be living now to speak of it? And why would I have dragged a whole cart full of barley up that *Gottdamn* hill just to tell him I'd not pay his tax? I was certainly not *that* drunk."

"It does sound hard to swallow," someone in the mob concedes.

"Everything is hard to swallow now," someone else complains, "without our beer."

"They burned your farm last night, you know," Brock tells Gundar gently.

"I'm not surprised," sighs Gundar.

"Well, we're not just going to stand for it, are we?" someone else insists.

"Please, don't cause yourselves more trouble on my account," Gundar replies stoically. "Winter's not for several weeks yet. I can build another farm."

"Who cares about your farm?" protests the other man. "I meant our

---

39 German phrase roughly translated into English as "Holy cow!" More literally as "God in heaven!"

beer! Winter's only weeks away, as Herr Barrel Mouth has just observed, and that beer's all we had to eat!"

This remark is met with cheers of outrage from the mob.

"With winter upon us and all our grain already tucked away up in the castle granaries, we have no way of brewing more!"[40] complains another man.

"And even if we could," someone else groans, "how would we survive the months required to brew it?"

"Where's he keeping it all?" asks another man. "That's what I want to know. Mad Gus can't stand beer, so he won't have many barrels up there."

"I have it from Hans Schloser, the carpenter," one man confides, "that Mad Gus has turned one of his granaries into a giant vat!"

"So *that's* why they tore down my barn last night!" exclaims another fellow. "Without a word of explanation when they carted off the lumber!"

"Same with my tanning shed!" complains the village taxidermist.

"They've made a beer vat from your *tanning shed*?" someone asks, aghast.

"He's poured *all* our *different* kinds of beer into a *single vat*?" gasps the man behind him.

"Has he no conscience?" cries a balding man with bandied legs.

"Has he no taste buds?" demands another.

"He has no *soul*!" booms out another man.

"It's… *sacrilege*!" sputters yet another.

"It's psychotic sociopathy!" shrills a young man.[41]

"It's just too much!" shouts a nearly toothless geezer near the front.

---

40 Most beer scholars agree that the real issue being skirted here by this exclusively male group is that most early brewers of beer were female (known as brewsters). The abduction of so many village women may have been a much bigger impediment to new emergency brewing than the late season or sequestered grain harvest.

41 An intriguing interjection for two reasons. First, such concepts of clinical psychosis would not appear in the rest of Europe until around the 19th century with the work and writing of Sigmund Freud. (Was he too, perhaps, a descendant of the Durn Valley?) Secondly, the speaker here makes this accusation of psychosis even as he and his companions exhibit such clear symptoms of full blown cenosillicaphobia (fear of an empty beer glass).

"For decades now, that monster steals our cattle with impunity! He burns our barns and houses! He drags our very wives and children from their beds at night and sells them into slavery! Okay, we can live with that stuff; life is never easy. But marching in and grabbing our *beer*? *That* crosses the line! I say the *time*—has *come*—to *take*—this *FÜCHENMEISTER*[42] DOWN!!!"

[*Sudden silence, punctuated after some time by a spate of quiet throat clearing from Mr. Dourtmundschtradel.*]

My… apologies, Herr Halifax, for that… outburst. Always, at this point in the story, I… This is the moment of liberation awaited by my longsuffering forefathers since even before their own births. The emotion… It is… rather distressing, *ja*? I… hope you will consider, possibly, deleting this embarrassing lapse in discipline from your recording?

RH: I will certainly consult my superiors, Herr Dourtmundschtradel, but I assure you, there's no need of apology. I sympathize completely.[43]

GD: *Danke*,[44] Herr Halifax. Your understanding does you credit.

RH: The honor is mine, sir. Shall we continue?

GD: Of course, of course. Where were we?

RH: Er… at the, uh, dawn of Durn's liberation, I believe?

GD: *Ja, ja*. Well. A *respectable* civic leader like Herr Brock would, of course, have found that old man's disturbing emotional outburst as unseemly as you and I do, Herr Halifax, and perhaps have worried also about potential consequences for himself and his establishment should any of Mad Gus's men happen to be lurking near enough to overhear the indecorous display of seditious sentiment developing inside. He quite properly insisted that the discussion be suspended immediately and taken "elsewhere".

Now, everyone in Durn, except, of course, for Mad Gus and his various

---

42 Another colloquial expletive.

43 Deft sidestep by a consummate professional who, with all deference to German sentiments about displays of sentiment, clearly understands the value of uncensored authenticity in oral history. Our respectful apologies to the late Mr. Dourtmundschtradel, and any surviving family members.

44 German term for "thank you", not to be confused with "dunken" which pertains in Germany, as in America, primarily to warm, soft, mouthwatering, God-I-wish-I-had-one-right-now donuts.

agents, knew very well what "elsewhere" meant. In times of extremis, one was likely to hear that so-and-so had gone "elsewhere" for a while, or that "the thing in question" might be looked for "elsewhere." In Durn, "elsewhere" meant that secret second cellar, which I have mentioned, underneath Herr Brock's inn. Thus, with knowing looks and crafty nonchalance, the hysterical mob sidled furtively down Brock's cellar stairs, and passed in single file through the slyly sequestered slot behind the curtain, cleverly concealed inside a false-backed barrel into Brock's secret second cellar to resume their rabble-rousing in greater safety.

Unfortunately, this space is said to have been no larger than eight feet in any direction, so one must assume the hysterical mob was packed inside quite tightly. The smell alone of all those rustic fellows jammed together in the darkness must have been appalling,[45] though they were likely far too angry at that moment to care much about such trivialities, *ja*?

At any rate, once all were pressed inside, their rebellious conversation was resumed.

"So," Brock commences sensibly, "how exactly do you bravos think that we, without any weapons, can hope to overthrow Mad Gus with all his henchmen and that cannon he is always polishing?"[46]

"Anybody ever seen him fire it?" asks a voice from near the back. "I'll bet it doesn't even work, or he'd have fired it at us long ago."

"You are volunteering, then," Brock counters, "to stand between it and the rest of us while we find out?"

"Our cause is just!" cries the old man with hardly any teeth. "God will surely supply us with whatever weapons are required."

I do not doubt Brock rolled his eyes, though no one would have seen it in the darkness. "And what kind of weapons do you imagine God would

---

45 Some scholars theorize that men and dogs were brought into partnership in ancient times by the fact that they smelled much the same when wet. Further research suggests that when dry, ancient men smelled worse, but this was likely no deterrent for dogs, who, as any layman knows, are only too glad to shove their noses into any heap of dung they pass.

46 This detail too, if not apocryphal, suggest the tale's origin must be much later than Herr D has indicated.

send us?" he asks wearily, having watched this kind of theater come and go in Durn too many times before.

A consternated silence fills their crowded refuge.

"Beehives!" someone exclaims.

"Beehives?" Brock asks. "Mad Gus's beekeepers will have many more of those up at the castle than we're likely to assemble here. What would we do with them anyway?"

"Doesn't matter," says another voice. "Don't need the hives—just a couple tubs of honeycomb, and take it to the castle as an offering to make amends for Gundar's blunder."

"I told you," Gundar protests. "I did nothing!"

"Hold your tongue, Gundar," scolds the first voice. "I'm not finished yet. Being such greedy bastards, I bet they'll tear into that honey right in front of us and shove it all into their faces while we look on, hungry, *ja*?"

"Which will accomplish what of any help to us?" asks someone else.

"Nothing," says the first voice, "'til we set the bears loose on them!"

"What bears?" asks Gundar, backed by many a concurring grunt.

"The woods are full of hungry bears this close to winter," he replies. "We just catch five or six of them, and sic 'em on Mad Gus and his collaborators when their greedy faces are all covered in our honey. They'll be torn to pieces."

"How are we to trap these bears without being mauled ourselves?" scoffs Gundar.

"And how are we to sneak them up into the castle?" asks another voice as scornfully. "Shall we hide them in our breeches while presenting Mad Gus with the honey, or just whistle for them once he has indulged this bestial sweet tooth you describe?"

"We could use weasels, then," says a new voice. "They're easier to catch, and small enough to hide—even in our breeches, if we have to."

"Are you seriously proposing that we kill Mad Gus with weasels?" Brock asks crossly.

"Just 'cause they're small don't mean their claws and teeth aren't just as sharp as any bear's," says this latest idiot, near drowned out by boos and raspberries from the others.

"Weasels care for sausage, not for honey," Gundar laughs. "So I think we know what they will use their teeth on first if any of us tries hiding them inside their pants."[47]

"A peace offering of goats then," says yet another voice, "with beehives stuffed inside them,[48] so that when the castle butcher cuts them open—"

"—all the kitchen staff is stung to death!" Gundar roars with mirth. "That will show Mad Gus who's boss in Durn. And how are we to get these beehives into goats?"

"Just wrap them up in trash, and leave them in the goat pen," says yet another man. "There's nothing goats won't eat."[49]

"Are we finished with this nonsense?" Brock snaps. "It's getting rather close in here."

But they weren't even near to finished, Herr Halifax. Someone next suggested they send a cauldron of soup up to Mad Gus, filled with poisoned parsnips, but everyone agreed that no one in the valley, least of all Mad Gus, could stand parsnips,[50] so not only would Mad Gus not eat them, but the village would be punished further just for sending him such an insulting vegetable. Another man suggested they persuade Mad Gus's own henchmen to insurrection by offering up the village women as a bribe. But a brace of others reminded him that the only women in their village not already kidnapped were the very ugly ones, suggesting he'd have thought of that if his own wife were not still safe at home.

---

47 This reference continues to confuse historians as it seems to suggest carrying sausage in one's pants was common practice at this time—an assertion supported by no other known medieval reference, and made all the more mysterious in light of the fact that the men in question here have made it clear they possess no food at all.

48 An idea likely inspired by accounts widely published at that time of the famous Trojan Horse, though it's puzzling that they didn't just adopt the Greeks' tried and true approach without alteration—unless perhaps the construction of Mad Gus's vat had left in its wake a village-wide lumber shortage.

49 There is, in fact, a firmly established if rather brief list of items which goats won't eat, including, but not limited to, bathroom cleanser, granite, jet fuel, haggis, marshmallow peeps, and any object larger than the goat which cannot be broken into smaller portions. Pretty much anything else though.

50 This detail is indisputably apocryphal. Parsnips are delicious.

It didn't help their progress any that with every passing hour each man there was becoming soberer than he had likely been in years. As things got hotter under everyone's collars, Brock began to fear they'd simply kill each other right there in the secret cellar without anyone's being the wiser. His only reassurance lay in the fact that there wasn't room to draw so much as a butter knife—which Durn's peasants *were* allowed to own and carry.

It was then that Gundar finally bellows, "Silence!" And, to Brock's amazement, silence falls. "*Men* of Durn," Gundar growls, "is it not time we all stopped living like Mad Gus's children here?" The silence stretches. "You know as well as I that there's no silly circus act by which to overthrow Mad Gus. If we truly care about our beer, then we must make whatever weapons we are able from our farming implements and from the branches of our trees and the sharp stones of our fields. Then we must march as one to Gus's gates, and fight like men until not one of his hired scoundrels is left standing to defend him. Are there not many more of us than there are of them?"

None of them were skilled enough at math to provide him with an answer. But, remembering, perhaps, how handily Gundar had managed to drag a fully loaded barley wagon clear across the valley and up to Gus's castle—or moved by how he'd walked away alive after whatever insult he had offered Gus to cause them all of these problems—they enthusiastically declared Gundar leader of their imminent rebellion.

Thus inspired, everyone rushed home and quickly fashioned bludgeons out of tree limbs, slingshots out of harnesses, scythes and pitchforks out of, well, scythes and pitchforks, and reassembled early the next morning at the village inn, where Gundar got them all formed up in rows, as befits a fighting force that fancies itself fearless in the face of any foe. When this was done, he shouted, as any good commander must, "Forwaaaaard *march!*" Whereupon, they all turned sharply, if in numerous directions, and, after just a few collisions and a minor shouting match or two, managed to get headed all in more or less the same direction.

Probably because they hadn't taken care to march up to the castle quietly enough, they arrived to find Mad Gus's gates shut tight against them. Atop the walls stood Gus himself, flanked by several dozen henchmen armed with swords and cudgels. Frowning down at them, Mad Gus yelled, "Whatever are you nitwits doing now?"

Gundar stepped forward and called up with great ferocity, "We've come for our beer, Your Lordship."

"No, seriously," Gus called back down. "What are you up to?"

Gundar exchanged uncertain glances with his men, unable to think of any answer clearer than the one he had just given. Looking back up at Mad Gus, he called, "With due respect, Your Lordship, you tend to make even the simplest conversations very complicated."[51]

"Well, let me try to be a little clearer then," Gus said. "*What...*" he started making bizarre hand gestures, which may have been some proto-attempt at sign language—or at Italian—"*are... you... NITWITS,*" he cupped both hands around his mouth for added volume, "*UP TO?*"

Gundar rolled his eyes, having had it up to here by then with Gus's poor communication skills. Instead of answering again, he grabbed a four-foot length of tree branch from a stout lad nearby, walked to Gus's lavish gates, and started pounding on them with it.

"Stop that!" Mad Gus shouted. "Stop that immediately! You're damaging the finish!"

Gundar kept on banging, having already knocked some impressive chips out of the fancy carving there.

"*I said—*" Gus started to repeat.

"I heard you," Gundar cut him off. "Did you hear me? We've come to get our beer back! Now open up this gate, Your Lordship, or we will knock it down—one small chip at a time, if that's what it takes. Could make it very hard to sleep in there tonight!"

"*Open my gates?!*" Mad Gus shrilled. "*Is that your wish, you lout? My gates open?*" He directed an outraged wave at his henchmen, who turned as one and disappeared. "*Fine then, I'll be glad to open up my gates, moron!*

---

51 Being new to the science of leadership, Gundar was clearly still unacquainted with standard diplomatic syntax used by seasoned leaders everywhere expressly to make even the simplest conversations complicated for the very prudent purpose of discouraging anything so reckless as decisive action.

Hope you're ready! Here it comes!"

Of course, Mad Gus could just have had his henchmen fire arrows down at Gundar's band, and slaughtered everyone in minutes, had he not years earlier declared bows illegal in his kingdom, even in the hands of his own men, fearing any weapon with the speed to reach him faster than he felt able to react. Given his own laws, however, it was now necessary for Gus's men to come down in person to dispatch the rabble.[52] Gundar and his men braced themselves as Gus's gates swung open and dozens of men in mismatching armor[53] swarmed out with a mighty hue and cry, bristling with weapons in various states of repair, but still more than equal to the job.

After decades of encountering nothing but the flaccid[54] resignation of hopeless, half-drunken serfs, however, Mad Gus's men were not at all prepared for the inconceivable sobriety and determination which Mad Gus's misstep had suddenly engendered. Nor, it turns out, is a standard, pre-owned sword or cudgel as effective as you'd think against heavy branches two or three feet longer, wielded by men who've been required, lo those many years, to use their arms for work more strenuous than drinking wine and whoring.[55] Gundar and his men were increasingly mystified by the strange clumsiness of all these so-called "seasoned fighting men", until they started noticing the stench of stale beer on their breath.

"Why, they've been making free with all our stolen beer!" somebody

---

52 Lord Augustus is credited earlier with having a cannon, which one must imagine capable of delivering its lethal payload faster than any man could react, if not with nearly the silent stealth of a bow. However, it appears that Gus had allowed just one such weapon in his domain, and reserved access to himself alone.

53 Further evidence of Lord Augustus's penny-wise, pound-foolish approach to leadership.

54 Unclear whether this refers to the villagers' limp resistance to harassment, or their general digestive condition, as either one might be consistent with a regular diet consisting almost entirely of beer.

55 Lord Augustus's men were also regularly required to beat up villagers, burn down buildings, and kidnap women and children, of course. But given the hitherto general flaccidity of response denoted earlier, it seems likely that none of those activities had required much more in the way of muscular exertion than drinking and whoring normally do. Quite possibly less.

shouted, which made the village men even more irate and formidable. Before the castle's tipsy henchmen quite had time to realize how badly they were losing and retreat, Gundar and his peers had forced their way inside the gates, and moved the brawl into Mad Gus's courtyard.

Once inside, strangely little effort seemed required to fend off half-assed feints and forays aimed tentatively at them from time to time by Gus's discombobulated force, now trying—rather badly, it seemed—to improvise guerrilla tactics inside their own stronghold. More urgent for Gundar and his band was the blessedly bitter, yeasty smell of beer that hung upon the air around them. Their heads swam with it, their mouths salivated, as they gazed about, trying to triangulate the lovely odor's source. It took their veteran noses hardly any time at all to home in on the second of Mad Gus's three huge granaries, built against the courtyard's farthest wall.

"Our *beer!*" shouted several men at once, as Gundar's motley army charged together toward the open granary entrance. The sad fact that none of them had thought to bring their steins along would not likely have impeded them from simply kneeling down and lapping it out of the vat. These were men more practical than proud. But here is what they found as they raced through the granary door:

Directly before them, filling more than half the room up to the ceiling nearly thirty feet above, stood an unimaginably large beer vat, its hastily constructed walls groaning audibly in the sudden silence. In front of this stood nearly every henchman Mad Gus employed, which helped explain the odd lack of resistance they'd encountered in the courtyard. And finally, dead center, out in front, stood Mad Gus beside his cannon, staring right at Gundar's rebel band, and smiling blandly.

In one hand Gus held a white lace handkerchief, with which, it seemed, he had been giving his beloved cannon a last-minute polishing. Without shifting eyes or smile from Gundar's men, Gus gave the cannon one last swish, and said, extremely quietly, to a henchman standing just behind the cannon, "Fire at will."

Of all the müdder füching[56] dirty tricks, thought Gundar, certain that he and his brother peasants were completely had. But in that instant, a lifetime of bottled rage fountained up inside him, and, no longer caring how few minutes long his life might be, he tucked his head defiantly, and charged straight at the cannon with a bullish roar.

Fortunately, Gus's fussy cannon was of the kind ignited by those silly six-inch fuses that burn down so slowly and dramatically in movies—which provided Gundar just sufficient time to close the gap and shoulder the cannon's barrel upward as it went off with a deafening boom. Gundar felt his hair part on one side as the cannonball whizzed past on its way to hit a heavy metal plate bolted just above the entrance to support a hanging pulley system, then bounce back to fly with nearly as much speed across the chamber toward the high vat wall, into which it slammed and stuck, not ten feet above the heads of Gus's startled henchmen. All of them turned now, looking up with open mouths to where the leaden ball hung half-embedded in the splintered wood. An instant later, with a tinny pinging sound, the cannonball popped loose and fell onto the upturned head of one unhappy henchman, who went down like a sack of sand. Where the cannonball had been lodged, a little fountain now appeared, spitting out a slender golden arc of beer, which splashed down onto other upturned faces among Gus's corps—igniting momentary envy in Gundar and his crew. Then, an ominous grumbling sound issued from the vat's straining wooden walls, rather like that of a stomach filled too full.

"*RUN!!!*" Gundar screamed, already racing for the granary entrance.

Being so near the door already, Gundar's men just made it out as the awesome vat gave way. Only Gundar failed to make it through in time, though he was so few feet inside that the tidal wave of beer just picked him up and spat him through the straining entrance like an olive pit. Gundar's wide-eyed men backed rapidly away, sure the granary's quaking front wall would collapse at any moment. But it held, causing most of that unthinkable tide of beer to rebound off its inside face and surge back toward where Mad

---

56 An archaic colloquial term for "mean" or in some cases, "mean to mother".

Gus and his henchmen lay broken and scattered now amidst the ruins of their ruptured vat. Afterward, it was surmised that the rebounding flood had gathered up all in its path and flung the load so forcefully at the already shaken building's rear wall that it gave way at once.

As a sodden Gundar climbed back onto his feet out in the courtyard, his men and the remaining castle staff stood frozen, staring in shocked silence. Then, when it seemed certain that the front wall would stand, they began to move—first slowly, then with greater speed—back toward the granary door. Inside, they found nothing left but a giant frame for open air where once the granary's back and the castle wall behind it had stood. Rushing to the vast gap's edge, Gundar and his men looked down—a long, long way—at the still roiling and foaming waterfall, which plunged even more precipitously than usual into the valley's sole outlet ravine, beside the steeply switch-backed trail that led one out of Durn and down into the wider world. There was no sign of Mad Gus and his henchmen. The great tide of beer, in combination with the waterfall's usual raging torrent, had washed them all away.

"*Mein gott in himmel!*"[57] Gundar murmured. "We are free." He turned, beaming at his brave companions. "We are free at last! To live however we wish! To eat all the food we grow! All the milk and cheese our cattle give us! To sleep nights without fearing for our homes or wives or children! To drink all the beer that we can make again—without fearing that some *dummkopf* in this castle might come take it all away! Do you hear me, brothers? *We are Mad Gus's slaves no longer!*"

[*Another lengthy pause, broken by the sounds of quiet weeping from Mr. Dourtmundschtradel. Then, after further sniffling, in a broken voice:*]

As you may imagine, Herr Halifax, a great cheer went up at this. Not just from the village men, but from the castle staff as well.

There were many weeks of celebration after that, for there was no end of food and drink stored up in Gus's remaining granaries and storerooms... I have no doubt it was... a very... *beautiful* time to be alive...

---

57 Yet another variation of the German phrase for "Holy Cow"—more literally translated as "My God in Heaven!"

RH: What a tale, Herr Dourtmundschtradel! I've heard nothing more astonishing in all my years of research. I assume they all lived happily ever after?

GD: *Ach*, no, Herr Halifax. Regrettably, they did not.

RH: Oh dear. Did Mad Gus come back after all? Had he survived somehow?

GD: No, no. Nothing half so dire as that. They sent a party down the riverbed to look, of course. Wanting to be sure. But all they found were planks of wood, several dead henchmen, and a lot of inebriated fish, still flipping onto shore in drunken confusion. It is presumed all other bodies, including mad Lord Stephenson's, lay tangled in the rocks and roots below the river's countless rapid shoots and pools. Mad Gus was never seen again.

RH: Then what went wrong for them?

GD: Alas, they could not bring themselves to end their celebration, Herr Halifax. They had been so miserable for so long, and risked so much to free themselves, that no one thought they should be made to work again—on anything. Without a dictator to organize their labor and keep the valley's complex civic logistics in motion, the peasants just ran out of goals, and food, and reasons to get up each day.[58]

RH: That's... so sad.

GD: Not entirely, Herr Halifax. Not ultimately, at least. Their inability to live without a dictator forced them all to leave in search of another one to give some order to their lives again. This search for new enslavement caused them to disperse all over Europe,[59] bringing the previously secret knowledge of beer's manufacture[60] with them everywhere they went. As I mentioned when we started, Gundar Dourtmund's journey ended here, in

---

58 A common syndrome easily observable at smaller scale whenever adolescent children are left home alone for longer than a day by too-trusting parents.

59 Where, happily, even minimal further research suggests they had little difficulty finding what they sought.

60 Again, doubt is cast upon this assertion by some scholars who point to evidence such as one 4,000-year-old Sumerian stone tablet inscribed with the words "Drink Elba Beer, the beer with the heart of a lion." Then again, maybe Elba's franchise had simply never branched out into Europe...

what would much later come to be Germany. It was here that Gundar met my many-times-great-grandmother, and we have been enjoying what he taught this country about brewing ever since. There are no better brewers in the world than ours, Herr Halifax.[61] How much more happiness can one demand of any ending, *ja*?

---

61 This assertion is vigorously contested by most British scholars, though it must be noted that the oldest acknowledged functioning brewery in the world is 900-year-old Bayerische Staatsbrauerie Weihenstephan near Munich. Coincidence? We think not!

About the Author

SHANNON PAGE was born on Halloween night and spent her early years on a back-to-the-land commune in northern California. A childhood without television gave her a great love of the written word. At seven, she wrote her first book, an illustrated adventure starring her cat Cleo. Sadly, that story is out of print, but her work has appeared in *Clarkesworld*, *Interzone*, *Fantasy*, *Black Static*, Tor.com, and many anthologies, including *Love and Rockets* from DAW, Subterranean's *Tales of Dark Fantasy 2*, Flying Pen Press's *Space Tramps: Full Throttle Space Tales #5*, and the Australian Shadows Award-winning *Grants Pass*.

Her debut collection, *Eastlick and Other Stories*, appeared in October 2013 at Book View Café; her first novel, *Eel River*, a hippie horror tale, was published by Morrigan Books one month later. 2014 will see the publication of *Our Lady of the Islands*, co-written with Jay Lake, and *The Queen and The Tower*, first book in The Nightcraft Quartet, from Per Aspera Press. Her editorial work can be seen in the anthology *Witches, Stitches & Bitches*, from Evil Girlfriend Media. Shannon is a longtime yoga practitioner, has no tattoos, and is an avid gardener at home with her partner Mark Ferrari in Portland, Oregon. Visit her at www.shannonpage.net.